SHATTERED FALLS

SHATTERED FALLS

WAYNE RUSSELL

First Printing, 2024
26 Infinity Publishing

For Rachael
With Love Forever, and then some.

1

The next one hundred and fifty kilometres felt like the most important distance Karen would ever travel. She wanted only one thing. To be with her children. She had her husband beside her, driving faster at times than he should, but always coaxed back to a safe speed by her words or questioning look. She knew David was doing his best to not drive angry and other than her father, he was the safest driver she knew.

She had always felt safe with him. Safe and loved, but now after what had happened, she...they needed to know their whole family was safe. Jake was just shy of four years old, and she could envision him at this moment, chasing chickens through the backyard of her parents' home. Rebecca, the independent nine-year-old would be sitting on the back porch with 'Grandma', watching and laughing as Grandad supervised Jake. Karen knew her kids were safe but knowing that, and having your arms wrapped around them were two different things.

David glanced away from the road for just a moment to study his wife's face and echoed her thoughts.

"They're ok babe, and we'll be there soon. Just over the mountains, and we'll hit Murrurundi, then it's a clear shot to Kurri. Couple of hours."

"I know. Just seems like an eternity...and that doesn't mean you should drive faster."

"I got it babe, and I'm sorry I was angry. It wasn't at you, but I guess you know that. Fact is, I'm still angry but I know what we're going to do about it."

Karen smiled and reached over to squeeze her husband's forearm. "I'm glad I've got you. I love you...but slow down just a little." Karen turned her gaze up the hill, at the oncoming traffic. "This part of the road has always given me the chills."

David nodded, lifted his foot off the accelerator and slid into the left lane.

"Thank you, baby."

She drew in a deep breath of air from the partially lowered passenger window and closed her eyes.

'Relax', she thought to herself. She had never been an anxious person and even though she had seen the signs of anxiety in herself at times, she had always been able to manage them. Until yesterday.

Yesterday David had come home from the mill, whistling some unknown tune, and leaving a trail of sawdust, to find her curled up in the corner of the kitchen, sobbing and trembling. When he had calmed her enough to talk, she had seen the concern in his eyes turn to rage. She knew he had always held back his emotions, but this seemed to be his tipping point and it had taken the next half hour for her to calm him.

And then, they sat, both together on the kitchen floor. Karen told him everything, and he listened, biting his lip in bursts of renewed anger at times but always holding it in. Then they made a plan.

First, they would head down to Karen's parent's house, where their children were spending the last few days of the summer holidays. Then tomorrow they would visit a lawyer. The brother of Karen's parents' neighbour. The appointment had been made and even just making that first step had lifted a weight off her shoulders but the thought of being surrounded by David, Rebecca, Jake, her Mum and Dad was the real therapy she was looking for.

A semi-trailer, double length overtook them as they headed over the last rise of the Liverpool Range, the sound of its gears shifting bringing her head back from her window to look out David's window. A line of vehicles behind the truck streamed past. She watched them, thinking how all those people likely had their problems, their own issues.

Her jaw dropped open as a battered white Commodore pulled alongside them.

"David." Karen pointed toward the other vehicle.

She knew the face and as David turned his head to look, he knew it as well.

"What the...?" David squinted at the car. The familiar face was looking directly at him and then a hand was raised and beckoned for them to pull to the side of the road.

"David, what's he doing?"

Before David had any chance to answer, Karen screamed as she looked once again at the car beside them. David looked as well and took only a moment to realise what was wrong with what he was seeing.

"You've got to be stuffing kidding?"

David pushed his foot down on the accelerator, and they lurched forward, the car beside them disappearing. The Commodore had more power and it gained on them again, pulling alongside.

The driver was now screaming at them, waving them to the side of the road but David refused the direction and focused on the road ahead.

And then the Commodore swerved. Metal ground against metal and in an instant Karen's vision filled with silver guardrail, yellow reflectors, flashes of grass, trees, and rocks and finally a canopy of blue sky through shattered windshield. Pain stabbed at her everywhere.

And then nothing. Blackness washed over them both. Washing away their pain and all their hopes. Shattering the worlds of everyone they cared for.

Her last thought was of her children. Her last thought was of Jake and Rebecca.

2

Fourteen Years Later.

The road ahead held a painful memory, something best slept through, but Rebecca knew that sleep would not come easy. The coach was warm enough, and the seats comfortable enough, but she had too much on her mind.

Outside icy rain occasionally spattered against the window and when it was quiet enough, she could hear the wind. Her Grandad called it a lazy wind, it only blew one way, straight through you.

It was mid-July, the dead of winter, late Wednesday evening and about a half hour north of Maitland. The coach trip would take just over four hours and would pull into Tamworth just after midnight. She had already booked herself into a hotel near the station. In the morning, she would wait for an old family friend to take her the final half hour of the trip and the start of a new life.

Right now, all she could do was sit and think, which was exactly what her Grandad had told her to do, although his words had been more like, 'giving you a chance to get your shit straight'. He was a man that liked to tell it, how it was.

Two months ago, her father's father, Pop had passed away. He had made it to eighty before his heart had finally given out. A heart attack one afternoon on the veranda of the local hotel and then two weeks in a hospital in Newcastle becoming less and less of the formidable man he had once been, before he finally decided he had had enough. His Will had left his house, small property, and a half share in the timber mill that he had started years ago to Rebecca and her brother. Jake was a few months short of eighteen, still in high school and in the care of Grandma and Grandad, her mum's parents. He would come up in the next school holidays to visit but now Rebecca just needed an escape from the troubled life that had engulfed her.

Outside the coach, the rain had gotten heavier. They had just stopped at Muswellbrook to pick up and drop off passengers and the frigid air from outside had been driven inside by the increasing wind. Rebecca flipped the collar of her coat up and pulled a knitted grey woollen beanie down over her ears. All she could think was 'God I miss summer', but summer and her memories of it seemed a million miles away.

The best memory she had was of summer. She had been nine years old, and her dad had been dragging her around on a boogie board and catching waves in the big, protected rock pool at Tuncurry. Mum had ventured into the water, carrying Jake on her hip, jumping up to stop the waves from getting her hair wet. Jake had laughed hysterically every time his mum had sworn as the waves slapped against her chest and splashed up at her hair. It had been the best Christmas holiday she had ever had and the last one she would ever spend with her parents. From then on, her life had been one of rebellion and depression, all of which she knew in her heart were rooted in the loss of her parents fourteen years ago.

Fourteen years ago, on the same highway she was now on, a red sedan had been sideswiped and forced off the road. It had hit a guard rail and flipped, plummeting down an embankment and ending up a twisted wreck of metal at the foot of the Liverpool range just north of Murrurundi. Rebecca's mother had died on the scene, her father two days later in an intensive care unit in Sydney, and that spot, where all their lives had changed, now lay less than an hour ahead of her. Rebecca could fell her anxiety kicking in, clammy hands, short sharp breaths, and tense muscles.

"Focus on your breathing" she muttered to herself, "Focus."

It took her a few minutes but after years of dealing with it through a dozen different types of pills, she had found her own way. A way that worked for her. Breathe. Deep controlled breaths that slowed her racing heart.

The anxiety eased and even though she knew that falling asleep would be a battle, she had to try again. She placed the small lavender scented travel pillow, that Grandma had insisted she take, up against the window and leant against it. Rebecca clenched her eyes shut and began trying all the tricks she had ever heard of to help her sleep. Counting sheep, clearing her mind, humming quietly but nothing worked. She opened her eyes and stared intently out the window at what little of the passing countryside she could see. It was not much, the distant rain-distorted light from a farmhouse, other cars and trucks going about their own seemingly untroubled lives and the never-ending flash from reflectors on the guardrail.

Rebecca turned and looked back around the coach. It looked like there was now less than ten passengers, but it was hard to tell as they all seemed huddled into their seats keeping warm and trying to sleep. Across from her sat an elderly woman, she had been on the coach before Rebecca had gotten on, and beside her, in the window seat sat a small boy. A boy who looked only about four years old, dressed in spiderman pyjamas, yellow rain boots and a red and white beanie. Apart from the driver and Rebecca he seemed to be the only other person awake on the coach, but unlike Rebecca he seemed intent on staying awake. Rebecca had heard the boy promise to the lady, who she assumed was his grand-mother that he would sleep, but as Nana had drifted off, the boy pulled himself up to the window and stared out, amazed by every snatch of light that caught his eye.

Rebecca could not help but laugh quietly to herself.

'Kids', she thought, 'if only things had worked out different. Some-one like you might have been sitting next to me instead.'

Rebecca thought back, dropping out of high school, the string of bad boyfriends, the trouble the last one had gotten her into with the police, and then she had gotten pregnant. When she had told her boy-friend, he had laughed at her and walked out the door, leaving her with a handful of bills and two flatmates who wanted her gone. She turned to the two people she knew she could rely on, Grandma and Grandad. Grandad had been the hardest one to tell, not because she feared him but because she had always looked up to him and seeing his face, knowing she had let him down had been hard. But Grandad had turned out to be her greatest ally. He had walked into the flat, packed all her gear in a duffel bag he had brought and driven her back to the house. He had told her he loved her and kissed her as he carried her bag into her room. Then when she had lost the baby two weeks later, he had held her in his arms for the longest time. Rebecca had even felt his tears fall upon her neck. And now here she was, under Grandad's instruction, trying to get her shit together.

CHAPTER THREE

3

Rebecca woke with a sudden jolt. Somehow, she had fallen asleep. She sat upright and looked around the coach, getting her bearings. The little boy in the window seat across the aisle seemed to have fallen asleep as well, his head resting on his grandmother's lap. It was still raining, and Rebecca had no idea where they were. Somewhere on the New England Highway but other than north of Muswellbrook it was a bit of a mystery. She stared out the window hoping to catch a glimpse of a sign, hopefully something that told her they were past Murrurundi and over the other side of the Liverpool range.

There seemed to be lights behind her, a town just passed, maybe that was Murrurundi, and the road would soon ascend the range and pass the site she wanted to avoid. She closed her eyes and whispered a quiet prayer that it was not. A truck passed, heading south, its brakes squealing as it slowed for the sixty zone of the town Rebecca had just passed through. She opened her eyes and in the light of the coaches' high beam she saw a sign. 'Quirindi Left, 2 Kilometres'. She was well past Murrurundi, past the scene of the accident and within about forty minutes of Tamworth. The lights behind her must have been Willow Tree.

She closed her eyes again and whispered a quiet thanks. When she opened them again, she found the little boy smiling at her from his seat across the aisle, almost as if saying 'It's okay.'

The next forty minutes passed quickly, the storm still raged outside and if anything, the wind had gotten worse. Luckily the hotel she had booked into was near the depot, but she doubted she would be dry by the time she managed to crawl into a bed.

The coach pulled to a stop beside the Train station. The little boy shook his grandmother, "Nanny we're here. Look I can see Poppy's car", the excitement in his voice equal to the relief Rebecca felt as she stood and grabbed her carry bag.

The boy turned to Rebecca as he walked down the aisle "Bye lady" he hesitated a moment, "you talk lots in your sleep you know."

Rebecca felt a wave of embarrassment wash over her, and was sure that she turned bright red.

The boy must have sensed something and said, "It's alright I won't tell."

Rebecca smiled at him and waved "Bye matey."

Outside the rain had slowed, but the wind was howling. The coach driver had on a heavy raincoat and offered a quick 'Goodbye' and 'Goodnight' to the passengers as he passed them their bags from beneath the coach. Half a dozen cars were waiting in the car park and in no time the passengers piled into them, the vehicles came to life, and they headed off, windscreen wipers madly swaying to keep the rain at bay.

Across the road Rebecca could see the Tamworth Hotel. She had picked it because it was close to the station and had no idea what to expect. Now it looked like a safe place out of the wind and rain, and that was all she needed. The driver looked up at her as he handed her the old duffle bag.

"You got someone picking you up."

"In the morning. Just going across the road to the hotel for the night."

"Okay. You keep warm and safe now."

The driver climbed back aboard the coach and watched Rebecca from the step.

"Do you want a hand?" he yelled.

"No, I'll be right. Thanks."

Rebecca pulled a hood from her coat up over her beanie, slung her carry bag on one shoulder and hoisted Grandads old duffle bag onto the other. The traffic was light, and she had no problem crossing the road, ignoring the pedestrian crossing, and running directly across to the hotel. She had planned to get in late and after a quick but loud knock she was let in. Fifteen minutes later she was in a warm room above the hotel. She hung her coat and damp clothes above the old oil heater to air dry and climbed into the bed. This time she did not have to find a way to get herself to sleep. It came quickly and despite the strange surroundings she slept soundly and without a thought of the troubled life she had left behind only hours ago.

CHAPTER FOUR

4

A knock at the door roused Rebecca from her sleep. She looked groggily around the room for a moment before calling out.

"Who is it?"

"It's your wakeup call Miss.", a young male voice, "It's eight AM. If you want some breakfast we're serving until nine."

"Ok thank you."

"No worries. Also, had a phone message for you. Paul rang and said he probably won't make it here until about midday. Problems with the road after that storm last night."

"Ok. Thanks again"

"Don't forget breakfast until nine."

Rebecca heard footsteps head along the hall and down the stairs. She threw off the covers and immediately regretted it. Even though she could see bright sunshine peeking through the curtains, it was still mid-winter and the air felt icily cold. She quickly grabbed a set of clothes for the day, towel and her toiletries bag and headed off to the common shower that was at the end of the hall. Luckily for Rebecca the lady that saw her to her room last night had told her that there was no one else staying in the hotel overnight, so she had the showers to herself.

The water was hot, and steam soon filled the bathroom. The mirror clouded, and Rebecca just stood beneath the water and let the warmth wash over her, losing herself to the sound of running water. She lost track of how long she had been in there when suddenly the water pressure changed, and the temperature dropped.

"Bloody Hell." Rebecca cursed loud enough to be heard and quickly jumped out of the shower, her feet slipping. She grabbed at the clothes she had hung on a wall hook and managed to steady herself, but the clothes fell to the floor and into a puddle of water.

"You have to be kidding."

On the floor lay both sets of clothes. Jeans, shirt, and pyjamas all soaked from water that had sprayed out from under the shower curtain and pooled on the floor. The only thing still hanging on the wall was her towel.

Rebecca dried off and wrapped the luckily large towel around herself as best she could. There was no way she was going to put on wet clothes when the temperature was what felt like five degrees. When she was happy that the towel felt secure around her, she poked her head through the door and checked out the hallway. Her room was three doorways down the hall, and it seemed to her, despite some noise coming from downstairs that nobody was around. Rebecca with key in one hand and her wet clothes in the other, made a dash for her room.

She made it halfway before a head poked up the stairwell, soon followed by a tall young man in a high-visibility vest.

"Sorry miss the showers going to be out for fifteen minutes or so. Trying to fix a leaking pipe in the kitchen, so no hot water at the moment."

"I know, I was in there."

"Oh my god. The kitchen guy told me no one was up here. I am so sorry."

"Umm yeah. I've sort of got to get some clothes on, so don't worry about it."

"Ok sure, sorry didn't mean to stop you. Sorry again."

Rebecca swung the door open and almost fell over her own feet and into the room. She closed the door behind her and dug through her duffle bag to find another set of clothes. After she had gotten dressed and had hung up her other clothes to air, she headed downstairs to catch breakfast.

The plumber was still in the kitchen and gave her a nod and smile. Rebecca was starving and ordered a full breakfast. She had not eaten last night, feeling nervous about the trip ahead.

The lady she had seen when she checked in last night came up as she was ordering.

"I heard about the shower, and I am really sorry. Breakfast is on the house."

"It's really okay, woke me up to tell the truth. Thanks for the breakfast." Rebecca turned to look for a table, "would it be okay if I hung out here till lunchtime, my lift is running late."

"That's fine honey, no one booked into your room until tomorrow. So where did you need a lift too?"

"I'm headed out to Shattered Falls, if Paul ever gets here."

"Ahh, beautiful little place out there. Tourists love it now, gone all crafty and bed and breakfast. Is your Paul from out there?"

"No, God no, he's not my Paul. He's an old friend of my mum and dads, he lives here in Tamworth. Maybe you know him."

The lady gave a little laugh, "Well it's a big town you know, but what's his name?"

Rebecca took a seat, "Paul Caplan."

"Well, that Paul we do know. He's in here several times week. Not good for business though, but he's a good friend to have." A young girl brought out a plate of food and placed it onto the table, "Enjoy your breakfast honey, and enjoy your time at Shattered Falls."

Rebecca finished her breakfast and went back up to her room to pack her bag. The clothes that had gotten wet were still a little damp, so she placed them into a plastic bag before putting them into the duffle bag. When all was packed, and Rebecca was ready, she grabbed her bags and headed back downstairs. It was now just after ten am and Rebecca found the pay phone in the hotel foyer. She should have rung earlier, and she knew Grandma and Grandad would be sitting by the phone waiting for the call, but it was good to have a morning to herself, even if it had been a bit hectic.

The phone only rang twice before it was picked up.

"Hey Ma"

"Becky are you okay. We were worried."

"I'm fine. The trip was long, well it felt long. I got some sleep on the coach and the Hotel is good. Paul is running late, but he should be here about lunchtime. How did you guys go in the storm?" Rebecca tried to get it all out as quick as she could. She knew Ma would ask a seemingly never-ending stream of questions, so best give her all the information upfront.

"The wind got up pretty bad, but everything is fine. Pa thought the shed roof was blowing off, but it was next doors screen door banging crazy. You want to say hi to him, I think he wants too."

"Thanks Ma"

Rebecca heard the phone get passed along.

"Hey my girl. Are you doing good?"

"Yeah Pa, I'm good."

"How was the road?"

Rebecca knew what he meant, the road in the hills north of Murrurundi.

"I slept through it, surprised myself, otherwise I would have been a shocker, but all good."

"Ok, I'll put Ma back on. Call us tonight okay."

"Ok Love you."

The phone changed hands again.

"It's me again Becky. Jake said to say Hi. He was running late for school this morning, blamed you for keeping him up late seeing you off."

"Little ratbag."

"He loves you, you know".

"I know Ma. I miss you all, already."

"Me too. Now you best get sorted before you get me crying. Call tonight. Love you"

"Love you too. Bye Ma."

Rebecca hung up the phone and took a breath. She still could not believe she was a few hours away from stepping out on her own. A home of her own in the country, well almost her own. Jake would own half but still she was about to take control of her life for a change, instead of it controlling her.

She had left her bags behind the bar and let staff know she would be back after a quick walk around. The last thing she wanted to do now was sit in a pub for the next few hours. She grabbed a bottle of water, slung her backpack over her shoulder and headed outside.

Outside the street was busy with mid-morning traffic. Delivery vans, small trucks and four-wheel drive vehicles seemed to outnumber the standard cars. Rebecca looked up and down the street deciding which way to head and spotted the plumber that had arranged her cold shower, loading his van a few cars away. He spotted her, smiled, waved and after putting a bag of tools in the back of his vehicle he wandered to where Rebecca was standing.

"Just wanted to say sorry again about this morning. I should have checked".

"It's really okay."

"So, you from Tamworth or just visiting."

"I'm from down south but moving up this way."

"Well, if you ever need a plumber give me a call." he fished inside his pocket and pulled out a business card.

'***Braye & Son Plumbing Services.***'

"I'm the 'and Son' bit, but seriously if you need help with any plumbing, I'll make sure you don't get ripped off."

"Well, it's always good to have a tradie on your side, but I'll be a bit out of town."

"That's no prob, we do Quirindi, Kootingal, Werris Creek. Even helped out at Gunnedah a few times."

"I'll be at Shattered Falls."

"Well, that's no issue, my aunt lives out there. So just call if you need someone, my names Craig."

"Rebecca. Thanks, Craig. Can you tell me where to get a decent coffee, the one I had in there wasn't crash hot?"

Craig gave a laugh, "Yeah there not renowned for it, about five doors that way should look after you." he pointed down the road, "Anyways I got to get movin', nice meeting you Rebecca".

"Thanks"

He turned and headed back to his van, giving Rebecca a quick smile before he jumped in the car and pulled out into the traffic. She watched him drive off and then turned and made her way to the coffee shop.

The coffee shop was a small bakery but as Craig had said, the coffee was good and the free newspaper that someone had left behind helped kill the next thirty minutes. People wandered in and out and the smell of fresh baked bread and fresh brewed coffee gave the place an old-fashioned feel.

Rebecca finished up a second cup and stood to leave, folding the newspaper, and pushing in her chair. She turned to the counter and offered a smile.

"Thanks for the coffee. If I get back to town, I will be back."

"No probs, you're welcome anytime. See ya again." the girl behind the counter nodded to someone behind Rebecca, "Hey Sergeant Caplan, you after coffee."

The voice that answered was friendly but still gave the impression of authority. "Nothing for me Angie, actually looking for this young lady." he put his hand on Rebecca's shoulder, and she spun around.

"Uncle Paul.", she screamed as she wrapped her arms around him and gave him a hug.

"Steady on girlie, I'm on duty, but it's good to see you too."

Rebecca let him go and stood back to look at him, "Uniform suits you, but you got mud on your pants."

"Yeah, I know, been helping clear roads since five this morning. Trees down everywhere. Sorry about being late."

"That's okay, I know you've got a job to do. I'm ready whenever you are to head out to grandad's place. Just got to get my bags from the hotel."

"I already got them; they told me you headed this way. We'll head out after lunch. Aunty Meg's got a feed waiting for us and I know she has been dying to see you."

Rebecca's smile faded slightly as she thought of Aunty Meg and asked, "How is she?"

"She puts on a brave face, but it hasn't gotten any better. She stays home most days now; pain makes it hard to walk. I hope you don't mind me swearing Bec, but this cancer shit is a real prick, but I know she's going to be smiling all week once she catches up with you."

Rebecca could hear his voice break when he spoke about the disease that had robbed his wife of her breast and still worked its way through her body. She did not want to cry and took a deep breath to centre herself.

"Well dopey, we best not keep her waiting then."

"Dopey? You cheeky bugger. You do know I'm a cop, don't you?"

They both gave a laugh.

"Ok, you best get in the wagon young lady. Dopey's ready to roll."

Rebecca had been in a police car before but not a Landcruiser. The big white vehicle had mud caked along its sides and mud spray right up to the windows. She climbed up into the front passenger seat, noticing her bag in the back seat and wound down the window.

"Yeah, sorry about the smell. The chainsaw leaked a bit of fuel. Anyways, five minutes and you'll be sitting in the kitchen with Aunty Meg. Now buckle up, the cops around here are bastards."

Six minutes later the four-wheel drive police vehicle pulled into a driveway in East Tamworth. Rebecca had been here before but not for many years. The brick and tile house had been a place where she had come for barbecues with her parents, and on sweltering summer days the backyard pool had been a favourite of hers. It seemed different now, darker, less alive.

A small white furry dog came running down the driveway, yapping like an old woman. Paul shook his head.

"Not exactly a coppers dog I know, but Peaches keeps Meg company when I'm away, and she's a good dog. Brave as all hell for her size. She chased a red belly black snake last Christmas, caught it, and broke its neck. Tough girl she is, but a big softie too."

Paul turned off the engine and they both headed inside.

"You need anything from your bags Bec?"

"No, I've got my backpack. All good."

"Ok let's get inside then."

A woman was standing inside the mesh security door, waiting patiently. She called through the door at Rebecca and Paul, who were standing in the driveway petting Peaches, as the dog jumped and barked playfully.

"Hurry up you two, get inside out of the cold air."

Rebecca looked up at the house, she recognised Aunty Meg's voice but heard the tiredness and pain in her as well.

"Coming darl, hope the kettles boiled."

After a click of a latch, the mesh door swung open, and Paul gestured for Rebecca to head inside. As soon as she saw Aunty Meg, she knew that things were not well, but despite her appearance Aunty Meg immediately left Bec with a feeling of love. She wrapped her arms around Meg's frail body and enjoyed that feeling of love, something that only a mother or grandmother could give you.

Meg let go of Rebecca and stepped back. In a quiet, but obviously cheerful voice she spoke.

"God, you look like your mum. Doesn't she Paul? So much like Karen it's almost scary."

"Yeah, I saw it too but...I didn't want to upset you Bec, but if you saw photos of when she was your age...it's uncanny."

Bec smiled at them both, "Don't be silly. It doesn't upset me. I've seen the photos, where do you think I got this hairstyle from. It's so good to see you guys. Now did you say the kettle was boiled?"

Rebecca did not need another cup of tea or coffee, but it was at least a way to shift the conversation away from her mum. Even after all the years it was still a gateway to the depression that had previously engulfed her life.

"How about we skip the cuppa? I knew you wouldn't have chance to eat properly tonight, so I made a roast. I will feel better if I know you have a good meal and your grandma made me promise to look after you." Meg smiled and headed to the kitchen.

"Let's eat girlie, then we'll head out before it's too late."

"Ok, but don't you have to get back to work."

"Got the rest of the day off. It's good to be the boss. Now c'mon before Megsie gets stroppy."

A home cooked meal with people Rebecca loved just like real family was just what she needed. The food was good, the conversation better. It was good to catch up and laugh about some of Uncle Paul's escapades with her dad when they were young. They had been schoolmates and best friends since before any of the women in their lives had come along, and even though it brought back painful memories, Uncle Paul kept her laughing.

"My god, how the hell did you manage to become a cop?"

"Well, me and your dad managed to never get caught, and even though we got up to no good it was never anything really bad, and when we found our loves, your mum and Megsie, we got settled pretty quick."

Rebecca went quiet and took a deep breath.

"Hey girlie we all miss them; just don't forget you are not alone."

"For once he's right Bec. You are not alone. Now who's for dessert? Apple pie?"

Even though she was full, Rebecca managed to eat two pieces of the home-made pie and after a few more laughs and a friendly argument over rugby league teams it quickly became mid-afternoon.

Paul stood up, "We're going to have to get moving. I want to get you settled in before sundown. You ready to go?"

Rebecca sighed, as comfortable as she was, she did want to get out to her new home and take it all in.

"Yeah, guess we best do it." She stood and walked over to Meg, "thanks for the feed, Aunty Meg. Thanks for everything."

"Don't need to thank me. Just don't be a stranger, visit when you can. It's only a half hour away."

"Love you Aunty Meg."

After a hug and a foil wrapped plate of leftovers was handed over, Paul and Rebecca bundled themselves back into the Landcruiser. It was just after two o'clock and it was at least a half hour drive to Shattered Falls. Dusk came early at this time of year and the nights were cold, so Paul wanted to get Rebecca there as soon as possible.

CHAPTER FIVE

5

The road to Shattered Falls headed east into the foothills of the Great Dividing Range. Winding its way up and down hills until it finally came to the river. From here the road hugged the upper banks of the Shard River, crossing it twice on old wooden bridges that remarkably had survived floods better than new bridges further downstream.

The land opened at one point at a place known as Ballroom Flat, an old mustering point for cattle and then the river valley closed in again, forcing the road to follow higher up close to the ridge top until it suddenly dropped off the ridge and followed the river again. Several roads headed off east back into the state forest and up the mountains to the national park. It would be quiet up there this time of year, unless it snowed, then everyone for hundreds of kilometres around would flock in for the weekend, just to see snow. It got busy up there in school holidays too, and there were always a few diehard fossickers after sapphires, or gold or whatever else they could dig out of the ancient volcanic mountains.

Rebecca could see the old willows along the river and knew that the town was around the next bend. They crossed a small creek, and they were there. The general store and petrol station on the left and the caravan park to the right, along the wide bank of the river. Further up was a crossroads with the pub sitting on one corner, the main road headed back west to the highway and the other roads led to Shattered Falls back streets.

They kept driving straight, past the old bank that now had a 'For Sale 'sign on its front window and past the public swimming pool that only opened in late spring and closed in early autumn.

At the next left turn, they headed off toward the mountains again and it was only a kilometre further on that they came to another turn off. This one marked by a sign. 'ords Timber Mill and Joinery'. The sign was old, and the F had worn off, but it still made Rebecca smile. This was her pops mill and another hundred metres down the road was his old house. Her new house.

The trip had been relatively quiet. A few comments about changes to the landscape and who lived where, but mostly quiet. The police radio had crackled to life a few times, but Paul turned it down low. He was off duty. Most of the trip Rebecca had just stared out the window and Paul had concentrated on the road, occasionally looking over to Bec to see if she was awake.

When he spoke suddenly, Rebecca jumped in her seat.

"Well, this is it Miss.... Sorry didn't mean to scare you Bec, but we're here."

The Landcruiser turned into the rutted driveway that lay in the narrow gap in the old wire fence and pulled to a halt in front of the old shed that had served as a garage.

Rebecca sat quiet for a moment, surveying the house. A small set of cracked concrete steps led up to a wide veranda that Rebecca knew circled most of the house. The front wire screen door was tattered and did little to keep the bugs out of the house, and behind it was the old white door, its top half a frosted glass panel with a white paint stain in one corner. The doorbell was one you had to twist and from Rebecca's experience it rarely worked.

She hadn't even realised Paul had already gotten out of the car until he opened her door.

"C'mon let's get inside and get a fire going. It's gonna be cold tonight. I'll grab your bag. You take this."

Paul reached out a closed fist to her and Rebecca put out her hand. He opened his hand and dropped a long key into her palm.

"Welcome home."

Rebecca's hand was trembling as she slipped the key into the front door. At first, it seemed to fail to catch, but she turned it back the opposite direction and heard the tell-tale click. She turned the handle and pushed the door open. It smelt musty but not in a bad way. The smells instantly brought images of her pop to her mind.

Paul was behind her with her bags.

"Yeah, smells a bit musty, but it's been mostly locked up for a while now. I came in yesterday and made sure you had all the essentials. Bread, milk, some fruit and veggies, a pantry full of stuff and some meat in the freezer. Your Gran and Meg gave explicit instructions." Paul raised his eyebrows, "Now your neighbours are good people. Karl and his wife Alexa are straight across the road, Mrs. Lewis is about five hundred metres back down the road we came in on, and through the week the mill will be open, and you know Nashy, any issues and he'll send one of the boys to fix anything."

Rebecca tried to take it all in but felt just a bit overwhelmed. It must have shown on her face and Paul put his arm on her shoulder.

"It's okay girlie. I wrote down everything you need to know and stuck it on the fridge. You check out the house while I put the kettle on and get the fire going."

Rebecca looked at Paul. "Thank you, Uncle Paul. I'll be okay. White with two for me."

"White with two it is. Your bags are in the bedroom, the big one. There isn't a bed in the spare anymore, your pop gave it to Nashy for some of the drifters he's got working at the mill. So, I hope you don't have a problem sleeping in your Nan and Pop's old bed."

"It'll be a bit weird, but I remember how comfortable it is. I remember Pop made it. Me and Jake used to build forts under it. We could almost sit upright under it, so I got no idea how he got into it when he got older."

"Think he spent a lot of nights in the recliner in front of the fire."

"Yep," she smiled, "that sounds like pop. Okay I'll go reacquaint myself with it all."

She headed down the hall from the kitchen to the bathroom, which stood at the back of the house. She remembered when the toilet had been outside, which had made those cold nights all that much more memorable, but Pop had had it installed inside years ago when Nan's hips had started to give her trouble. It sat in the corner of the bathroom where once there had been a water heater. There was an old free-standing bathtub, a pale green sink, spider webbed with cracks, and a big mirror. Rebecca just knew that behind that mirror would be Pops big shaving brush, the soap he frothed up to shave and the cutthroat razor that Jake had nearly cut his finger off with. There was a grey shower hose that connected to the bath tap hanging over the baths side.

'Exactly as I remember it.' She thought to herself.

The laundry was still outside, a fibro shell around a concrete slab, with an old Whirlpool. Older than Rebecca.

Across the hall from the bathroom was a spacious room that Rebecca knew was full of all the 'treasures' Pop had collected over the years. Stuff he had dug up, things he had found on his aimless walks and every card, drawing and collectable piece of his life that his wife, son, daughter in law and grandkids had ever given him.

Further up the hall were the two bedrooms, on opposite sides of the hall. The main bedroom with its gigantic bed and across from that what had been her dad's room, then hers, and eventually hers and jakes when they slept over. For the past fourteen years it had been just another empty room, a stack of old newspapers, a wardrobe and dresser.

At the front of the house was the kitchen and living room. Paul was still in the kitchen, stirring the cup of tea like he was ringing a bell.

"Sit down in the front room Bec, I'll bring the cuppas out and get that fire started."

The slow combustion fireplace took up an entire wall of the front room. A worn but comfortable looking brown faux leather lounge sat opposite the fireplace; a coffee table still covered with Nan's slightly stained, crocheted doilies between them. In the corner Pops recliner looked like it was waiting for him. Rebecca could imagine him sitting in it, snoring but ready to jump up at the slightest noise.

"White with two for you girlie."

"Thanks Uncle Paul."

Rebecca took a seat on the lounge and took the cup of tea from Paul. They both sat their cups on the doilies and Paul went to work on the fire.

It took him about ten minutes, two trips outside to find dry wood and half dozen swear words but the fire kicked in and the room flickered with the cosy glow of the flames.

"Ok, now I best get that cuppa into me and get heading. I got to get home and have a feed and a nap before I sign on for the night shift."

"Uncle Paul, you should have said something. I could have got a lift out here."

"Don't be silly. I wouldn't feel right," he gave her a long look. "Speaking of which, how are you feeling. You going to be alright."

"Yeah." Rebecca's face changed to a big smile and for a moment Paul just stared. "You know what, for the first time in a long time I think I am going to be alright."

"Ka...," Paul stopped himself "Bec I really got to get moving. The phones working, and all the numbers are on the fridge. Check in with your Grandma and Grandad. I'll drop back in on Saturday, see how you're doing."

They both stood, and Rebecca gave Paul a hug.

"Thanks for everything."

"No problem girlie. See you Saturday."

Rebecca stood at the front door and watched as the Landcruiser reversed out the driveway and disappeared up the road. The sun was low in the sky, and she could feel the chill of the coming night. She stepped back inside, locked the door, looked around, listened to the silence, and screamed. Not from fear, just from relief. Finally, things were going her way.

The afternoon quickly turned to dusk and the darkness that was rural New South Wales soon enveloped the house. Rebecca hardly noticed as she busied herself unpacking, getting herself some dinner, phoning Ma and Pa and soaking herself in a hot bath.

It was about 9.30 when she finally stopped and stood at the back door with a hot cup of coffee in her hands and looked out into the darkness. She breathed in the chilly air and exhaled, laughing as she remembered how she and Jake had played at making 'smoke' come out their mouths in the near freezing air.

For fifteen minutes she stood there, clad only in a loose tank top and a pair of Bugs Bunny boxers, revelling in the cold that bit at her bare skin. A loud crash turned her attention to the garage and adjoining shed. She couldn't see what it was, but she was sure one of the many possums must have jumped from a nearby tree and scampered off across the tin roof. The bush and hills that lay toward the back of the property would have a fair population of them.

She looked up the hill and into the darkness. A flash of light caught her eye, a quick red flash. There were plenty of tracks up there, so more than likely someone out hunting rabbits or something similar. Headlights shone her way for a moment, and then she heard the tell-tale roar of a four-wheel drive heading off further into the night.

'Time to call it a night' she said quietly to herself and headed back inside.

CHAPTER SIX

6

On a forestry trail about a kilometre up the hill he sat in the car and stared at what had been an abandoned house for most of the year, but now there was a girl standing at the back door. He could see her face clearly through the old binoculars. Cup of coffee in hand, short shorts, and a tiny top. He gasped and accidentally put his foot down on the brake. He swore to himself, imagining how easy it would have been for her to see the flash from the brake light. Now lifting the binoculars back to his eyes, he took one long last look at her face. It couldn't be true.

"Holy Shit."

He started up the car and headed off into the night.

7

Friday morning came with a heavy fog and temperatures just above freezing. The fire that Uncle Paul had lit for her had kept the house cosily warm all night but now just a few embers and a glowing half log remained. Something had woken her, a truck maybe, but as soon Rebecca had opened her eyes, she felt wide awake. She swung her feet over the side of the bed and let them dangle there, feeling for the floor, but she had to slide further to the bed edge before they finally reached. As soon as they touched the old floorboards, she drew them back.

"Whoa, that is icy." Rebecca made a mental note to invest in some slippers and maybe some rugs.

Light was filtering in through the torn blind that had hung in the bedroom window for the past fifteen years. Grandma's homemade curtains hung there as well but Rebecca had not thought to draw them over the night before.

The sound of another truck rumbling along the unsealed road finally encouraged Rebecca to climb out of bed. She stepped to the window and peeked through one of the larger tears in the stained grey blind. Outside she saw the flash of a taillight in the thick fog. Rebecca knew it was probably a logging truck heading off to the state forest and that it would rumble back, fully laden later in the day. She fumbled through the duffel bag that she had yet to unpack and found her track pants and a hooded jumper, quickly pulling them on and following with a thick pair of socks she had borrowed from Grandad.

She had never been one for breakfast, but coffee was a must. Rebecca wrapped her arms around herself as she wandered down the hall to the kitchen. She took a deep breath of the chill morning air and noticed immediately that it smelt somehow different to her memory. Mornings here had always smelt of hair cream and black tea, but with Pop gone those smells would never return.

The kettle seemed to be taking forever to boil and Uncle Paul had only bought her some cheap coffee, but she needed a caffeine hit to start her morning. While she waited for the old kettle to break the morning silence with its piercing whistle, Rebecca walked to the back door and swung it open. The freezing air rushed inside, shaking away whatever sleep from her eyes that still hung there. The fog was still thick, but she could see the trees in the back yard and small patches of light blue sky above. Once the fog cleared, she knew it would be a bright and sunny day.

Looking at the old wooden veranda, covered in a film of water from the morning mist she noticed small animal footprints.

'Possums', she thought, 'Cheeky buggers but damn I must have slept. I didn't hear a thing.'

Rebecca was about to turn back and head to the kitchen when she noticed something else. Another footprint but larger and not some wild animal. It was a print of a work boot. She stared at it for a moment, trying to figure it out. Her mind racing at possibilities but arriving at only one conclusion. Someone had been prowling around the house while she slept. She felt her heartbeat quicken and almost fell over as the kettle suddenly let loose with its scream.

"Shit", she muttered through deep breaths and then stepped out onto the weathered old boards of the veranda to have a closer look.

It was a single boot print, right beside the concrete blocks that made up the steps down to the backyard. Beside it more prints from the possums and now drips of water from the eaves. She thought it strange that there was only one footprint and stepped onto the first step to look for any others that might be on the old cement path but stopped and took a mammoth sigh of relief when she saw and finally understood what had happened.

One of Pops old boots lay on the grass directly below the footprint. One of the possums must have knocked it during the night, leaving the mark that had given her a bigger fright than she needed. Rebecca looked out into the backyard to the trees that were becoming more visible through the fog, before shaking her head and muttering.

"Little bastards."

She now needed that coffee more than ever and the kettle was still screaming. As she headed back inside, she turned one more time to the back yard and yelled.

"Game on Possums. Game on."

Suddenly something crashed heavily against the shed right at the back of the yard and as Rebecca watched, a figure, clad in heavy, dark clothes and a grey beanie ran from the shed and disappeared into the fog.

8

She drew in a deep breath, frozen in place, staring at the backyard, listening to the kettle scream, wanting to join in with it. After a few moments she realised she had stopped breathing and gasped in a lungful of the chill morning air. The icy air clawed at her throat, and she gave a chesty cough as she staggered back inside.

'Call Uncle Paul', was all she could think.

Her fingers tingled and seemed not to be able to do what she wanted them too. She clenched her fist three times and grabbed the handset that hung on the kitchen wall. Slowly she punched in the numbers that had been written in black marker on the notice board stuck to the front of the fridge. It rang three times before it was answered.

"Sergeant Caplan."

"Uncle Paul, Uncle Paul. There's someone in the backyard. Someone creeping around the house."

"Whoa Rebecca. Slow down. I can hardly hear you. What's that noise? Is someone screaming?"

"Oh shit. It's the kettle. I'm sorry."

Rebecca stepped back and pulled the kettle cord from the wall. Almost knocking the boiling water onto the floor.

"Ok that's better. Now what the hell's going on there?"

"There's someone in the backyard. I saw them."

"Ok listen up. I want you to lock the door, sit and have that coffee it sounds like you're making. I'm an hour away, but I'll ring Nashy and get him over there straight up. Okay."

"I'm sorry. I sound like a scared little girl."

"It's okay. Now I'm going to hang up and ring Nashy. You go lock that door."

"Ok. Thank you, Uncle Paul."

"I'll be there as soon as I can."

The phone line closed off and Rebecca hung it back up, before heading to the back door and locking it. She checked the lock twice, pulled on the handle and rattled the lock again. When she was confident it was secure, she crept back into the kitchen and made the long over-due coffee. Grabbing the steaming mug, she wandered back down the hallway and sat with her back against the now locked door. She lifted the mug to her mouth and took a quick sip, inhaling the coffee infused steam, and closing her eyes to help settle herself.

She took another longer sip of the coffee, feeling the burn on her lips and spat it out as something slammed heavily against the front of the house. A banging, repeated banging and then a yell.

"You in there Rebecca? Rebecca it's Cameron Nash. Nashy. Paul rang me said you needed help. Rebecca?"

She pushed herself up from the cold floor, realising she was clench-ing the hot coffee mug in her hand and not even noticing that it was scalding her palm. As she hurried back down the hall, she almost slipped on the spilled coffee, but caught herself with one hand on the wall.

"Shit.", she murmured to herself before yelling out toward the front of the house, "Coming. Sorry Nashy. I'm coming."

Rebecca almost threw the coffee mug into the kitchen sink before making her way to the front door. Opening it she felt a wave of relief as she saw the familiar face of Nashy. His pudgy, stubble covered face was red and his breathing in short gasps.

"Shit girl. What's going on? You okay? I feel like I just ran a marathon getting over here. The way Paul was going on I thought you was being murdered."

Rebecca almost felt guilty for all the fuss. Behind Nashy stood two other men.

"There was someone in the backyard. Down behind the shed. I'm sorry. I just got scared."

Nashy turned to the two men behind him.

"You two go check it out. Be careful." The two men began walking down the side of the house, one of them stopping and picking up a sizable stick that had fallen from one of the old gums, "Good idea Matthew, you see anyone, hit first, ask questions later."

With a grunt the two men disappeared.

"Now you, young lady are going to make me a hot cuppa and tell me what's going on, before I have a heart attack, and don't tell your Uncle I said to hit first."

"Thank you Nashy. I know I probably overreacted but…"

"Don't be daft, but you sure know how to settle into town don't ya."

Rebecca gave a quick laugh, feeling stupider by the second.

"Ok. Come and get your cuppa."

Rebecca held the door open for Nashy, and he made his way to the kitchen. He had been in the house a hundred times and knew his way around better than Rebecca.

"Tell you what girlie. You sit down, and I'll make it. You'd probably make me coffee anyways. I drink tea. You want one?"

"Yeah, but I really need a coffee."

"I can do that. Let me guess. White with two?"

"Yep."

"Ok now what the…. what happened?"

Rebecca told Nashy about the morning, with Nashy adding his 'yeps' and grunts as she did. She watched him as he made the tea and coffee and noticed that he had put on a lot of weight since she had last seen him. His legs were short and clad in what Rebecca assumed was an old set of overalls. A dark green, woollen jumper full of holes was stretched over his chest, looking like it would break at the seams any moment.

He finally turned and placed two steaming cups on the table.

"There you go missy. Well, whatever is out here Matthew and Karl will sort it out." He looked at the expression on Rebecca's face, his eyes screwing up. "What are you looking at?"

"Your jumper looks a bit small."

"Hmmpphh. Okay, okay I put a bit of weight on. I used to be a ball of muscle you know, but since I been running the joint, I don't get out as much. It's all office and books and phone calls."

"Sorry Nashy. Sorry about everything."

"No problem. You settling in okay, apart from the strange happenings in the backyard?"

Before Rebecca could answer, another knock came, and the front door swung open. It was one of Nashy's men, the one he had called Matthew.

"No one out there now Miss, but there's a loose panel of tin on the back of the shed. Looks like someone's been sleeping in there."

Rebecca smiled at Matthew, noticing now just how blue his eyes were.

"It's Rebecca, and thanks for coming over."

"Uh, yeah Matthew. Nice to meet you."

"Ok you two enough with the flirting. Matthew, you, and Karl get back. That saw on number two needs replacing before the first truck gets back. I'm going to stay right here till Paul turns up."

"I wasn't flir...Ok sorry miss...sorry Rebecca."

"Back to work, number two saw. I'll be there in an hour or so."

Matthew wandered back towards the door, nodding to Rebecca as he went. Rebecca heard the door close and turned to Nashy.

"He seems nice."

"You're his boss missy, one of them anyways. Don't go getting involved with the staff. Distracts 'em."

"Ok... for now anyways. He said someone's been sleeping in the shed...what the hell is going on? Who's sleeping in the shed?"

"Actually, I got an idea who. If I'm right, then you got nothing to worry about, but we'll wait till Paul gets here before we check it out."

"What? Who?"

"Wait for Paul, but right now tell me what you been up too. How's Jake and your Grandma and Grandad going?"

"Nashy. This is my place now, mine and Jakes, and I want to know what's going on."

"For chrissakes girl, Paul will sort it out. Just be patient. Now drink your cuppa and wait for him to get here. You're as stubborn as your Pop."

Rebecca looked Nashy in the eye, rolled her eyes and drank the coffee. After a few minutes of heavy silence, she finally gave in and broke the mood.

"Grandad and Grandma are doing fine. Getting older, but they look after themselves. Grandad still swims laps in the pool every day, winter or summer."

"He's a mad old bastard...No disrespect, but cold is cold."

"Jake, well he's seventeen now, finding every opportunity he can to get into trouble. Nothing serious though. Wagging school, sneaking out at night, but he's doing good at school... when he goes, and he's good with engines. I reckon he'll be a mechanic or an engineer when he's finished school."

"Always jobs for good mechanics."

Rebecca sat her empty coffee mug on the table.

"Nashy, you don't have to wait with me. I won't go out there, I promise. I'm just going to have a shower and wait for Uncle Paul."

"You have your shower, but I'll be waiting right here till Paul gets here." Nashy proclaimed as he pushed his finger onto the table in a way that Rebecca knew was serious.

"Okay, okay. I'm showering."

She stood, turned into the hallway and headed to the bedroom. Rebecca pulled a toiletries bag from the duffel and wandered to the bathroom.

The tap squealed as she spun it on, and she had to wait almost a full minute for the water to turn hot. After another minute of adjusting the temperature by playing with both taps, she finally found just the right mix and climbed into the bathtub and held the cracked, grey shower hose above her head.

'Well that's almost like cracking a safe.' she thought as she avoided bumping the carefully adjusted taps.

The water was hot, and the warmth quickly steamed up the room. She washed and as she rinsed her hair, she found that a hook had been screwed to the wall just above head height. Rebecca smiled as realised what her Pop had done. A clip on the shower hose fit snugly onto the hook, and the stream of water from the showerhead now flowed onto her without her having to hold it. She stood in the water, feeling the heat soak into the muscles of her shoulders, helping loosen the tightness from the stress of the morning. Finally, she turned the taps off and climbed out of the bathtub onto the wet floor, her feet feeling the chill of the water that had splashed across the tiles.

"Ok, add a shower curtain to the shopping list I guess."

The towels hanging on the rail were soft to the touch, and Rebecca wrapped one around her as she wiped the mirror with the back of her hand. She took a moment to stare at herself, contemplating the morning's events and it was then, while staring into her own eyes that she realised that despite everything that had happened, her anxiety had not surfaced. She gave herself a smile and finished towelling herself off, pulled on the clothes that she had hung on the back of the door and did her best to dry her hair with the now clammy towel.

Rebecca wandered back down the hall but Nashy was nowhere to be found. He had turned on the radio and some talk back host was rattling on about live cattle exports and then erratically shifting the discussion to 'Ice' and a B and S ball on at Gunnedah next weekend. She turned it down, half tempted to turn it off and listened. The hacking cough led her out the front door, where she found Nashy sitting with a cigarette hanging from his lip.

"Nashy, you need to give those things up."

"I have, or at least that's what the missus thinks." He winked at her. "Just between me and you okay."

Rebecca looked down her nose at him in her best schoolteacher gaze.

"Ok but think about quitting."

"Yeah I know. Not as easy as that though. Just part of my daily ritual for so long, I wouldn't know what else to do...Anyways, got a message from Paul, he'll be here in about five minutes. Must have driven like a mad bastard."

No sooner had Nashy taken another long draw on the cigarette, then the mud smeared four by four came barrelling along the road, skidding to a stop in front of the house. Paul wasted no time jumping out of the car and barging through the front gate. He was obviously concerned. The look on his face could almost have been mistaken for anger, but when he spoke both Nashy and Rebecca knew it was his work face.

"Ok Nashy. What the hell's going on?"

Nashy knew Paul well and did not take the tone personally, but Rebecca just stood and watched the two exchange words.

"Someone's been sleeping in the back shed. Rebecca must have caught them leaving and scared herself silly."

"Who?"

"Could be one of the boys that come down from Queensland for work. We didn't have beds for 'em and I thought they were staying at the pub."

"Seriously Nashy. They can't be breaking into property. Let's go check out the shed."

Paul stopped and finally looked at Rebecca, his face changing from work to Uncle.

"Sorry Bec. I should have asked how you were."

He stepped up onto the veranda and wrapped his arms around her, hugging her protectively.

"I'm fine. I was stupid. Overreacted and now everyone has had to go out of their way to look after me."

"It's okay Bec. It's okay."

Rebecca had to push with her shoulders to encourage Paul to release the hug.

"Sorry Bec. You had me worried. Now let's check that shed and I'll be having a chat with whoever got this shit all stirred up."

"I don't want anyone getting in trouble. Not for just needing somewhere to sleep. Don't arrest them."

"That'll depend on any damage they've done. C'mon. Get the keys from on top of the fridge, and we'll see what's what."

"Ok. Let me get some shoes on. I'll meet you there."

Rebecca hurried back inside, grabbing at the key ring loaded with keys on top of the fridge before she headed back down the hall. She noticed that there were still dots of coffee on the hall floor and quickly grabbed the wet towel from the bathroom and gave it a quick wipe across the old floorboards. She left the towel on the floor, scrunched up in a pile and went back to the bedroom and pulled on her runners.

By the time she made her way back out the front door, down the side of the house and across the backyard, which she noticed needed to be mown, Paul and Nashy were squatting at the back of the shed. Paul was holding up the loose sheet of corrugated tin, like he was turning a page on a magazine, and both were staring into the darkness of the shed.

Rebecca jangled the keys to get their attention, and they stopped mid-sentence and turned to her.

"About time young lady." Paul called to her as he stood and held out his hand.

Rebecca tossed the keys toward him, just as Nashy decided to stand up. The bunch of keys hit Nashy in the side of the head, and he fell back on to his backside. Swearing as he fell.

"Shit girl. What the...Bloody hell."

"Sorry, Sorry."

Nashy climbed back to his feet, and was about to scold Rebecca, when Paul gave him a look that made him go quiet.

Paul bent down, grabbed the keys from the damp grass and walked toward the front of the shed. There was an old wooden door on the side of the shed, painted a faded and patchy red with bits of plywood peeling away from its base. Paul found the correct key amongst the pile and cracked the door open just enough to peer inside with one eye.

"You two wait here till I call you. Understand?"

They both nodded, and Paul opened the door wide and stepped inside. Rebecca watched the darkened frame turn from pitch black to white as Paul found the light switch and flicked it. A minute later he called out.

"Righto. It's all clear."

Rebecca stepped inside first and Nashy followed, still dusting dirt and grass from his pants, and muttering under his breath. The shed was just over two car lengths long. A pair of swinging doors were bolted together by a heavy chain, the curved shank hanging loosely from two of the chain links. The swinging garage doors Rebecca knew opened back into the yard she had just come from. In front of her, covered in an old and dusty calico sheet was the car Pop had had since he was twenty-five. It was known as 'The Beast' to Jake and Rebecca, and she knew that underneath that protective cover it still shone just like it had when he had first bought it. It was Jakes now. As much as she admired it, she knew Jake had fallen under its spell from the first day he had sat behind the wheel with Pop many years ago.

Further down toward the back of the shed, the walls and some of the empty space in the centre of the shed were filled with shelving, and in turn the shelves were crowded with boxes. Cardboard boxes, plastic tubs, old milk crates. Spaces between the boxes were peppered with glass jars and piles of yellowed paper. Pop had been a hoarder but in a good way, not like the hoarders of rubbish Rebecca had seen pop up on current affairs shows recently. She knew that everything in those piles of paper, glass jars and boxes was part of her, and her family's history.

She saw movement from beyond the shelves and Paul stuck his head into one of the few gaps on the shelves.

"Down here you two."

Rebecca and Nashy followed the voice and found Paul standing over a sleeping bag and lantern, laid out near the back wall of the shed. One of the shelves had been pulled away from the rear wall at an angle, with an old sheet of wood standing between it and the loose sheet of tin that was the back wall of the shed.

"This is where he's been sleeping. Even got a little gas stove there." Paul pointed to a small gas bottle under the shelf. "Any idea who it might be Nashy?"

"Yeah. There's a couple of young blokes down from Queensland. Didn't have room for them at the mill. I thought they had found rooms at the pub."

"Well at least one of them has been here, and Queensland sounds about right."

Paul had bent to check the sleeping bag and held up an old jumper. The image on the breast 'Chinchilla Bulldogs RLFC'.

Nashy took one look at it and grunted.

"Bloody Sedgewick. He fed me a story about staying at the pub." He shook his head. "He's a good kid though. Don't think he meant any harm. Just struggling for a quid. Go easy on him."

"Well Bec. It's up to you. It is trespass and you're well within your rights to have him charged."

Rebecca looked at Paul wide-eyed.

"I don't think he's done any damage and like Nashy said, he just needed somewhere to sleep. So…. it's okay, but he can't stay here."

Paul looked Rebecca in the eye, "Fair enough. I'll talk to him and warn him off. I'll tell him to come get his stuff, nail that shed wall up and come apologise to you."

"Okay. I don't want everyone to start thinking I'm a troublemaker."

"Righto then. You, young lady go put the kettle on. Nashy you introduce me to this Sedgewick character."

"His names Tate. He's a good kid Paul."

"Well let's just make sure he stays that way. I'll be back in twenty minutes for that cuppa Bec."

9

Exactly twenty minutes later Paul walked back in the front door and straight into the kitchen. He pulled out the old padded chair from under the kitchen table and collapsed into it. Rebecca slid the cup of tea over to him and sat in the chair opposite.

"Well young lady, that guy won't be giving you any more trouble. Scared the crap out of him I did. He'll be over with another guy soon to repair the shed and collect his gear."

"You didn't need to scare him; just tell him he can't stay there."

"He's just a kid. Couldn't be older than nineteen. He'd get scared if you looked at him sideways."

"Bit young to be out on his own, isn't he?"

"Said he had to leave home. Dad kicked him out. I'll run a check on him to make sure, but he won't be a problem."

Paul took a long drink of the tea and a deep breath.

"You okay Uncle Paul."

"Long night."

"Work?"

"Nah. Meg had a bad night."

"Oh my god. Is she okay?"

"Let's just say she's not getting any worse."

Rebecca was lost for words. She could see the tiredness in his eyes and the slouch of his shoulders, and to some extent sense it in his spirit. She stood up, walked behind him, and put her palm on his shoulder, gently squeezing.

"I'm sorry for making you deal with my crap this morning. I know you have better things to do.", Rebecca apologised.

"It's okay Bec, and honestly I haven't seen Meg so happy in a long time, even if she is sick. Catching up with you yesterday has done her the world of good."

Rebecca gave a little smile, "I'll ring her later."

"She'd like that, just don't worry her with what happened here. She worries enough about you already…. and now young lady I have to get moving." Paul stood, pushing the chair back as he did, its legs screeching as they slid across the linoleum floor.

Rebecca walked out to the front of the house and waved goodbye to Paul, watching as the Landcruiser threw up dust and disappeared down the road. She was still staring down the road, watching the mist burn off when she heard someone cough behind her.

"Rebecca. This is Tate Sedgewick.", Nashy stood in the front yard casually pointing at one of the two men standing beside him. Tate looked young, even for the nineteen years of age that Nashy had mentioned. His gaze was centred on his feet, which he was nervously kicking at the edge of the concrete block that made up part of the front path. Rebecca studied his face and could just see the beads of sweat on his top lip, hidden within the downy whiskers of a teenager's first attempt at a moustache, or what Grandad called 'Bum Fluff'.

"Tate. You got something to say to Miss Ford."

Tate lifted his face but couldn't meet Rebecca's eyes. "Sorry Miss." The words came out muted, barely louder than a whisper.

The other man spoke. "C'mon Tatey. You can do better than that. Look the lady in the eye and speak up like a man."

Rebecca looked at the new voice and was immediately caught in the shining blue eyes and felt a smile creep across her face. The man was older than Tate, maybe a year or two older than herself and despite the cool of the morning wore a sleeveless blue work shirt. Rebecca knew she was staring, and it was only a yell from Nashy that stopped her.

"TATE. For chrissakes apologise properly and get the shed fixed." Nashy turned back to Rebecca and spoke in a quieter voice. "Rebecca this is Matthew, the other one from Queensland. You met him this morning. He'll make sure Tate gets the shed fixed" and then he raised his voice again, directing it at the two men "...and then the two of you can get back to bloody work."

Nashy turned and started back down the road to the mill, cursing under his breath as he pulled a cigarette from his pocket and lit up.

Tate tried again, his voice now louder and a touch more genuine. "I'm sorry for all the trouble Miss Ford. Really sorry, and thanks for not making the cops charge me."

"It's okay really. You just scared me to death."

"He won't be doing anything like that again. He'll be sharing a van with me down at the caravan park, and I'll make sure he doesn't." Matthew seemed to have taken a big brother role for Tate and Rebecca couldn't help but admire his attitude.

"Ok we best get to work Tate. We'll let you know when it's done Miss Ford."

"Thanks Matthew, but it's Rebecca."

"No worries."

The two headed down the side of the house and Rebecca noticed the tool belt hung over Tate's shoulder.

Matthew turned back to her before they disappeared into the back yard and looked at her, "and by the way Rebecca.... it's Matt."

Rebecca went back inside and set about tidying up the kitchen, then found a mop and bucket to wash the hallway floor. When she had finished, she took a seat in the kitchen and grabbed the phone. She was about to ring Aunty Meg when there was another knock on the door.

Outside she found Matt waiting on the veranda, with Tate standing at the fence line still looking like a scolded child.

"Sheds all fixed Rebecca. We put the big shelf back up against the wall too, and Tates got all his belongings, so no more need to worry. Any other problems, just let Nashy know and one of us will come over."

"Thanks, so much Matt. I know it had nothing to do with you. Tate is lucky to have a good friend like you."

"Not really a friend. Hardly know the guy, but us Queenslanders got to stick together." Matt went quiet for a moment, just giving Rebecca a smile, almost as if he was studying her. "Anyways, we got to get back before Nashy goes off his head."

"Ok, thanks again Matt."

Rebecca watched as Matt and Tate both turned and began to head back toward the mill. Rebecca felt an urge to yell after them and hesitated a moment.

"Matt." The two men stopped and turned, looking at Rebecca.

"Where can a girl get a decent feed on a Friday Night?"

Matt's face was suddenly lit up by a huge grin.

"Well Friday nights I usually have a sit down at the pub. Not a five-star establishment but it beats the sausages and beans I cook up in the van the rest of the week. You're welcome to join me if you want, as long as you don't mind Tate tagging along."

Rebecca almost said 'No thanks' straight away but the smile on Matt's face was infectious, and she felt herself smiling as well.

"Ok."

"See you there at seven then."

Matt turned around again walking over to Tate, who punched him in the shoulder and spoke through quiet laughter. "Seriously. You got a date?"

Matt slapped Tate in the back of the head and the two of them headed once again back to the mill.

Rebecca stood on the veranda watching them for a moment and jumped ever so slightly when the phone rang inside the house.

"Non-stop action here, isn't it?" She mumbled to herself.

A deep voice on the other end of the phone blurted out a line before she could even say hello.

"Have you checked the children?"

"What?"

The line crackled with a sound like radio static before a different toned voice spoke.

"Ma'am we've traced the call. It's coming from inside the house."

"Jake, you little asshole."

"Hey sis. Whatcha doin'?"

"Why aren't you at school? Does Gran know you're at home?"

"Whoa...what are you? A Narc. She knows Becsta. I'm home sick ...or hurt."

"What have you done now dimwit?"

"Skateboard accident. Tree ran out in front of me. Twisted me ankle, scraped some bark off, but the girls dig scars you know. Gives me the 'gangsta' look."

"You are such a dufus."

"Yeah I know...but just wanted to chat and there's something you need to know."

"Really?" Rebecca rolled her eyes.

"Serious for a tick sis. Okay. I was talking to Renee at Woolies." Renee was an old school friend of Rebecca's.

"And?"

"She was talking to one of Zak's mates." Rebecca felt herself draw a deep breath. Zak was her old boyfriend, the one that had gotten involved in drugs and run out on her when she had gotten pregnant.

"Yep, that crazy piece of shit. He knows Bec.... He knows where you are."

The remainder of the call continued with Rebecca ignoring any further mention of Zak. Jake must have sensed the apprehension in her voice and avoided bringing it up again. Instead he had what seemed like a million questions about the house, the mill and one other thing. Excited as he was about owning half of the house and property, and part of the mill, he only wanted to know about the one thing that Pop had specifically given to him in the will.

"So...Bec...Did you check it out? The car...My car."

"I went to the shed with Uncle Paul." Rebecca was careful not to mention anything about why she had gone there in the first place.

"Is it okay?"

"I didn't take the cover off, but I'm sure it's fine."

"Fine. It's a 1951 FX Ute. It's a classic. How is that fine? It's awesome."

"Okay, okay. It's awesome. So, when you coming up?"

"Couple of weeks. Grandad wants to come up and see how you're doing, so we'll all be coming."

"That would actually be great."

After more small talk, some immature brother to sister insults and a 'you hang up first' standoff, they finally said their goodbyes.

10

It was almost noon and Rebecca was beginning to feel hungry, but she had a call to make. She wanted to check in with Aunty Meg just like she had promised Uncle Paul. The phone was answered almost straight away, as if the call had been expected.

They spoke for the next half hour and even though Rebecca could hear the smile in her voice, she could also sense something else behind it all. It sounded like someone that had accepted their fate and abandoned hope. By the time the call ended Rebecca felt exhausted herself and felt the need for a mid-day cup of coffee and something to eat.

She stepped to the pantry, opening the door, and sighed as she looked inside.

"Seriously Uncle Paul, where did you shop? Okay time to go buy some stuff myself and get some real coffee."

Rebecca grabbed a smaller ring of keys from on top of the fridge, threw on a jacket, grabbed her purse and headed outside. The garage near the front of the house had a lock painted red on the side door, and she knew that it matched the red key on the ring. The shed with Jake's Ute was further toward the back of the yard. The front garage was just two rooms, one big enough to park a car in and a workshop behind that. When she stepped inside there was plenty of light coming through the old windows, and she smiled when she saw Pops car. It was a white Suzuki four-wheel drive. A Suzuki Sierra and Rebecca knew it was a manual, which was fine with her. She had driven it a few times before. Once she had driven Pop to Newcastle for Grandma and Grandads fortieth wedding anniversary, and then back again two days later. They had driven the long way that time, via Wauchope and back along the Pacific Highway which added almost two hours to the trip and Rebecca had caught a train up there and back, but Pop understood, and it gave them time to chat about everything.

She jumped in and was surprised when it started first time but then remembered that Pop would have had it no other way. The garage door was one of the few luxuries that Rebecca had been able to convince Pop to install. She pressed the button on the keyring and the door rolled up. She reversed out and turned around in the front yard before pulling out onto the road.

11

The drive into town only took five minutes, which had hardly been long enough for the heater to kick in. She pulled into a parking spot almost in front of the store, locked the car and climbed out.

The main street was quiet, a few cars parked along it and not another person visible. She stepped through the rainbow-coloured plastic strips that hung over the front door of the store and immediately felt at home. Apart from a change of paint on the wall and the neon that lit the glass fronted fridges, the store seemed exactly as it had been almost fifteen years ago. Rebecca closed her eyes for moment, taking in the smell of freshly baked bread, and she half expected that when she opened them, she would see her oldest friend come running through the door from the residence out back.

She didn't have to open them.

"Oh my god. Rebecca, Rebecca Ford."

Rebecca opened her eyes and spun around. Standing behind the counter, still sporting what Rebecca swore was the same ponytail from all those years ago stood Tracey Pearce, the friend she had just imagined, several years older but still a welcome face.

Tracey yelled, "MUM. Get out here. It's Rebecca Ford. MUM. MUMMMMM."

"Hi Tracey."

"Don't you Hi me bitch. Get here and give me a hug." Tracey stepped from behind the counter and wrapped her arms around Rebecca. "Oh. My. God. It's been forever. We were such besties. You should have come visit me sooner." Tracey let Rebecca loose from her grip and yelled out again. "MUM."

An older woman stepped through the residence door, and Rebecca recognised her as soon as she saw the striped tunic wrapped around her waist.

"Hi Mrs Pearce."

"Becky Ford. Now there's a whole bunch of memories and aren't you the spitting image of your mum." Mrs Pearce stood and stared at Rebecca for a moment before turning to Tracey. "And you, young lady, don't you go calling ANYONE a B word in my shop."

"Mum. We've been calling each other bitches since we were eight years old." Tracey wrapped her arm around Rebecca's shoulder, "and I don't think we're going to stop now. Ain't that right Becky."

Rebecca feeling a touch overwhelmed by the enthusiastic reunion could only manage "I guess so."

"I was so sorry to hear about your Pop. Mr Ford was, well everyone loved him. He was such a sweet old dear, and he loved you, and your brother. Broke his heart when your mum and dad passed."

"Mum. Seriously. Do you have to be such a downer?" Tracey gave her a mum a stern look. "Bec. You and me are going to have a bite to eat and catch up, Mum can watch the shop. Okay Mum?"

"Yes. Of course. I'm sorry Becky. I didn't mean no harm. You girls go have some time to yourselves."

"It's okay Mrs Pearce. Umm...I was going to get some things to fill the cupboards."

"You just write me a list. I'll get it sorted for you." Mrs Pearce pulled a pencil from the front of her tunic and pushed it along with a small notepad toward Rebecca. It took her a few minutes, but she scribbled a list of things she wanted, all the while Mrs Pearce watching over her. She was sure that the supervision made her forget some things but if she had decent coffee, she could get the rest another time.

"That should do it." Rebecca handed the note and pencil back. "Uncle Paul got me some stuff, but..."

"Yes. Don't think he had any idea when he was in here earlier in the week. I'll get it sorted. Go catch up."

Tracey reached out her hand and grabbed hold of Rebecca's arm.

"C'mon. We'll sit out on the back deck, while the suns still shining. C'mon."

For the next two hours Rebecca sat on the deck that overlooked a long yard which dropped away suddenly at the far end to the river. Massive weeping willows hugged the deeply eroded riverbank. The heavy fog that had blanketed the countryside earlier had now burned off and the plains that stretched out beyond the river were dotted with bunches of what Rebecca assumed were cattle and occasional houses.

Tracey had put together a lunch of crusty bread rolls and a creamy pumpkin soup, which Rebecca had noticed was listed on chalkboard out in the shop as a 'Mum's Special Lunch', but it was just what she needed to fill her empty stomach and shake off the stress of the morning.

"Thanks for the soup Trace. Your mum still makes the best pumpkin soup, just never ever tell my Grandma I said that."

"Yeah it's good. One day she might even give me the recipe."

"You haven't changed a bit."

"Tonight. What are you doing tonight? I want you to meet Tony. My boyfriend."

"Well...I'll be at the Pub having dinner."

"What? On your own?"

"No. No. Two of the guys at the mill. Long story but they're sharing a meal with me tonight."

"A date. You work quick."

"It's not a date. Just making friends. I know it sounds a bit weird, but they are nice guys."

"Well, I tell you what. Me and Tony will meet you there as well. Make it a bit less weird for you."

"Ok. Let's lock it in then.... Bitch."

"That's more like it."

After more catching up, laughter and general time wasting, the girls finished up and Rebecca paid for the groceries that Mrs Pearce had organised for her. She got a big hug from both Tracey and Mrs Pearce and as she was leaving noticed one thing on a shelf that she grabbed and paid for before leaving.

"Is this for you, young lady?" Mrs Pearce gave her a motherly look as she asked.

"No. No but I know someone who needs it."

"Let her be mum. You're such a busy body."

For that comment Tracey got a glare, which she just laughed off.

"Ok Bec. See you tonight."

"See you then."

12

Rebecca climbed back into the car and headed toward home but instead of continuing to her house she turned down the road that went into the mill. It was almost four o'clock, which she knew was knock off time, and she wanted to catch Nashy before he called it a day. She parked the car beside an enormous, weathered log that lay along the length of one of the larger sheds that made up the mill. Rebecca remembered trying to climb it when she was young. She had never been able to manage it and looking at it now, she doubted she would have any more luck today.

Stepping inside the mill she smelt the sawdust and the burning fuel from the old diesel driven motors that powered the saws. A set of metal stairs were to her left as she moved inside the shed, and she headed up them to the office that overlooked the work area. Nashy was on the phone and gave Rebecca a questioning look, raising his eyebrows and squinting his eyes. Rebecca just shrugged her shoulders and waited patiently for him to finish the call. She stepped to the big window that looked over the mill, its outside covered in a thin film of sawdust and webs, but still clear enough for her to make out the men below. It looked like they were cleaning up, with two men sweeping down the aisles with wide brooms and another two pulling dust covers across the machines. She heard the phone being placed down and turned around just as Nashy stood.

"What is it now?"

Rebecca laughed. "Nothing. Honest. Just came to say thanks and to give you this." She placed a small packet onto the table. "I grabbed it at the store."

Nashy just stared at it for a moment before picking it up.

"Seriously girl? Not you too." He tore open the pack and lifted it to his nose.

"You're not supposed to inhale them."

"I know, but most of this stuff smells like shit. Truth is I've almost picked up some myself......OK. I'll try it but no bloody promises."

Nashy popped out a strip of nicotine gum and threw it into his mouth. His face twisted in a grimace for just a second, and he gave a cough, before finally giving Rebecca a sly grin. "I'll try."

"Good, and now I'm outta here. I'll drop in Monday and see if I can help out here doing something."

"Not much to do. Been quiet. The joinery shop is open tomorrow. We get a few people from out of town come in looking for handmade furniture and stuff. Might be able to help out there, I'm not fantastic with customers."

"OhhhKay. Guess I could give it a go."

"Anyways if you turn up you turn up, if not that's okay too. Nine thirty start."

A bell rang throughout the mill and Rebecca knew that it meant it was knock off time.

"I'll be there."

"Sounds like a plan. Oh, and by the way, I hear you're going to the pub tonight. Don't ask how. There are not many secrets around here. It gets rowdy there later so be careful."

"I will Nashy. I'll see you in the morning."

Rebecca almost felt embarrassed but headed down the stairs before the flush showed in her cheeks. As she headed into the parking lot, she saw a few of the employees heading off home in their utes, four-wheel drives, motorbikes and even one jumping onto a pushbike. One of the four-wheel drives slowed down as it passed her, its passenger window rolling down. Grinning at her was the familiar face of Tate, and he gave a casual wave before the driver lent forward and yelled out.

"See ya later Bec."

Rebecca could see that it was Matt and waved back as the car drove off, leaving her standing in what was now a deserted car park. Only Nashy's old Commodore and her Suzuki remained. Even though it had just turned three in the afternoon the sun was getting low and the evening chill was beginning to set in. Rebecca climbed back into her car and drove the short distance home.

As soon as she stepped inside, she headed to the bathroom and began to fill the bath. The water seemed to be taking ages to fill the tub, so she turned the radio on in the kitchen and turned it up loud, put away her groceries, found something to wear to dinner tonight amongst her small wardrobe and brought some firewood inside. When she stepped back into the bathroom, the bath was still only half full.

"Bloody hell. You wouldn't want to be dying for a bath. Water pressure is crap. Might have to call my Plumber friend."

She sat on the side of the bath, dangling one hand in, testing the temperature, and adjusting the taps to suit with her other hand. The radio was blaring songs from before her time, but she knew the tunes well. Her mother and father had always had music playing wherever they were. The car, home or out on a picnic, and they always sang along. Right now, she found herself singing and tapping her foot to 'Sugar Sugar' and surprising herself that she knew all the words.

The bath finally filled, and she slipped out of her clothes, climbed in, and let the heat soak through her. The old tunes on the radio continued and Rebecca slid down further into the bath, just her head sticking above the water. For a moment she thought she was going to fall asleep, as her head nodded forward but a splash of water on her nose kicked her back awake. Not wanting to drift off again, she quickly washed her hair and slid under the water, scrubbing the shampoo from her brown hair. As she popped her head back above the water, she found herself engulfed in silence. The radio had gone quiet and the lightbulb in the bathroom had gone out.

"Seriously."

She climbed out of the bath dried herself off, wrapped the towel around her chest and pulled on the pair of slippers that had been amongst the things she had bought at the store today. She knew the power box was on the side of the house opposite to the garage and headed out the back door. Even though she was in the country she did not want to take any chances of going out the front door and having someone drive by and see her half-dressed. There was a line of mature citrus trees along that side of the house, and they would block anyone seeing her, beyond that there was an overgrown hedge of camellia that nobody would have any chance of seeing through. Rebecca made her way onto the veranda and was surprised at just how dark it had gotten, and cold.

"Well I'm out here now. May as well get this done."

The veranda that circled the house made it easy for her to get around to the power box, and she squeezed the towel tightly under her armpit as she lifted the tin cover upward on its hinges. She balanced the cover on her head and peered inside. The circuit breakers were new, and she closed her eyes and gave a quick thanks that she was not dealing with older breakers which would have meant fiddling with wire and threading it through the old ceramics. She looked over the three breakers and found that they had all flicked over. Rebecca wasted no time flicking them all back one by one and listened carefully to see if the radio came back to life. It did and as she was standing right outside the kitchen wall now it sounded even louder than it had before. She jumped enough for the power box cover to bounce on her head and her hands flew up to protect her scalp. The towel however fell and not wanting the metal cover to cut her head, she let the towel fall, catching the cover instead, and putting it back in place. Then she picked the towel up and wrapped it around her again. She stood there for a moment until she started laughing. Laughing as she walked back inside.

13

Behind the Camellia hedge he stood. Not needing to hide himself. Standing in complete silence, hidden on the untended side of the hedge. Watching through the remnant of a path that had at one time been a track from the old house to the mill nearby. Moments earlier he had pushed through the hedge on that old path, flicked the breakers and pushed back through the hedge. Scratching his face as he did. He watched as she walked back inside laughing.

All the time thinking to himself. 'It just can't be.' Before skulking back along the old track to the mill.

Rebecca now fully dressed, sat on the old couch on the back veranda, a steaming cup of coffee warming her hands and watched as the light slowly disappeared and was slowly replaced by a sky full of stars. She began thinking of the events that had led to her sitting here. Despite the tragedies involved with her parents and her pop, she was glad that she was here. She felt the urge to pinch herself to make sure it was not a dream and did just that. Unbelievable as it was to her, finally her luck had changed and all she could think was 'It just can't be.'

14

The Shard Inn Hotel, perched on the rise that was the main street of Shattered Falls, looked quiet. Now anyway. Rebecca knew it would get rowdy as the night progressed, but she did not intend to stay much beyond sharing a meal with her new and old friends. Friends which at the moment were yet to arrive. She wandered in, casually eyeing the décor which looked almost as it had in 1867 when it had first been built. Pop had told her stories about the hotel on one of their drives back to Newcastle, and she remembered some of it as she now ordered a lemonade and found a seat in the beer garden beside a tall gas patio heater.

The original owner had built the hotel when gold had been discovered in the nearby streams and set his mind on making his fortune from the gold miners that he believed would flock to the area to make their fortune. The miners did flock, and they did pour their money into the cool ales and fortifying spirits, and he would have made his fortune, had it not been for one fact.

Edward Turnidge, the hotels founder, had lost the Pub in a game of cards not six weeks after he opened the doors. Since then, generations of the Nixon family had run the hotel through good times and bad, and it was Evan Nixon that stood at the bar right now. Rebecca watched as he left the bar and headed toward her, a look of concern on his face.

"You're young Rebecca Ford if I'm not mistaken."

"Hi Mr Nixon. Yep it's me."

"You know we were all fond of your Pop. It was a dark day, the day he collapsed out front. We thought we'd lost him then and there. I'm so sorry for your loss but I'm so glad I knew him. A true gentleman he was."

"Thank you, Mr Nixon."

"You here alone tonight?"

"No. I'm going to check out your menu with some friends if they ever get here."

"Well, when they turn up, round of drinks is on me. Enjoy your night Rebecca."

"Thanks Mr Nixon. There'll be five of us so don't feel like you have to do that."

"As long as you don't all go for the top shelf, I should be okay."

Evan headed back to the bar, spoke to the other bartender, and nodded toward Rebecca.

Five minutes later Tate and Matt sauntered in the door. Matt stopped for a moment, looked around and spotted Rebecca through the door that led to the beer garden. He slapped Tate on the back and pointed toward her, smiling, and laughing together as they headed toward her.

"Evening Bec. I see you found a seat."

"Hi Matt., Hi Tate. Yeah, not sure though, it might get a bit cold out here."

Tate piped up suddenly, "Snow tonight they reckon. Town'll fill up with Snow-droppers tomorrow if it does."

Matt laughed, "Tate, you are a dead set idiot. Snow-droppers is perverts that steal undies from your clothesline. Not snow tourists."

"Yeah, but it sounds cool."

Rebecca looked Tate dead in the eye, straight-faced and asked, "You're not a snowdropper are you Tate."

Tate's face dropped, the grin he had been carrying since he walked into the pub disappearing.

"No, I...I'm not...I was only..."

"It's okay Tate I'm only mucking around..."

Tate took a deep breath and sat down at the table.

Rebecca was unable to resist one last jibe. "But if any of my undies go missing...".

Matt gave a deep, infectious laugh and Rebecca joined in. Tate sat quiet for a moment before joining in himself, "Funny bastards aren't you'se."

Another group of people ventured into the beer garden. An older couple with two young boys tagging behind them, who were soon joined by a middle-aged man and woman. Matt gave the older man a nod, and he nodded back.

Rebecca gave Matt a questioning look. "Someone you know?"

"Not really just some folks that have been staying at the caravan park this week. I was telling them how to get up to the falls and best places to go up in the mountains."

"You seem to know the place pretty well for a Queenslander."

"We used to come here when I was a kid. Originally lived out Kootingal, but dad moved back to Queensland when I was still young. Only came back to sort out some stuff and earn a few quid."

"Me too. I mean I used to live in Tamworth when I was younger. I left too."

Tate rolled his eyes. "Shit you two. Enough flirting. Who wants a drink?"

"Be nice Tate or you'll be sleeping *under* the van." Matt narrowed his eyes and gave Tate a glare.

"If you guys can wait just a few minutes I've got the first round sorted. Just got to wait for my friend to get here."

No sooner had Rebecca mentioned her friends, then did Tracey stride through the door, a tall bearded man trailing behind her. Tracey stopped for a moment looking around until she spotted Rebecca, then gave a piercing yell "BEC", before dragging the hipster looking man over to the table.

"Well don't you look cosy? Hi guys I'm Tracey, Rebecca's friend."

Rebecca smiled and slid along the seat to make room for Tracey. "Tracey this is Matt and Tate. They work at the mill."

"I've seen you two in the shop, haven't I?"

Matt answered. "Yeah. Nowhere else to buy anything here. Unless you want to drive into Tamworth."

Rebecca looked up at the bearded man still standing at the end of the table.

"Hi."

"Oh, shit sorry. This is my boyfriend Tony."

Everyone said their hellos and Tony turned around to grab another chair to sit at the end of the table.

"So now can we get a drink?" Tate sounded like an impatient child.

Rebecca gave Tony a smile, "Tony would you mind going to the bar. The first round is sorted, just tell them it's for me."

"Yeah no problem. What you drinking?"

Everyone rattled off a drink, and Rebecca watched as Tony's eyes closed and he was obviously making a mental list.

Matt stood up at the same time as Tony. "I'll come with you mate."

Tate stood up too, "and I'm off to the dunny."

Rebecca and Tracey suddenly found themselves alone at the table as the boys headed off. Tracey grabbed Rebecca's wrist.

"Soooo. What's the deal here? You got your eyes on one of these two. Tate seems like just a kid, but Matt. He looks a bit of a catch."

"Trace. We only just met today, so settle. They both seem nice, even if Tate did break into my shed."

"What?"

"I'll tell you later, but Matt, he's been a real gentleman, but just a friend. So far anyway."

The boys were back from the bar before Tracey and Rebecca had a chance to take the conversation any further. Drinks were handed around the table and the talk began to flow a little more freely. Music, not too loud started to drift out of the front bar and the friends had to raise their voices a little to be heard.

Matt put his hand on Tony's shoulder and turned to Rebecca, "Bec, did you know Tony's a ranger. Looks after half a dozen parks around here."

"A ranger. That would be so awesome. Working in the bush all day. Animals and stuff."

"Not as awesome as it sounds Rebecca. Lot of office work involved, and when I do get out in the mountains, some of the people I get to deal with are a real pain in the arse, but yeah it's got its good points."

Tracey slid her hand over Tony's arm, "and he knows some really beautiful places that I'm sure no one else has ever been to. Well, that's what it feels like anyway."

Another group of people wandered into the beer garden, found themselves a table and started reading a menu. Rebecca looked over to them and then grabbed one of the menus that sat in the middle of her table.

"Maybe we should order. Don't want to be waiting all night."

Tracey grabbed a menu too, "Yeah. The food's good here, but sometimes takes a while."

Matt looked around the room. "Anyone seen Tate?"

"He went to the toilet when you two headed over to the bar." Rebecca craned her neck and scanned the room as well.

Tony half turned in his chair, looking toward the bar. "Is that him out in the front bar?"

Matt had his back to the bar and turned around in his seat. His knee resting on the bench seat as he looked toward the bar. On the far side of the bar he saw the mop top locks that could only belong to Tate. Matt waved his hand to get Tate's attention and then beckoned him to come join them. Tate nodded and finished talking to someone out front before traipsing back through the door and back into the beer garden.

"What's up?"

"Time to order. So, get here and get ordering."

"You know, my brother used to tell me what to do all the time, Matt. I don't much like him either."

"Shut up ya silly bugger and sit down."

"Fair enough, and just so you know there's some bloke out front tried to sell me some pot, and other crap. I told the barman to keep an eye on him."

"Good call. Don't go getting involved with him. Don't even let on you ratted him out. Last thing we want is a crazed drug dealer hammering on the van tonight."

Tony looked back toward the bar again. "Was he a local?"

"Nah don't think so. Never seen him before. Not dressed for the cold weather and looks rough as a pig in the scrub."

"Ok. Let's forget him and order some grub. What do you like the look of Bec?"

Rebecca looked over the menu again. "I might go the Scaloppini."

Tracey joined in "Oh yeah. It's really good. Make that two."

"Ok. Suddenly I'm the waiter, but that's okay." Matt leant slightly over the table toward Rebecca, "and by the way Bec, Tate will be paying for your meal. Least he can do after the stunt he pulled in your shed."

Everyone turned to Tate, expecting a sharp comeback "Yeah righto, but I'm not paying for yours."

Matt stood up, "Well if everyone's good I'll get the order started. Scaloppini for you Bec."

"Yeah. Thanks Matt. No pepper."

"Got it."

Tony and Tate stood as well and the three of them headed to the bar to order the meals. Rebecca and Tracey found themselves alone at the table once again.

"Tony seems nice, and he's got a good job. Your mum would be happy with him."

"She is, all except for the beard. She said it reminds her of an old boyfriend."

"So, is it serious?"

"I think so. Well yes, it is serious."

"Damn. You look so happy. Makes me jealous."

Tracey looked over at the boys at the bar. Tate seemed to be arguing over the price of something with Matt.

"You'll get you turn Bec. Looks like you're on the right track."

"Maybe. We'll see."

The boys wandered back over to the table, Matt and Tony carrying another round of drinks that an unsmiling Tate seemed to have been forced to pay for. Matt and Tony passed the drinks around the table, and they all sat back down and began chatting again.

Twenty minutes later the food made its way to the table. Scaloppini and vegetables for the girls and steak and chips smothered in horseradish chili for two of the boys. Tony was the only odd one out, having ordered a spinach and fetta frittata.

Matt gestured to Tony's meal "You a Vegetarian Tony?"

"Sort of."

Tate snorted, a chip hanging from his mouth. "How the hell can you be sort of a veggie?"

"Just my diet. One week off meat, one week on."

"Whatever floats your boat Tony. I reckon you got to feed the man meat. Salads for rabbits." Tate sucked the chip into his mouth whilst he spoke to Tony, ducking under a head slap that Matt aimed at him. "Too slow Bozo."

Rebecca kicked Tate's leg under the table. "Yeah but the good guys work in pairs."

"Oww. Shit. Okay, okay. Sorry already. Are you guys gunna eat or what?"

The conversation quietened slightly as they all began to eat, but the noise from the front bar more than made up for it as it became rowdier.

"Sounds like the normal Friday night crowd has turned up." Tracey said, raising her voice to be heard over the din.

"Nothing wrong with a bit of noise." Rebecca smiled as she spoke.

"True. Just don't spend too much time out the front bar. Get some ferals in here sometimes."

"Pop liked it here."

"True, but I don't think he did Friday nights."

Matt stopped for a moment and pulled his phone from his pocket, excused himself and walked to the rear of the beer garden. Rebecca watched as he talked on the phone, his face losing its usual jovial look.

Tony finished his meal, stood, and walked to the bar, returning a few minutes later with glasses of lemonade for everyone.

Tate stared Tony in the eye as the glass of lemonade was laid down in front of him.

"What.... The..."

"Almost time for the road. Don't want anyone getting done for drink driving."

"I walked...and what are you? My mother."

Tate was about to get up when Matt's hand fell on his shoulder.

"Tony's right Tate. Time to call it a night. Sorry everyone I got to go."

Rebecca looked up at Matt, concern showing on her face. "Is everything okay?"

"Yeah. Just some stuff I got to sort out. Didn't mean to rush you."

"It's okay Matt. I was done anyway, and I've got to work in the morning"

Tracey mouthed 'Work' at Rebecca.

"I'll tell you about it later. So, if we are all done."

The noise out in the front bar suddenly turned to yelling and screaming.

"Just when the party started." Tracey grabbed Tony's hand "Best we go I think."

Matt stepped up to Rebecca as they all began to move for the door. "Sorry Bec. I'll see you Monday."

"You sure you're okay."

"Yeah. Yeah. Have a good weekend. Sorry again."

Matt grabbed Tate by the shoulder and the two of them headed out the side door. Rebecca watched them walk out and did not notice Tracey standing beside her until she spoke.

"What was that all about?"

"I have no idea."

"You going to be right to get home."

"Yeah I'm fine. Thanks for coming out with me."

The yelling from the front bar suddenly spilled into the beer garden. A tall, gaunt man stumbling through the door and knocking over a table. The crowd in the front bar cheered and the obviously drunk man began to swear as he turned to return to the bar. Rebecca looked at him, his eyes sweeping over the diners in the beer garden, but not fixing on any one person. In a quiet voice she calmly asked Tracey "Is it okay if I sleep at your place?"

"Umm okay. Why? What's wrong?"

Rebecca drew a deep breath and realised that she was clenching both her jaw and her fist. She released them both, only now feeling where her nails had dug into her palm.

"That guy. The one that fell through the door."

Tony had joined them, "That's the one Tate said tried to sell him some stuff."

"Yeah that sounds right."

"Who is it Bec? Bec, my god your trembling." Tracey wrapped her arm around Rebecca's shoulder.

"His name is Zak. He's my ex."

15

Tracey drove Rebecca's Suzuki and Rebecca back to her house, which turned out to be a studio at the rear of her parents' home and shop. Had it not been for the fact that she was feeling nervous having seen all the bad parts of her teenage years stumbling not ten metres away from her, she would have told Tracey that it looked more like a Granny flat than a studio. Tony sat in the back seat; his big frame cramped up in the small leg space. No one spoke on the two-minute drive that felt like an eternity. Tracey drove the car into the back yard, and they all quietly moved into the studio.

"You want a coffee Bec?"

"Umm no thanks. Is it okay if I just crash somewhere?"

"Sure. Tony can you fold out the couch? I'll get some blankets."

"Thanks Trace, Tony. I'm just a bit shocked."

In just over fifteen minutes the couch was converted into a bed. Sheets, blankets, pillows, and a thick doona. After sitting with Rebecca for a short time, arm around her shoulder and not saying a word, Tracey stood up and said goodnight.

"Thanks Tracey. I'm sorry. I'll talk to you tomorrow."

Lights were turned out as Tracey and Tony retired to the bedroom. The studio went quiet and Rebecca's mind began to race. Why was he here? It was obviously about her, but what did he want? Money. More than likely, he must have heard about the inheritance. And he was still into drugs, dealing drugs. In the morning she would call Uncle Paul. He would fix it, but maybe she should stand up instead of relying on him all the time, but he's a drug dealer. She began to feel overwhelmed.

The question. Why? Running through her head over and over again. Things were starting to go her way. Why now?

Why?

Somehow, she fell asleep and somehow, she did not dream.

CHAPTER SIXTEEN

16

Where was she? She was supposed to be here. He had knocked and banged on the door, but no one had answered. After that, it had not taken much to open the bedroom window. It was old and slid up in jagged movements, screeching and whining as the old wooden frame caught and rubbed.

The house was cold, freezing cold. There should have been a fire in the old fireplace, should have been smouldering embers keeping the house warm but the air, the walls, the floor, the whole house was like the inside of a freezer. Where the hell was she?

Should he wait? No. She would scream if she walked in and found him there and then it would all be ruined. No, he would have to do this properly. Climb back out the window, walk away. Come back another time.

This would work. He knew it would. He remembered her face. A face he had kissed more than once. It seemed a lifetime away, but they had had a chance once, even if she had left, and then he had ruined it all. Destroyed any chance they had, but now...now it was a fresh start. They would be together. Even if, he had to do things outside the law. She would be his.

17

Morning broke dimly over the town. Where earlier in the week there had been heavy fog, now there was low unbroken cloud. Not dark like a rain cloud, these were pale white and looked more like balls of cotton than clouds. Rebecca opened her eyes and pulled the doona from over her face. A deep breath of the morning air, even the heated air of the studio bit at her lungs. Today would be cold and more than likely there had been snow last night.

Rebecca climbed out of the fold out couch bed. She had fallen asleep still in the clothes she had worn last night. Socks still on her feet, which proved to have been a good decision when her feet met the floor. She found her shoes and jacket and made her way out into the small kitchen, stepping quietly, not wanting to wake Tracey and Tony. On a sheet of note paper, she quickly wrote a note.

'Heading home. Got to work in the shop at the joinery this morning. Catch up later. Thanks for everything.'

Once outside, she was shocked at the chill. There was no breeze to add iciness to the air but there was no need. The temperature was several degrees below zero, and she could feel her cheeks tighten as she pulled her shoes on and buttoned up the jacket. She made her way quickly to the car which started first time, surprising her in the freezing weather. She knew that the sound of the engine would wake them, but she needed to get home. As she turned the car in the yard and headed out the driveway, she caught a glimpse of a light turn on in the kitchen.

"Sorry Trace." she muttered over the heater which she had turned up to full to warm herself.

The drive home took less than five minutes and the heater had still not warmed the car. She knew the house would be just as cold, or even colder. Her stupid fears of her past had taken control of her last night, and she hated herself for it. Time to take control again.

She went straight to the fireplace and focused on warming the house. Tinder, kindling, large and small wood. It only took her a few minutes until a small flame began to lick at the small sticks, and she fed it carefully. The flames growing and growing until she was happy that it had taken. She stood back, grabbed a small log, and placed it into the flames and smiled as she felt a wave of pride.

"Well I've got that shit beat. What's next?"

She filled the kettle and almost flicked the switch to turn it on but changed her mind. She remembered she was still wearing the clothes she had gone out in last night. Slept in them in fact and just that thought made her feel itchy and uncomfortable.

"Shower."

The water was thankfully hot, and she felt the morning chill wash away from her as the steam filled the room and the water ran over her shoulders. She let it run while she ran through the previous night in her head. Zak had obviously been in town looking for her and tried to score some cash selling whatever it was he was into now. Which meant that eventually he would come knocking on her door. It would not take too long to find out where she was staying, not in a small town like this.

'Maybe', she thought 'I should pack up and leave. Go back to Grandma and Grandad's. Find a place of my own down there.'

Rebecca felt the water begin to cool, and she knew then that she had been in the shower too long. She turned off the taps, grabbed a towel and stepped out into the steamy room. She wiped away a small patch of misted over mirror and looked herself in the eye, surprised to see her own steely grey eyes. For a moment she could have sworn she was considering her mother's eyes. That was all she needed to bring a smile back to her face and a renewed sense of resolve.

"You know what sister. Stuff you Zak, this is my place and you don't scare me."

While she got into some warm clothes and made her first cup of coffee for the day, she began to work out just how she would go about ensuring that her ex moved on, but everything kept coming back to Uncle Paul. He could make life difficult for Zak around town, and she knew Zak was a coward when push came to shove. As soon as she could, she would do what any law-abiding citizen would do. She would call the cops, or Uncle Paul at least.

Nine o'clock came and she made the call. It was short, and Uncle Paul did not say much but promised he would sort it out. She felt the weight lift from her as she hung the phone up and hardly even noticed the winter chill outside as she jumped into the car and drove the short distance to the joinery.

18

Nashy was already there, sweeping the floors of the joinery and moving some furniture around. Rebecca surprised him when she stepped in the door and then again when she gave him a hug.

"What's that for girlie? You know I'm married, don't you?"

"You're hilarious"

"And you're early. I don't open the doors for half an hour yet."

"Yeah I know. I just wanted to get busy and besides I need to check out the merchandise. Make sure the stuff I'm selling is top-notch."

"You know it is. This stuff is the best."

Rebecca looked around the room. Her eye was drawn to a chest of drawers, she remembered they were called Tall Boys. The deep brown stain, the shine of the finish and the intricately carved mouldings, stood as testament to Nashy's words.

"Yeah. I know. You and the boys do amazing stuff with lumps of wood."

"Yeah but not half as amazing as the stuff your Pop could make. He was a true artisan with any piece of wood he put his hand too. Taught me everything I know. Your dad was pretty good too. Both were top notch themselves."

Rebecca tilted her head and smiled as she looked back at Nashy.

"And you seriously have to ask why you get hugs?"

Nashy laughed and pushed the broom up behind the counter.

"Girl. It's good to have a smiling face like yours around. Let's open early."

For the next few hours Nashy showed Rebecca how to use the till, gave her a tour of the shop and a few pointers on the products. The first customers didn't come in till about ten and Nashy took care of them while Rebecca watched on. The next lot she took on herself with Nashy standing nearby mouthing words which on several occasions almost made her burst into laughter. By twelve o'clock she had made three sales and Nashy another six.

As Nashy locked the front door he turned to Rebecca.

"That Girlie...was awesome. You are a natural...almost."

"So, I got the job?"

"Ha...yeah you got the job. Can't say no to my business partner anyways. So that's it for the day, you can go. I'll lock up and besides I got to go the loo."

"Nice. You really know how to spoil the moment."

"Sorry girlie. Just telling it like it is. Now get out of here before I have second thoughts about your future employment."

Rebecca was home by quarter past twelve and was making herself a toasted cheese sandwich when she heard a car pull into the drive-way. She looked through the front window and saw that it was Uncle Paul and quickly went to turn off the grill before heading out front to meet him.

A cold breeze had sprung up from the south and Rebecca zipped her jumper up under her chin, as she stepped to the opening car door.

"Uncle Paul. You didn't have to come over. I'm alright now. I just wanted you to know what was going on."

"I know. I know, but if anything happened...well girl...let's just make sure nothing happens...besides I needed to drop off some things for you."

"Some things." Rebecca raised her eyebrows. "Have you got some more home cooking for me from Aunty Meg?"

"No, but I reckon if she had known I was coming over I could have filled your fridge."

Paul reached across the front seat of the car and grabbed a plastic bag.

"This, Miss Bec is for you." Paul smiled as he handed over the bag.

Rebecca wasted no time reaching inside and pulling out a mobile phone box. An iPhone.

"Uncle Paul. I can't take this. It's too much."

"It's not new...and you can owe me...and I'm not leaving here until you've got the rest of it set up. One of the guys at work did most of it, you just need to put your own contacts in there. My number is already there...and we set it up, so I can track you. Some 'Find My Friends' thing. You can turn it off if you want, but while that twit's in town...let's just be safe."

She opened the box and removed the phone while Paul went to the rear of the car. She didn't even notice as he opened the tailgate and hoisted a bag onto his shoulder. It was only when he whistled that she looked up and saw what the other 'thing' was that he had brought.

A dog, which Rebecca immediately recognised as a German Shepherd jumped down from the tailgate, seeming to land awkwardly on its back leg and followed Paul as he walked back to Rebecca.

"Bec. I'd like you to meet Sarge."

"You're kidding. A police dog?"

"Retired. She was in a car accident. Nearly lost one of her back legs, but she's a fighter. Not fit for the force anymore, but I reckon she'll make a good guard dog for you...and she needs a good home. Win, win if you ask me."

"I don't know how to look after a dog."

"Feed her," Paul patted his hand against the bag of dog food on his shoulder, "and keep her company. All her medicals are covered. Vet number is in the phone."

"You've got his all worked out, haven't you?"

"Yep. So, no argument."

"Ok. I guess."

"Sarge. Come here and met Rebecca."

Rebecca leant down on one knee while the dog came and sniffed her hand for a moment and then licked her face.

"I think she likes me."

"Of course, she does. She's trained to do what I tell her."

"And you told her to like me?"

"I told you, she's a police dog. Follows orders...and even if you don't know how to look after her...she knows how to look after you."

Sarge was nuzzling against Rebecca's chin and almost knocked her off balance. A smile had crept across Rebecca's face, and she knew that despite her reservations, Sarge and her would be best friends.

"I'll put the dog food in the laundry, and you can show Sarge the house, then we need to talk."

Paul headed inside while Rebecca watched him.

'We need to talk.' She thought on his words. 'Sounds ominous.'

"C'mon Sarge, check out your new digs."

Once inside Rebecca put the kettle on, while Paul went to the laundry and put down the dog food. Sarge began a long, slow patrol of the house, sniffing everything as she went. Rebecca let her go and explore while she made the cuppa's and reheated her lunch.

"Ok miss. Dog foods in the laundry...ahhh...cuppa would be great. Thanks."

Paul sat down at the kitchen table, lifted the steaming cup to his mouth and eyed Rebecca's toasted cheese sandwich. Rebecca caught his gaze and swung a protective palm over her lunch.

"No. I'm starving Uncle Paul...well I guess I could go halves with you."

Sarge came into the kitchen, sat at the edge of the table, and gave the sandwich the same fixed stare as Paul had only moments earlier.

"Oh my god...Okay. Thirds it is."

"No. Don't feed her any of that shit. She's got her dog food, it's proper vet stuff. You eat the sandwich. I've only got time for this cuppa and then I've got to go anyway."

"Sorry you had to come out."

"I did some checking. That dickhead seems to be a bit of loose cannon. Drugs and small-time crime. Done a couple of years. What did you see in him miss?"

"I was stupid. No other reason I can think of. He gave me some attention and I fell for it."

"Well he doesn't seem to be still in town. I spoke to Evan at the Shard. Seems he stirred up some trouble with some bad people. If he's smart, he won't be back, but first sign of him...you ring me. That's what the phones for. I've promised a lot of people I'd watch out for you...your mum and dad, they were the world to me and...well..."

"It's okay Uncle Paul. I know I can count on you if I need to... but I want to try and find my independence. Did my first shift at the mill today.'

"You're just like her you know. Trying so hard to be someone, losing sight that you already are."

"Mum?"

"Yeah...Okay. You do your thing girlie, but just know I'm a phone call away, and don't be surprised if I turn up out of the blue now and then."

"Wouldn't have it any other way."

"That's settled then." Paul lifted the cup to his mouth and drained it, wiped his lips with the back of his hand and stood, "and now I should shoot through."

Sarge followed Paul as he walked to the door and Rebecca was close behind the two of them. The dog gave a small whimper as Paul closed the screen behind him and looked at the two girls.

"Be good...and you Sarge... you make sure she does."

Rebecca let her hand fall to the top of Sarge's head and gave a little scratch. The dog looked up at her and sat, something that Rebecca took to mean she was happy to stay.

The Landcruiser drove off and suddenly it was just the two of them. Two girls, both of whom felt like they had found a new home, despite whatever they felt unsure about.

The rest of Saturday afternoon involved a couch, a warm fire, and a footy match on the TV. Sarge, obviously content fell asleep curled up on one end of the old blanket covered lounge with Rebecca's arm resting on her neck. Rebecca however stayed awake and watched her team lose, with Sarge waking once or twice when Rebecca yelled at the ref as the close calls didn't go her way.

19

The sun had gotten low in the sky and a cold breeze begun to sound through the dimming light of the late afternoon, forcing Rebecca to make the decision to go outside and replenish the firewood supply. Sarge followed her sniffing the cold earth of the back yard as they walked the short distance to the woodpile. It had gotten dark quickly and the first stars now glistened in the twilight sky. Rebecca loaded up the old washing basket that sat beside the pile with as much wood as she could carry, making sure she had a mix of different sized logs. As she lifted the full basket to her hip a beam of light shone down the side of the house, she heard a car door slam, and she placed the basket back down. Sarge gave a low, rolling growl and walked slowly to the path beside the house.

Rebecca walked up beside the dog and squatted down to scratch Sarges head.

"It's okay girl...Lets go see who it is before we go all Cujo."

Before the two of them had made it up the side of the house, they heard the banging on the front door and a girl's voice.

"Hello... Bec...Hello. Answer the door, it's friggin' freezing out here."

Sarge barked twice and the voice out front changed pitch.

"Shit...there's a dog...Tony honk the horn. Tony? For chrissake...Tony honk the horn."

Just as Rebecca made it to the front of the house, a car horn let out two piercing blares and Tracey gave a scream as she spotted Rebecca and the low dark figure of Sarge at the side of the house.

"Tracey. What the hell...what are you doing here?"

"Sorry I didn't mean to scream…just wasn't expecting a dog…is it yours?"

"Just an added piece of security from Uncle Paul. This is Sarge."

Sarge stood beside Rebecca and seemed to understand that Tracey was a friend, but her gaze was focused on the vehicle in the driveway, unsure of whomever was inside.

Rebecca put her hand on Sarges head as she heard the low growl.

"It's okay girl. It's okay. They're friends"

Sarge sat down but still watched warily as the car door opened and Tony stepped toward the girls.

"Whoa. Looks like she means business."

"Yeah. Sorry Tony, now that she knows your good guys, she should be okay, just don't go trying to stab me."

"Deal"

"So, what are you two doing here?"

"Seriously girl. You left this morning in a bit of a hurry and after last night…well I was worried and when I'm worried, I make sure Tony's worried too."

"Yep, she does." Tony quipped.

"So, we bought some Chinese and a Movie."

Tony held up a bag in one hand and a DVD in the other. "Hope you like Black Bean, Spring Rolls and Adam Sandler…You do have a TV in there don't you."

"Yes…I have a TV. Running water too."

"Running water. Good. Might need to wash up if we decide to stab you."

Sarge growled and stood up but eased off when Rebecca began to laugh.

"Well let's get inside and dig in, before it gets cold, if it's not already. Long drive from Tamworth."

"It's warm but only just. Microwave might come in handy." Tracey added.

"Lucky, I got one of them too…just have to get electricity now." Rebecca turned and stepped to the front door and led her friends inside.

Sarge stepped in front of them all and quickly found her place in front of the fire.

It wasn't long before with fire, friends and a furry bodyguard, Rebecca felt that she had recovered the security that she thought she had lost only the night before. The Chinese and movie seemed to be over quickly and in no time, it became coffee and cards. A game of 'Bullshit', with rules that seemed to change with every hand they played. The game dragged on for hours and had them all in fits of laughter.

It was after midnight that Tracey and Tony finally decided to head home but not before making plans for the morning.

"About 10.30. Be up and ready. Tony knows this awesome place up in the park. You'll love it, but dress warm, might be more snow tonight."

Rebecca looked back at Sarge asleep on the couch.

"What about Sarge? I can't leave her alone. Not on her first days with me."

Tony smiled, "Its okay. The rangers a softie. As long as she behaves herself it'll be fine."

"Ok 10.30 then, and thanks for tonight...I really needed it."

Rebecca saw her two friends out to their car and closed the front door as their taillights disappeared down the road.

"Well Miss Sarge...", the dogs ears pricked up, "that was fun, but I think it's time for bed."

Sarge climbed down from the couch and headed toward the back door and sat and Rebecca understood instantly.

"Ok...toilet break for you too."

Rebecca stood and waited for a few minutes, looking out at the darkened hill that lay behind the house. Everything seemed so still, so quiet and calm. She stared into the dark and sucked in a lung full of chill air. The cry of a bird broke her stare from the night landscape and Sarge came running back up the steps.

"Ok girl. Let's call it an evening and get some sleep. Things are looking good. Safe even."

If only she had known that hours before, while Adam Sandler had been telling bad jokes, and she had been wiping plum sauce from her chin, a car had been sitting up the hill in that darkened landscape. The same car that had sat in the same spot before. The same person that had sat there before.

Watching.

Plotting.

20

Sunday morning came cold and crisp. Clouds told the tale of snow on the mountains and Rebecca took the advice of her friends and dressed warm. Even an old beanie of her Pops came out, smelling of naphthalene and the musty smell of a wardrobe drawer.

Sarge had spent the night sleeping on the foot of the bed, curled up and to Rebecca's surprise snoring like a wood saw. The dog had stayed there fast asleep, even after Rebecca had gotten up, showered and made her first coffee. Only after the smell of bacon began to waft down the hall did Sarge finally come wandering out.

"You have a big night girl?"

Sarge sniffed at the table and then wandered back down the hall to the back door, scratching at the floor.

"Ok. Toilet break."

When the back door swung open, Sarge did not hesitate to run out into the cold but Rebecca took a step back when the icy but light breeze washed over her face.

"Don't be long young lady. It's freezing."

Rebecca turned back down the hall, leaving the door open and made her way back to the kitchen. Despite the dietary instructions that Uncle Paul had given her, Rebecca placed two strips of bacon into Sarges bowl and waited. After only a few minutes she heard the pad of paws coming down the hall, which stopped and almost had Rebecca investigate before she heard the door shut and the click of claws begin again as Sarge once again made her way into the kitchen.

The short-cut bacon disappeared almost instantly and when Sarge turned to look at Rebecca, she was sure she saw a huge grin on the dog's face.

"You are priceless.... You ready for a day out?"

Sarge tilted her head, giving that look that meant 'I have no idea what you are saying...but I like the bacon.'

For the next half hour Rebecca set about cleaning up after the night before and getting ready, all the while aimlessly chatting to Sarge. She never expected an answer from the dog and jumped when Sarge finally gave a low growl and bark.

"You talk too much miss. You better not be doing that today...and I'm guessing that bark was for a car coming up the road."

Rebecca checked the time on her new phone.

"Only twenty minutes late."

The sound of car pulling into the driveway was quickly followed by a door slamming, a horn honking, and a female voice.

"Settle down already. I'll get her."

Rebecca scratched the top of Sarges head.

"C'mon girl, lets go join these two comedians."

Rebecca beat Tracey to the front door and Sarge almost knocked both over as she shot by them and waited at the back door of Landcruiser.

"Well she's keen." Tracey gave Rebecca a quick hug. "How about you Bec? Sleep okay?"

"Like a rock. So, did Sarge...but she's more of a snoring, farting rock."

Tracey turned and yelled toward the car.

"Wind down the window...she's a farter."

Rebecca saw Tony raise his eyebrows as he reached for the window controls.

"Not Bec you dag...Sarge."

"Seriously Trace, you're so embarrassing."

"Yeah well paybacks a bitch. Now come on. Let's go. We got lunch ready and the perfect spot."

Rebecca buckled herself into the backseat and Sarge lay down on the seat beside her.

Tony turned his head to look into the backseat as he began to reverse out of the driveway.

"You two ready? We could be in for a bumpy ride."

Bec pulled at her seatbelt, ensuring it was tight and rested her hand on Sarges head.

"Ready to rock."

The trip took them back through town and onto a tarred road that headed up into the mountains. The slope dropped away dramatically on one side of the road but gave glimpses of the valley and town below, through breaks in the straggly gums. It soon became a dirt road and the trees turned to plantation pine all planted in lines that gave geometric views into the deeper parts of the forest. The corrugations on the road sent a rhythmic shudder through the car.

"Is this the bumps you meant?"

"Oh no, no, no. This is just the warmup."

And on saying that Tony turned from the dirt road to a narrow track that quickly became hidden amongst tall pines.

Rebecca looked over Tracey's shoulder at the track ahead.

"Is this where you bury all your victims?"

"Ha...he smells like that's what he's been up too sometimes."

"Trust me girls. It's worth the ride."

The track became bumpier, and they slowed down considerably to negotiate some of the bigger ruts. At one point they had to stop as Tony got out and pushed a large fallen branch out of their way, and again when he unlocked an old gate.

Rebecca looked deep into the trees as they stopped and caught a glimpse of a white patch.

"Oh my god. Is that snow?"

"Yeah. Tony said there might still be some up here. Some places got a little fall last night."

For the next fifteen minutes Rebecca scanned the trees beside the car, finding an ever-increasing amount of snow on the ground. The car topped a small rise and the forest opened to a small meadow.

Tony brought the car to a halt in front of a large log.

"Here we are. Ashton's Glen. This is almost the headwaters of the Shard river, and guaranteed we are the only ones here." Tony held up the key he had unlocked the earlier gate with.

"So why is it locked up?"

"There's a couple of old ruins of a homestead up near the top of the paddock and some Aboriginal significant sites hidden down near the stream. So, now it's off limits to the public. I check on the place from time to time but the main reason I come here is to check on Tubbs."

"Who or what the hell is Tubbs?"

They all climbed out of the car, Sarge included and Tony climbed on top of the log and gave a whistle.

"Do me a favour Bec." Tony looked down to Sarge and Rebecca noticed the more serious tone in his voice. "Just keep an eye on Sarge."

"Yeah sure." Rebecca looped her palm through Sarges collar.

Tony gave another whistle and clapped his hands.

"Here he comes."

Tracey wandered down to the end of the log and around to the other side of it. Rebecca followed, still holding Sarges collar and when she saw what Tony had been calling too, she gasped.

"Oh my god it's so cute"

Dawdling through the low grass came a small wombat, obviously a juvenile. Sarge whimpered when she caught its scent, not menacingly. She seemed just as curious as Rebecca.

The wombat paused, half obscured behind a hummock of grass, having itself caught the scent of the dog, but as Tony jumped down from the log 'Tubbs' began to edge forward again. It stopped at Tony's feet, sniffing at his shoes. Tony reached into one the zippered pockets on his jacket and pulled out a zip lock bag. Inside was what seemed to be a mixture of diced fruit and vegetables.

He knelt and emptied part of the bag onto the ground, which 'Tubbs' wasted no time in devouring.

"She loves this stuff. You guys come around slowly. She's tame...that's the problem, but first sign of Sarge going crazy, you need to put her in the car. Promise me. We've already lost her brother."

"Ok. Promise. I've got hold of her." Rebecca firmed her grip on the collar but Sarge seemed to understand and sat quietly tilting her head and examining the small wombat.

With one hand on Sarges collar, Rebecca reached out and touched the top of the wombat's head. Its hair felt coarse and wiry to touch and Rebecca felt compelled to scratch it behind the ear, which the wombat seemed to enjoy.

"She's gorgeous isn't she Bec. Tony has brought me up here a few times when he's been keeping an eye on her."

"She is gorgeous. You said she had a brother."

Tony stood up and looked over the meadow, "Yeah. Something got him. Maybe wild dogs, or a fox. Their mum got hit by a car and I found them, they were old enough to fend for themselves but not street smart if you know what I mean. 'Crockett' just disappeared one night. All I found was a bit of bloody fur and a scared 'Tubbs'. She was hiding under this log, poor girl, but she's doing good now. Knows what to do when she's in trouble."

"Crockett and Tubbs. Is that from that show? The one with Don Johnson."

"Yeah. Some guy was talking about old theme songs on the radio just before I found them, and then he started playing the Miami Vice music."

"Couldn't you have given her something else. Tubbs isn't very feminine."

"Trust me she ain't very feminine."

Tubbs had now wandered toward where Sarge was lying with her muzzle on the grass and Rebecca, Tony and Tracey watched carefully as the two animals gave each other the once over. Sarge looked up at Rebecca questioningly.

"It's okay girl, she won't hurt you"

Sarge lifted her head from the ground and sniffed the wombats face and for a moment it looked as though 'Tubbs' was about to take an exploratory nibble on the dog's nose, but she turned and walked away back to Tony. She knew there were more treats in his pocket and as far as she was concerned, Sarge was just a big wombat. Nothing to see there.

Sarge took the rejection gracefully, sat up on her hind legs and nuzzled Rebecca. It was only a small nudge but enough to throw Rebecca off balance and onto her butt.

"Thanks a lot girl."

Sarge apologised by licking her face.

"Ok ladies. It's time for lunch. I've fed one of you." Tony gestured toward 'Tubbs', "now the remaining trio, if you would like to step back toward the car, I'm sure we can rustle up a picnic blanket, some sandwiches and a flask of Coffee."

With blanket, sandwiches, and coffee the group made their way to a small grassy ledge above the creek. The water flowed over rocks and cascaded into a small pool, that Tony confidently told them was 'home to Platypus and a 'shitload' of yabbies'.

For the next hour they sat chatting, laughing, and taking in the bushland sounds. At one stage Rebecca had to stop herself from falling asleep as the warm, winter sun played over her face. She kept thinking about 'Tubbs'. An orphan that lost her mother in tragic circumstances and deep down she knew she was thinking about herself.

"Ok folks. Time to move out. Pick up all the crap. I don't want any rubbish left behind. Stretch your legs if you need to but in twenty minutes we are out of here."

Tony headed back toward where hey had last seen 'Tubbs' and surprisingly Sarge followed him.

"Hey Tony. Looks like you've made a friend." Rebecca yelled.

Tony turned his head, saw Sarge following him and smiled.

"C'mon girl. Let's check her out one last time."

Tracey stood and began packing up their gear. Chatting to Rebecca as she went.

"He's really good with animals. They all seem to connect with him. Like 'Tubbs'...and now Sarge. Who only last night was ready to attack him if he looked at you the wrong way."

"You found a good one there."

"And mum adores him. I think he's the one."

"I hope you mean future husband."

The smile on Tracey's face told Rebecca all she needed to know.

"Oh my god. It's happening isn't it. When?"

"We've talked about it...but he hasn't asked yet...don't worry, you'll get an invite."

"An invite. I'm shooting for a seat at the big table."

"Anything is possible if you play your cards right."

The two continued chatting as they finished cleaning up and were soon joined by Tony and Sarge as they all headed toward the car.

Rebecca took a poke at Tony "That'd be right. Turn up after the cleanings done...almost acting like a married man."

"Got to get in some practice, don't I Trace."

They all climbed into the car. Tony opening the door for Sarge and gesturing for her to get in. The dog and man acting like they had been lifelong friends. Something that Rebecca thought weird but could only smile about.

The trip back down the mountain was broken by a few stops as Tony checked gates and performed quick drive-bys of some of the camping areas. There were a few tents dotted amongst the pines and when they reached the major camping ground at The Pane, they all stopped and made use of the facilities,

The Pane was an old dam, built during the gold rush days by an American mining company. At one stage over a thousand people had lived on the site, or so Tony said, but right now it consisted of three caravans, around ten tents and several swags.

The Pane itself stretched down a small valley. Protected from the wind on all sides it was usually a mirror-like sheet of water, hence the name The Pane. Like a Pane of glass. It was at its widest around ninety metres wide and nearly two hundred long. At its far end was a rough dam wall, with water running through a narrow causeway toward the falls.

The falls were those from which the town below had gotten its name. They dropped eight metres in a wide spanning sheet of unbroken water, much like The Pane from which it had originated, but then a jagged outcrop of rock broke the sheet into a mass of splintered cascades that fell down another seven metres to the creek below. This was Shattered Falls and down below the creek flowed into the Shard river.

Rebecca remembered coming here with her parents and sometimes Pop, for picnics, a swim on a hot summer's day or just for somewhere to go. She made a mental note to come back here soon. Just to walk down to the falls, to remember the good times and just because she could.

It was mid-afternoon when Tracey and Tony drove back into Rebecca's driveway. After some goodbyes, and a rough cuddle between Tony and Sarge, Rebecca found herself once again in the country quietness of her home.

As soon as they were inside Sarge curled up beside the fire, even though it had died out. It was like a message to Rebecca and she knew she had to get it going soon anyway. It would be another cold winter's night.

21

Monday morning came with a wind-blown rain. Nothing fierce like the storm that had hit the area just over a week ago but enough to make a trip outside awkward and bitterly cold. The radio had reported that this weather was expected to last all week. Rebecca had gone into the mill early Monday morning, early for her but the mill had already been operating for three hours. She tried to help in the office but could not seem to find her place. She felt like a third wheel and eventually Nashy sent her home because 'there weren't nothing that needed doin'.

Rebecca had to agree. Nashy seemed to have the place running smoothly without her and there were things she wanted to do. Things that she knew would likely take a while and possibly send her on a series of emotional ups and downs.

She got the fire roaring, boiled the kettle, made a coffee, and opened a packet of chocolate biscuits, and then she set off out into Pops shed. For in Pops shed lay boxes. Boxes filled with family history. Links to her parents, photos, newspaper clipping, letters and more. One or two boxes at a time she lugged inside and began the lengthy process of sorting, some were just trash, like the menu from a Chinese restaurant that used to be down the road or the phone book from nineteen ninety-eight. But some were treasures, some painful treasures, like the picture she had drawn for Pop when Jake had been born. Mum, Dad, baby Jake and Rebecca all crudely drawn in front of a big tree. And some were just painful but necessary reminders, like the newspaper clipping she held in front of her now. The report told of a crash, one dead and one critically injured. It did not tell of the two children that would never see their parents again. It was an almost impossible job, not just physically but emotionally, but Rebecca committed herself to it and gave herself a time-frame of the end of the week to have most of it done.

Wednesday just after lunch, was when she found her mothers diary, and any chance of clearing the shed by weeks end, disappeared.

22

The diary was bound in red leather, about the size of a paperback novel and thick. Thicker than it was meant to be with bits of paper, ribbon and an assortment of other things poking from the edges, either marking pages or being stuck in, like pressed flowers. Embossed in gold on the front was one word, 'DIARY' in a font which made it almost unreadable. Written in a black marker above the embossing was another word in handwriting that Rebecca had seen before. 'Karen'. At the base, a finishing touch, written on a piece of fabric tape, and in letters bigger than any of the other writing. 'PRIVATE'. All of it was tied tightly shut with an old thin length of leather shoelace. Probably one of dads.

Rebecca held the diary in her hands, almost cradling it like a religious relic. Turning it over and studying it intently. She pulled it to her face and pressed it to her cheek, and for just a moment she smelt perfume. She closed her eyes and breathed deeply, hoping to catch the smell again, but it was gone. She held it, just touching, feeling, imagining for the next half hour, but she dared not open it. She wanted to, but...she also did not want to. It was a struggle that she knew she would eventually lose, and the book would open, and a flood of emotion would come pouring out. Should she? She should. It would be okay, wouldn't it? Damn, this was hard.

The question was put aside when her phone rang. The sudden sound sending her hand flying across the table, along with her most recent cup of tea, a jar of chocolate covered peanuts and a small pile of newspapers. Sarge woke from her slumber in front of the fire to find that she was now wearing a lukewarm cup of tea. It hardly bothered her as she sniffed at her coat and turned so that it would dry facing the fire.

Rebecca pulled the phone from where she had it stashed in the front of her bra. She knew it was not entirely healthy to carry it there, but she rarely had pockets. As she answered, she stood, grabbed the diary, and headed toward the kitchen.

"Hello"

"You at home Rebecca."

"Is that you Nashy?"

"Yep. Sorry. It's me Nashy."

"Sounds like something's wrong." Rebecca's voice changed from surprise to concern.

"Nah. Nothing wrong. Just if you're not busy I could use a hand. I've got to shoot through and was hoping you could man the phones and help lock up."

"Umm...yeah. No problem. You got a secret rendezvous...anything I should tell Liz."

"Chris-sakes don't be starting rumours like that. She would rip me apart."

"Sorry, just kidding."

"'S'Ok. I got to run Liz in to Tamworth. Got a Doctor's appointment I forgot about."

"I'll be there in fifteen. Don't worry about anything, between me and the rest of the gang there, we'll keep the place running ."

"Ta. I owe you one."

23

Rebecca made it to the mill in twenty-five minutes. Nashy had already left, and Tate met her in the car park with a note.

"He said give you this, or he'll kick my arse."

"Umm okay. Can't have you getting your arse kicked now can we."

Tate did not hang around to chat. He disappeared back into the mill and was soon lost to Rebecca's view amongst the sawdust and noise. She wandered into the mill and headed straight upstairs to the office, took a seat, and folded the note open.

'Sorry to make you come in on short notice. All I need is someone to handle the phone in case it rings. Not expecting any calls but just take a message if there is any. Also, please double check the lock up. 4 o'clock is knock off. The senior boys Karl and Tom can take care of it, but they don't have the code for the security system. Could you please turn it on? It's your dad's birth date, just the six numbers. You know without the 1900 bit. Will talk tomorrow.'

Dads' birthday. Nashy knew Rebecca had a steel trap memory for birth dates, number plates and things like phone numbers, so he knew he did not have to write it down. She folded the note and threw it into the small garbage bin at the end of the desk and then lent back in the chair and waited for something to happen. Nothing did and without the distraction her mind went back to the Diary. She had left it sitting on the kitchen table and now cursed herself for not bringing it with her. Thoughts crossed her mind of opening those first pages or flipping it open somewhere random, and losing herself in her mother's thoughts, but now she was here in the mill. On duty and she would not let Nashy down.

She began to pace the length of the small office, looking down onto the mill floor through the big window. Small piles of sawdust sat along the outside of the windowsill, and it frustrated her that she could not clean them away. Everything was frustrating her at the moment. The slow passage of time, the smell of the saw engine running and the monotonous sound of metal clanging.

Down below she could see the work team. Tate looked like he was wasting time off in the corner, and she scanned the other heads scattered throughout the space. She spotted Matt and found herself staring, which she thought he must have sensed when he turned and looked straight up at her. He turned to one of the other workers, seemed to yell something and pointed up toward the office. The other man nodded, and Matt began to walk toward the stairs that headed up to where Rebecca was standing.

She felt her pulse quicken and started breathing in short sharp bursts. "A panic attack. Now. Seriously.", she muttered.

She turned away from the window and went to flick her hair with her fingers but smacked the back of her hand against the corner of the desk. Hard.

"Shit. Damn. Shit."

Matt stepped into the office just as the last expletive flew from her mouth.

"Sorry. Am I interrupting something?"

"No. I'm sorry. Just smashed my hand." She flicked her wrist, trying to shake away the pain and then clenched it and finally squeezed it between her arm and chest, "and it bloody hurt."

"You okay? For a moment there I thought you were taking the role of Nashy just a bit too seriously. He's got a bit of a mouth on him."

"It's okay. Nothing broken. No blood."

"Good, because I don't know where the accident report forms are."

Rebecca sat back down. Still clutching her hand in her armpit.

"Listen I wanted to apologise about disappearing the other night after dinner."

"I guessed something was wrong. You took that phone call, then got all serious."

"Yeah. My...mum. Just some issues had to shoot home for."

"Back to Queensland?"

"Yeah. All sorted now. You know what families can be like. My mum is a panic junkie, any little thing can turn into a big thing with her."

"Lucky she's got you to sort things out then."

"Yeah. Sorry...I...I heard about what happened to your parents."

"Oh...that was a long time ago." Rebecca caught her breath and swallowed the lump in her throat.

"Still can't be easy when a dope like me talks about their own mum or dad. That accident would've...well, would've messed me up for a long time."

"Like I said, it was a long time ago. Think I've dealt with all the pain now and come through it a bit stronger."

"Yeah. I reckon you have. Anyways I owe you dinner, so we'll work that one out sometime."

"Sounds good to me. Now time for you to get back to work. I'm part boss you know."

Matt did not know whether to take her seriously or not, but he knew there was work to be done. "Yeah. Sorry. I'll get back to it then." And he turned and headed back down the stairs.

Rebecca caught him with a yell that turned him around at the top of the stairs, "Matt...Thanks for the apology."

Matt just nodded and went on his way. Rebecca took a deep breath 'Whoa', she thought 'That could have been awkward. Not sure what all the parents thing was about, but it wasn't as hard to hear someone else mention them as I had thought it would be."

She sat, staring idly at the desk in front of her. Thinking random thoughts, trying to eat up the last hour of time before she had to ensure the mill was locked up. She doodled on a bit of paper, aimlessly drawing little flowers and balloons, and then stood up and began to examine the jumble of yellowed sheets of paper stuck to a small cork notice board beside the door. A calendar from 2016 was half covered by an Emergency Exit poster and several more Health and Safety posters. A receipt for Tim Tams and Tea bags with the total circled in yellow high lighter and the words 'Owe Karl' scribbled at the bottom. Pinned next to it was the cover from a mobile phone box and a note printed in big black letters. 'Missing Phone. Property of Nashy. No Reward.' The phone looked ancient to Rebecca, an old candy bar style and the date that Nashy had typed at the bottom of the note confirmed its age. The note had been printed fourteen years ago.

"Your bloody hopeful Nashy. Not likely to find that now." Regardless, she found herself looking under and behind the office furniture just in case they had only had a 'boy' look.

Then the landline rang. It startled her, and she closed her eyes for a second before she answered.

"Hello. Ford's Timber Mill."

"Well done. You got the name right." It was Nashy.

"Haven't you got better things to do?"

"Just checking things are okay."

"Things are okay. Are you two finished with the Doctor already?"

"Nah. Just waiting. Liz is in there."

"You should be with her you know."

"Bloody hell. No. Women's issues."

"You're a charmer, but seriously you should..."

"Love to chat but here she comes. Thanks for coming over again."

"Nashy before you go. You mind if I ring home from here?"

"Course not. Say hi to 'em from me. Now bye."

The phone went dead, and Rebecca wasted no time in making the call.

It seemed to ring for an eternity, and she had decided to hang up and call back another time, when finally, it was picked up. The voice on the other end sounded hesitant but Rebecca knew instantly that it was Grandma.

"Hello. Who is this?"

"Grandma. It's me. Rebecca."

"Oh, thank god Beccie." She was the only person that had ever called her that, and the only person she could ever imagine saying it, and she loved hearing from her...but not anyone else.

"You sound all flustered. Something wrong?"

"Oh. I was just reading in the paper about the scammie people. The ones pretending to be from the Tax office and trying to get our money...and then the phone rings...and my heart...well it just jumped a beat. I didn't know what I was going to say to them. I didn't want to be rude but ...anyway it's not them. It's my Beccie."

"You are a classic Grandma. I miss your strange little ways."

"Strange?"

"Good strange. My kind of strange."

"Ok...I think. I miss your strange ways too young lady. Really. I really, really miss you. Just the boys around the house now. It's all motors, beers, farts and jokes that go over my head."

"You should come up soon. We can have a good old chat in front of the fire...Oh, and guess what. I got a dog, or Uncle Paul got me a dog. Said I needed security."

"Security? Is there something I should know?"

"No, No. It's okay. Just he didn't like me being alone, and he had to find a home for an old police dog, well not old, just...out of the force."

"He's a good guy to have on your side."

"He is. So, how are you?" Rebecca knew that asking that was sometimes asking for trouble, because sometimes Grandma would tell you. Tell you every little thing.

"It would be a long phone call if I told you, but mainly I'm fine. Few aches and pains but my hearts strong and I still got my wits. Grandad, well he's another story. Had to threaten him with no footy on Sunday afternoon TV to get him to got to the doctors and after all that it's just gout. Too much beer in his early days. Catching up with him now."

"Trust me I know what he's like, but he's my rock."

"Mine too Beccie. Mine too."

"What about Jake?"

"Nothing wrong with him. Bit of attitude sometimes that I wish there was a pill for, but he's a softie, and he'd do anything for you, you know. He misses you the most I think."

"All the more reason to get the lot of you up here for a visit."

"Soon. Jake and Grandad are changing the brakes on the car this weekend and weekend after that we should get up there."

"Really? You just gave me the biggest reason to smile since I've been up here."

"Well can't talk all day Beccie, and you probably got a bunch of things to do."

"Yeah. Locking up the mill today. Guess I best start finishing up. Love you Gran."

"Love you too Beccie."

"Tell the boys I miss them."

"Bye my girl."

'Bye Gran."

Rebecca checked the time. Three forty-five. Fifteen minutes till lockup, and she could hear the machines winding down on the mill floor. She looked down and saw Tate pushing a big old broom down the aisle between the saw benches. Benches were being dusted off and old, stained sheets of what Rebecca knew was calico were being thrown over the top of machinery. The team seemed to have a system for clean-up and lockup because right on four everything was done, and Karl was walking up the stairs to the office.

"Hey Miss Ford."

"It's okay Karl, you can call me Rebecca."

"Well...maybe. Have to see about that...So, the boys are all done, and they'll be out of here quick. All the doors are locked up, so all we need to do is shut down the lights and the mains power to the machine bay, then you can set the alarm."

"The switches up here?"

"Yep. Beside the window is the machine bay switches. Just that big switch will turn 'em all off and lights are just below that. I'll show you."

Karl stepped past Rebecca and flipped the big yellow switch and quickly followed that by running his hand up over the line of light switches. They all turned off except the office light and one above the stairs. Through the window the machines were now doused in shadows.

"Office lights at the door and the stairs light is by the front door, next to the alarm panel."

"Well, that was easier than I thought. Let's go then."

"Right you are Miss Ford...Sorry. Rebecca."

They made their way out of the office, turning the lights out as they went and stopped at the alarm. Rebecca punched in the six digits on the worn key panel. The numbers that she needed to hit were almost worn away, compared to the seemingly untouched other numbers. It beeped three times as she pushed the 'SET' button, and she looked at Karl for confirmation she had gotten it right.

"Yep. That means you got about two minutes to exit the building or it'll start blaring. Nashy...sorry Mr Nash does that every now again."

The two of them stepped outside and Rebecca watched as Karl locked the door and then placed a big old padlock on a chain across it as well.

"That seems like a lot of security."

"We got broke into about five months back and since then Nashy has stepped things up a notch...Ok that's all done. So, if your good I'll be on my way. Got soccer training for the kids."

"Oh yeah sure. How old are they?"

"My boys are twins. Eleven."

"Ok. Hope they have fun. I'll have to catch a game sometime."

"Only junior soccer team in town. Saturday mornings, every second one down at the oval. Other than that, we could be anywhere. Gunnedah, Tamworth, Quirindi. You name it. See you Miss Ford."

Rebecca laughed to herself as Karl climbed into his Ute and drove away. He just could not call her Rebecca without stumbling through the Miss Ford.

24

The trip home was over before she knew it. Living next door to work had its advantages. Rebecca stepped back inside to find Sarge sitting at the fireplace, lazily watching the embers. The dog turned its head and acknowledged Rebecca with a low, friendly bark and padded across the room to get a scratch on the back of her head.

"What'cha been up to girl? Watching soaps?"

Sarge just looked up, urging the hand that still rested on her neck to continue scratching.

"Not talking, I guess. How abouts a walk down the back yard. I didn't even consider you might have wanted a toilet break."

Rebecca headed for the door and before she had even made it halfway down the hall, Sarge had rushed past her and was standing whimpering at the back door.

It was still cool outside and as the two of them stepped down onto the grass, Sarge took off to find some privacy. Rebecca just stood and drew a deep breath of the cool air into her lungs. She noticed the grass was beginning to look a bit long and knew she would have to get the old mower going and make a start on tidying at least part of the back-yard on the weekend or it would become unmanageable. She wandered further down the yard, which was more like a paddock. There were three more sheds back down there and one of them she remembered had the garden tools and mower. She was sure it was the small one with the roof painted green. The other two sheds had just always been there, and she could not recollect ever being in them. That, she decided, would be a mystery to solve tomorrow. A vague memory of Pop talking about Nan's kiln and pottery gear came to mind, but she could not be sure.

Sarge came bounding back across the yard and went straight up the steps and sat at the door. Rebecca raised her eyebrows at the dog.

"You, young lady have become soft. Too comfortable in front of that fire aren't you."

With Sarge curled back up in front of the fire, Rebecca began to prepare for dinner, turning on the television to catch the early news. She stopped peeling carrots when she heard mention of a fire at nearby Willow Tree. Overnight the Bowling Club had burnt to the ground. Vision showed firemen trying to contain a massive blaze but by morning only a charred pile of remnants were left. Police were investigating.

"My god. That place went up. That'll keep Uncle Paul busy.", then back to preparing dinner.

The night fell quickly, as it always did in winter. The sky had cleared, with only patchy cloud breaking a chilly, but star filled sky. Rebecca stopped to gaze up at it as she retrieved another load of wood for the fire. She knew that no one in the city would ever see the milky way like this, a splash of blazing white, dotted across the heavens. Sarge sat and watched her from inside, smartly staying within the warmth of the house, until Rebecca came back inside and closed the back door.

Dinner and dishes were done, the fire was roaring and soon it would die down to the slow burning embers that would keep the house warm all night.

'Time', Rebecca thought, 'to open that Diary.' She grabbed it from the kitchen table and found the sweet spot on the old couch, or more precisely the only remaining sweet spot. Sarge had claimed one end of the couch.

"Where to start girl. Beginning? Or open anywhere?"

After a moment of thought she closed her eyes and found a page somewhere near the middle, opened it up and let the words take her back to her mother.

'OMG. He thinks he's good at soccer. Cute in those shorty shorts but can't kick straight. Lucky Paul picks up on his weaknesses. But still his eyes are just mesmerising. They won the game but only just. No thanks to David. Narromine plays dirty (so do we but I'm biased). Celebratory drinks at the coach's place and then late-night drive back to the share house in Tamworth. Paul spent most of night talking to Meg. GOOD. Stop him giving me and David a hard time.'

Rebecca looked at a clipping from the newspaper that had been stuck into the Diary and folded over. It was a soccer team holding up a trophy, the only time they had ever won. She could make out her Dad and Uncle Paul. None of the other faces looked familiar, but then she saw the coach. It was a young and fit Cameron Nash, according to the list of names below the photo, better known to everyone as Nashy.

"See Nashy, get off the smokes and beer and you could be back to this." She knew Nashy couldn't hear but it was good to break the silence, even if it was with her own voice.

"How about some music Sarge?"

Sarge opened her eyes and looked down over her long snout at Rebecca, which Rebecca decided to take as approval. She walked to the kitchen and turned on the radio. It was partway through some song she had never heard before and she thought it sounded like rubbish, so she turned the dial slightly to the left and immediately stopped when Van Morrison started up with 'Brown Eyed Girl'.

"That's more like it."

She thumbed through some more pages, finding herself looking at the pictures, more than reading anything, but something caught her eye on a page in the back half of the diary. Something that made her stop and look closer.

'I'm scared, but what the hell do I do. He could hurt someone. But I need to tell someone. Do I tell David? Do I just hope he goes away? David would go crazy and I don't think he would end up on the winning side. Is it my fault? I didn't lead him on, did I? I should have made it clear years ago at that end of year footie do. Wish they'd never won that shield. More trouble than it's worth.

I have to tell David. I have to.'

"What the hell? Was someone on dad's soccer team giving mum a hard time? Stalking her maybe." Rebecca checked the date on the entry and turned back a page trying to find more information, and then remembered the photo of all the players that had been in the winning team. She flicked back until she found it and started reading the names and as she lifted the page, the aged glue must have finally given out and the clipping fell to the floor.

And then the lights went out.

25

The room was bathed in the orange glow of the fire, which meant that she was not left in complete darkness. There was a torch in the kitchen drawer, which she grabbed, and she began cursing quietly to herself as she ventured back outside to the fuse box. After a few minutes of flicking and checking the fuses it became apparent that the fuse box was not the issue. She walked to her front veranda and looked across the street. No light from the house across the street. Karl and Alexa's house, she remembered from what Nashy had told her earlier but not Karl from work. They were an older immigrant couple. European but she could not remember whether they were German or Dutch. She could see a flashlight at the side of their house, bobbing up and down as she guessed they were checking their fuses.

Now confident that it was not just her house that was blacked out, she returned indoors and to the warmth of the fire. Sarge had barely moved since she had gone outdoors, and only opened her eyes when Rebecca stood in front of the fire to warm her hands.

"Well girl. Looks like a blackout and who knows when that will be back up. So how about we call it a night."

Sarge seemed to agree and was already nuzzling her head into the cushion and falling back asleep. Rebecca loaded a few more logs onto the fire to burn slowly through the night, grabbed the diary and headed for the bedroom. Within twenty minutes she was under the blankets, but sitting up, two pillows behind her back, reading. A small battery powered lantern sat on the bedside chest, punching out just enough glow to make out the words in the diary. She turned a few pages, hunting for clues, but there seemed to be no more mention of the person. She decided to read on but as always when she chose to read in bed, her eyes began to flutter. They became heavy and no more than five minutes later she fell asleep. The diary falling onto the bed beside her.

The house was dark. They all were. Blackout. It made this easier. The door was not locked. Country people rarely took the security precautions that city dwellers did, but he was surprised by the set of eyes that greeted him as he stepped into the dimly, fire lit room. The dog sat on the couch and looked straight at him. It gave a low growl, but he pulled back his hood and retrieved a pellet of food from his pocket, flicking it toward the couch. The dog sniffed it, looked again at him, then without hesitation ate. When it was done it looked at him for more and when it saw that there was none, it once again tucked its head into the couch and went to sleep. 'Dogs' he thought to himself, 'were easy.'

The kitchen was pitch black but shadowed light filled the hall. As he moved slowly toward it, he saw that the light came from the bedroom. His feet slid slowly across the old floorboards, catching an old rug with his boot heel. He stopped for a moment, adjusting his vision to the shadows, and listening intently for any movement. There was none.

A squeak from a floorboard twisted his face into a pinched grimace but still there was no other noise. He continued till he stood at the door to the bedroom and saw her. Sitting, pillows behind her back, neck slumped to the left and a lantern beside her, that seemed intent on fading away to nothingness any second. Boldly, he stepped closer till he stood beside her, listening to her breathe, watching the way her hair fell across her face, moving slowly with every deep exhale. On the floor beside her, dropped or cast away like a piece of rubbish lay a small book. Red leather. He picked it up and saw the words on its cover. Diary. 'Might be something about me.' He selfishly thought and stuffed the book into the pocket on his jacket. He leant forward wanting to be close, perhaps even wake her with a kiss.

'Could I be that bold'

A touch closer, almost with his lips touching her cheek and then the house was blindingly filled with light. Music blared from somewhere, but he did not wait to find out where. He fled. The back door swung open easily. The dog began barking and she yelled. He was gone, heart beating faster than it had any right to. He fell heavily as he misjudged the last step and took a moment to regain his senses and then ran up the side of the house. Light streamed through the window and music blared. The blackout was over.

"What the ?" Rebecca jumped from the bed; her neck ached from the position in which it had been held for the last few hours. The radio was blaring in the kitchen and Sarge was going mental in the front room. She threw the covers off, not knowing what was going on. Her feet clenched as they walked up the hall, the floorboards icily cold. Only when she reached the kitchen did it finally register to her what was happening. The power had come back on, and when it had gone off all those hours ago, she had failed to switch off any lights or the radio. Now that failing had come back to jolt her awake.

She turned the radio off and turned to find Sarge standing beside her in the kitchen door.

"Sorry girl. That was my fault." Rebecca knelt beside Sarge and wrapped her arm around her neck in a huge hug. "Forgive me?"

Sarge answered by licking Rebecca's chin and Rebecca caught a whiff of some pungent smell on the dog's breath.

"What have you been eating? Smells weird." She looked at the dog's muzzle but saw nothing out of the ordinary. "Let's get you a drink."

Rebecca grabbed a glass of water for herself as she watched Sarge drink from a bowl. The old battery powered clock on the kitchen wall showed that it was just after one am and despite the excitement of the night so far, she still felt tired. As she chatted to Sarge aimlessly, she punctuated every sentence with a yawn until she finally declared, "Stuff it girl. I am dead tired. How abouts you? Back to bed?"

Rebecca checked the fire one last time before heading back into the bedroom. As she wandered down the hall, she noticed the back door slightly open.

"Damn. Must have left that open. Anyone could have gotten in there. Lucky I got you girl."

Sarge had already jumped up onto the end of the bed and had curled herself up. Rebecca was about to climb in herself when she remembered the diary and began to search the floor and bed covers for it. She stood upright, scratched at her wrinkled brow as she tried to imagine where it had fallen.

"Oh well stuff it. Find it in the morning. Too bloody cold.", and then curled up tightly, one of them unaware of the night's intruder, they both fell back asleep, oblivious to the fact that just a kilometre down the road a car was screeching away, driven by a man who had made his mind up to come back again. And again, until she was his.

26

The wind woke Rebecca from a deep sleep. The interrupted slumber of last night had meant she had not forced herself to get up when the alarm had gone off. Instead, she had rolled over, hit the button, and snuggled back down under the covers. Why she had even bothered resetting it, after the power had come on escaped her, but it was just what you did. But now it was nine thirty, and she could hear gusts of wind screaming outside. That alone would not have gotten her to rise from bed, but something was banging against the side of the house, something metal, and she hoped that a sheet of roofing had not come loose.

After putting on a few layers of clothing, she finally ventured outside. Despite the time it still seemed quite dark and the state of the sky told her why. A massive storm was brewing and if the wind did not blow it over the range quickly, it would likely dump some heavy rain before the day was out. She continued outside, investigating the clanging metal noise she had heard, and which was even now screeching and banging as she rounded the corner of the house. She saw it immediately. A metal downpipe hung precariously from the dislodged gutter. The pipe was bent almost in half, partway down its length, and she doubted it would be able to be fixed. A replacement pipe seemed more likely. Now she needed a tradesman, a plumber and it dawned on her that she knew just who to call.

She grabbed the business card stuck to the fridge and found herself saying the numbers out loud as she punched them into her phone and waited for it to ring.

"Braye's Plumbing. Angela speaking."

"Oh, hi Angela. My name is Rebecca. I live out at Shattered Falls, and I've got a bit of a problem with some guttering and a downpipe. So, I was hoping someone could come out and look. I don't think it's a big job, just think it could be an issue if we get a big storm."

"Let's see who is available. Have you used us before Rebecca?"

"No, but Craig gave me your card and told me to ring if I needed help with anything."

" I think we can get someone out there around lunchtime. Don't know if it will be Craig, but since it might storm later today, I think it best we get someone out ASAP."

"I appreciate it."

"Ok I just need to get address details and phone number...and payment is due at time of work for new customers. It's just policy."

"Umm...yeah that's okay. I can arrange that."

"Ok then Rebecca. Thanks for calling Braye's."

"Bye"

Rebecca walked back outside, giving Sarge a moment to run out into the backyard. She stood at the top of the steps, feeling the strong breeze kick her hair up into the air. As she waited, she looked down at the worn grass beside the back stairs and spotted something that she was sure had not been there before. She stepped down, bent to the ground, and picked it up. It had been pushed into the ground as if something heavy had landed atop it. It had more than likely been there when she had come outside only moments before, but she had been focused on finding what was making the scraping noise, but it had not been there yesterday. She held it up to her face looking for any clue to its origin but found no markings and then her phone rang, and she put the small, black flashlight into her pocket.

"Hello." Rebecca answered tentatively, not recognising the phone number. After Uncle Paul had given her the phone, she had spent time entering the names and numbers of almost everyone she knew, so that when they called their name would pop up and some even had photos. This one however was just a number.

There was silence on the other end of the line, then a groan and a brief, muttered expletive.

She tried again, "Hello'"

"Hello...Sorry...Hello...umm this hands-free thing is rubbish. Let's start again. Hi Rebecca, this is Craig from the Plumbing service."

"Oh, hi Craig. Sorry I rang and used your name, but you did say to ring if I needed help."

"Yeah, it's fine, really. We can use all the business we can get. Listen Angela said you got a busted downpipe and gutter."

"Is that something you can fix?"

"Sure. Just ringing to let you know I should be there in about two hours. Just finishing a hot water system repair and I'll be on my way."

"That's great. I was worried with the storm coming."

"Well don't worry. I'll take care of it. See you in two."

Once back inside she placed the small torch on top of the fridge, made some tea and set about solving the other mystery of the night. The whereabouts of her mother's diary. Firstly, she checked the floor of the bedroom. Down on hands and knees, head poking under the bed. Peering into the dim light, struggling to find any shape that resembled a diary. She had a thought and went back to the kitchen, returning moments later with the small torch. The light from it gave life to the shapes under the bed. A pair of old slippers, plus one lonely boot; a small box, possibly a shoebox; and the old chamber pot that she hoped had not been used in a long time; but no diary. Next, she searched the bed, lifting the pillows and shaking them vigorously, pulling back the quilt, blankets, and sheets. Searching every inch of them as she went. In the end she pulled them off the bed. A change of sheets was due anyway. Finally, in desperation she pulled the mattress from the bed. Its weight surprised her. Comfortable but extremely heavy. Still no diary, but she did find an old yellowed envelope. It had been tucked under the mattress, sitting atop a metal slat and almost in the middle of the bed.

The view now gave her a clear picture of what lay under the bed. Lots of dust, the box (which ended up containing a bunch of old plastic flowers and a note 'They ran out of real ones. Love you always') and the collection of boots and shoes, but still no diary.

Rebecca grabbed the old envelope, frustrated that the diary had still not been found. As she opened the envelope and looked inside, she closed her eyes and shook her head.

"You silly old bugger."

She reached in and pulled out a wad of fifty-dollar notes. She knew Pop had liked to hide money in the house and possibly in the shed, but she had thought he had stopped that years ago when she had roused on him before. 'Never know when I might need it. When anyone might need it and the banks...don't trust 'em. Not when you're depending on em.' She could almost hear him say those words. In all she counted out six hundred and fifty dollars.

It took her mind off finding the diary for the moment, and she did have the task ahead of remaking her bed. 'Maybe', she thought 'This will come in handy for the plumber.' She looked up, waved the money, and gave a nod. "Thanks Pop."

Putting the bed back together was more of an effort than taking it apart. Rebecca took the opportunity to rotate the mattress. Judging by the indentations on the base of it from the slats, she doubted it had ever been turned. New sheets, new pillowcases, and an extra blanket, and in just over half an hour, despite the cold she had worked up a sweat and a worrying muscle pain in her left shoulder. But still, no diary. Her mind began to come up with extravagant explanations for its disappearance. Rats, or maybe Sarge had chewed it up somewhere, or did she dream the whole thing, was there ever really a diary. She threw her hands into the air and for the moment gave up. 'Maybe' she reasoned, 'I just need to stop looking and it will come to me.' So, she did, but it did not.

She stepped outside again, needing some air and a bit of space to stretch her arm. Sarge followed her out and ran off as usual to do what dogs needed to do.

"Hope you're not going to shit out a diary. I'll be very cranky if you do."

Her phone gave a buzz and a message flashed onto the screen.

[15 minutes. In town now. Gutter will be fixed in no time. Craig@Brayes]

She typed back a message.

[OK. C u soon]

She yelled across the yard to Sarge. "C'mon girl. Time to get presentable. We're getting a visitor."

She barely had time to wash her face and change out of her pyjamas when a van pulled up in the driveway. Sarge began her barking and Rebecca had to calm her. The barking grew in intensity as if she sensed danger, and it was only when Rebecca commanded her to sit and be quiet that she stopped.

Craig knocked on the front door and Rebecca answered immediately. Craig wore a hi-vis jumper and a pair of mud streaked pants. His boots also were laden with their own fair share of mud.

"Hi Rebecca. Sorry didn't get here sooner."

"Oh, that's alright. It doesn't look like the rains going to hit us anyway. It's all blowing over the mountain."

"Yeah. Radio said Coffs Harbour was already getting a drenching. So, whereabouts is this gutter issue."

"Yeah. Ex police dog, and she's been told to guard me with her life. So, don't take it personally. I'll come out and show you the downpipe."

Outside the clouds had started to thin out. The wind still blew ferociously, sending Rebecca's hair flying into her eyes. She held it back as she pointed down the side of the house to the gutter and downpipe, which swayed even more dramatically now with every gust of wind.

"Looks like it's just about to fall off. I can fix it, but it will just be a PVC pipe and a few adapter fittings and should be able to get the gutter seated back up there properly. Just have to ask one thing."

"Ok." Rebecca creased her brow, wondering just what request was about to come. "I've got cash to pay, so you don't have to worry about that."

"Ha. No, No. Just wandering if you would be able to steady the ladder. This breeze is likely to send me flying if it catches me at just the wrong time."

"I can hold the ladder. Just don't drop anything on my head."

"It's a deal."

Craig returned to his van and came back a few moments later with a ladder and a belt full of tools. Once the ladder was secure against the side of the house, he looked Rebecca straight in the eye.

"You got this?"

"Trust me, I got this."

'Ok then my young Padawan."

"Padawan. Don't tell me you're a Star Wars fan too."

He gave her a bemused look as he stepped up onto the later, "Isn't everybody?"

The wind gusted again, and Rebecca put one foot against the base of the ladder and braced her arms along its side, as Craig reached the higher rungs. She looked up, squinting her eyes as if that would protect should anything fall, but all she saw was his behind as he reached his arms up unto the gutter. As Craig pulled a hammer from his belt, he caught her upward gaze.

"Stop looking at my butt."

"I wasn't looking at your...Ok...I'll stop looking at your butt."

"Ohhhhkay...I was actually just kidding...didn't think you were looking at it."

"Enough butt talk okay, I'm embarrassed enough."

"Deal. Let's change the subject then. The gutter has just come loose from a couple of clips. I should be able to get them back on for now, but it probably should be replaced sometime soon."

Rebecca heard the hammer bang against the metal gutter several times, but she did not dare look up. She heard Craig strain and grunt as she guessed he was putting the gutter clips back into place and then a yell of pain and a curse.

"Look out."

Rebecca stepped back quickly as a hammer fell to the far side of the ladder. It would have missed her, but survival instincts had taken over for just a second. The ladder wobbled and Rebecca moved quickly back into position to secure it.

From above Craig yelled. "It's okay. Just me coming back down. Sorry about the hammer. Caught my finger on the edge of the clip."

"Are you bleeding?"

"Nah...just nearly pulled my fingernail off. Stings like a ...stingy thing."

Craig stepped down the last few rungs and stood beside Rebecca on the grass. He shook his finger, and then squeezed it in the palm of his other hand. After a moment he released it, stretched out his fingers and they both saw a bright bruise growing under the nail of his pointer.

"You want me to get some ice?" Rebecca asked concernedly.

"Nah. It's okay."

"Good 'because I don't think I've got any anyway."

The final remark set them both laughing. "Mind if I just sit a moment. Let the pain ease."

"No problem. Back veranda is just the right size for sitting on."

Both set off to the back yard, sat down on the old wooden planks that made up the veranda and let their legs dangle down to the grass below. The bulk of the house shielded them from the worst of the breeze. Still, whirling gusts of errant wind came screaming around toward them every few minutes, sending Rebecca's hair flying across her face.

"You should tie that up. Your hair I mean. It's pretty but not built for handling this wind."

"Well that was a roundabout way to give me a compliment."

"You're welcome. So, you all settled in since I saw you last. It's been what...about two weeks?"

"Yeah about that, and yes I think I've found my place in the world. Beats the city hands down, and the sky, especially at night, those stars...well there are no words."

"I know, right. Just makes you want to lay out under it and stare up all night."

"How's the finger now?"

Craig stretched out his palm, turned it over, back and forth a few times and then clenched his fist. "I reckon I'll be able to keep it."

"You sure, because I think there's a pair pretty sharp garden shears in the shed that would cut right through it."

"Now that just sounds evil. I think you're supposed to do the crazy laugh when you say things like that."

"I'm laughing on the inside."

Craig just gave a huge grin and stood up, "Ok, best get this job finished then."

Rebecca followed the wounded plumber back to the ladder and gripped its frame as Craig once again climbed up.

"Let's see if we can't get this old downpipe off now."

He made his way toward the top of the ladder, stopping when he was just above the broken downpipe and pulled a nail from a twisted bracket that was supposed to have held the pipe in place. The pipe now hung on just one lower bracket and it dropped slightly lower so that the opening was now level with Craig's face. He peered inside.

"Well this would have been useless anyways. Looks like a tennis ball or something wedged a bit further down inside."

He pulled a screwdriver from his belt and poked it into the opening of the pipe.

"Must have been here for a long time. It feels all soft. Almost like tissue paper. I reckon I could push the screwdriver right through it.... Ohhhh Shit.... RUN."

Rebecca looked up and saw Craig barrelling down the ladder, two and three steps at a time. Jumping the last section to land heavily on the grass.

"I SAID RUN.... WASPS."

Rebecca let go of the ladder and ran, as instructed. Craig's foot caught the ladder and made it topple onto the downpipe, which in turn now fell. Fell directly onto Craig's head. Rebecca could hear the hum of the wasp's wings but kept heading for the front of the house, covering her head with her hands as she ran. Craig however now had his shirt caught on the bent bracket that still clung to the ladder. He struggled and pulled hard, ripping the shirt, a shredding tear that Rebecca heard over the sound of the wasps, but it was what she heard next that made her stop and turn. Craig gave three huge screams of pain. Howls that she was sure would be heard by her distant neighbours, and then the obligatory swearing, that invariably accompanies a wasp sting.

"You little striped bastards. Shit, Shit, God damn, Shit."

Rebecca ran back to him, grabbed him by the hand and half led, half dragged him to the back veranda and in through the back door to the relative safety of the house. Once inside she could stop and take the time to look what damage had been done to Craig. He was clasping his hand across the top of his other arm. Rebecca pulled his hand away, ignoring Craig's pained moans, so that she could see. His shirt had been torn open there when he had attempted to escape the clutches of the downpipe, and the wasps had taken advantage of the entry point. One of the wasps was smeared across the reddened flesh on his upper arm, with two swollen stings getting redder by the second. A third sting showed on the back of the hand that had been clenching his arm. She led him into the bathroom, turning on the tap in the sink and throwing a towel into the basin. She wiped the stung areas with the wet towel, applying some liquid soap to ensure she removed as much venom as possible. She looked Craig in the eye.

"Hold the towel over the sting for a moment. I'll find something cold to put on it."

"You got no ice remember."

"Maybe I keep some for special occasions...or maybe a pack of frozen peas will do just as good. I'll be right back."

Rebecca went as quickly as she could, hoping that there was a pack of frozen peas in the freezer. There was. She grabbed the peas and a frozen pack of corn as well and rushed back to Craig. She found him now sitting on the floor, the towel wrapped tightly around his arm, strangely smiling at her as he came back.

"What's so funny?"

"You think maybe they could be radioactive wasps. I could turn into a superhero. Climb up walls, hide in drainpipes and stuff."

"You are delirious."

She squatted down and removed the towel, wrapped it around the peas and placed it back on the stings on his arm. "Now put this one on the back of your hand." She pushed the corn into his hand as she tied the towel off.

"I don't like corn."

"Then no dessert for you."

Craig closed his eyes and lent back against the wall and closed his eyes.

"How's the pain now?"

"Not getting any worse, or better...but the back of my head feels a bit achy too. The pipe must have caught me there. Happened so quick. I don't remember it all."

Rebecca made Craig bend his head forward and felt through his hair until she found the lump.

"Yep. You got a massive egg there. Maybe I should check you for shock...back in a sec."

Rebecca went to her bedroom where she had left the little black torch, she had found in her yard earlier. As she bent to pick it up from the bed, she heard a crash as something hit the tiles in the bathroom.

"My god. What Now?"

As she re-entered the bathroom, she found Craig head down in the sink gulping down mouthfuls of water. Above him the bathroom mirror had been slid to one side, revealing bottles of old medication. Pops old tablets.

"What are you doing now?"

"Sorry I needed something for the pain. Panadol, Nurofen, something."

"So, did you take anything?"

"Yeah some of these and that one."

Rebecca read the bottles and packets that Craig had indicated. Paracetamol and some type of antihistamines.

"How many?"

"Umm four of the Paracetamol ones and a couple of the antihisty thinghies."

"Bloody hell...That was stupid...I don't think that's a good mix."

"I'm gunna sit down."

"Ok, but not here. Out in the lounge room."

Rebecca led Craig once again. Sat him down on the couch and turned on the torch.

"What's that for?"

"To check your eyes."

"What...did they take my eyes? Wasps took my eyes? Look quick, make sure they're there."

"Ok. You're starting to scare me. Just open your eyes and look at the torch."

She waved the torch in front of his face a few times, checking his pupil dilation and tracking, but it all seemed normal.

"Hey." Craig announced, sounding groggier and groggier by the moment, "That's my torch. What'cha doing with my torch?"

"Found it."

"Ok. Do you have any more corn? I think I like it now."

"Think we best get you to the doctors."

"Doctors? Let's go baby, I'm driving."

"Umm...No. We'll go in my car. You can pick yours up tomorrow."

"You think I can. Did they make me strong? The radioactive wasps...so I can pick up cars."

"No...I didn't mean...Holy Shit. You need to rest."

Rebecca called to Sarge, who in all the commotion she had forgotten about. She turned and found the dog standing behind her, just watching, cocking her head from side to side, almost looking amused at the situation. In fact, Sarge had been shadowing her the whole time, or more precisely watching Craig. Watching, doing her job, protecting. Craig was after all, a stranger and there was something else. Something that Sarge just could not make out, but it worried her. Rebecca grabbed a few of her things and went outside to open the garage and saw that the driveway was blocked by Craigs van. She went back to Craig, who now seemed to be playing Incey Wincey spider with his fingers.

"I need your keys. I have to move your van."

"Ok, but you be home before midnight young lady."

He fumbled in his pocket and pulled out the keys, which Rebecca grabbed. "You know if this wasn't so serious, you would be quite funny."

She walked out the front door once again, the screen slamming shut behind her. From inside she heard Craig yell "BINGO" and Sarge gave a muted bark.

The side door of the van was still open, and she moved to slide it shut. Looking inside she was surprised by how neat it was. Everything seemed to have a place. As she began to slide the door, she noticed a black torch hanging from a holder on the wall of the van. A torch that looked identical to the one she had found earlier. Another the same hung beside it and beside it an empty socket that looked like it would hold yet another torch.

The door slid shut, and she went around the white van and climbed into the driver's seat. Instead of reversing out, she turned the steering wheel and parked the van on the grass in front of the house, locked it up, opened the garage and brought the Suzuki out onto the driveway.

'Now' she thought to herself, 'the tricky bit.'

She was surprised how easy it was to get Craig to the car, strap him in and get Sarge into the back. She had been expecting to struggle to get Craig to walk down the stairs and step up into the car, but he did it with a minimum of fuss. She climbed into the car herself, started it up, turned down the radio and began the at least half hour journey to Tamworth Base Hospital. She could have tried one of the doctors at the medical centre, but she just did not know how serious it all was.

It was mid-afternoon and the wind had finally died away as they headed out of her front gate. Craig looked at her, then looked into the rear vision mirror at his van for a moment, then turned back to Rebecca.

"You stole my ladder didn't you."

'No. You can get it tomorrow or whenever the Doctor says you can drive."

"Ok, because I need my ladder, but you can keep the torch."

"Are you sure this is your torch?"

"I think so. I bought two of them last week. Bunnings had a crate full of them. Three dollars. Lots of people bought 'em. I could go for a sausage sandwich."

"Soon. Soon. Just rest."

"Ok. Thanks, pretty lady."

Rebecca was not sure if he was being sincere or if it was the tablets and head knock talking, but it did make her smile.

Before they left town, she made one last stop. Tracey was behind the counter as Rebecca walked in with Sarge by her side.

"Bec. Mum don't usually let dogs in the shop."

"I'm really sorry, but could you look after her for a while. I got to make an emergency dash to Tamworth."

"Emergency?"

Rebecca explained the situation and Tracey took it all in and before there was even a chance to ask questions Rebecca ran out the door with a final pat on Sarges head and a "Love you both."

Tracey and Sarge just looked at each other both thinking the same thing, 'What the f...'

27

The drive took longer than she had expected. By the time they had gotten to Tamworth it was just after five and the roads were buzzing with end of day traffic. Craig had lent against the window, breathing deeply most of the trip but Rebecca had refused to let him go to sleep. She had kept the conversation flowing, encouraging Craig to talk most of the time and occasionally both had sung along to songs on the radio. Rebecca learnt a great deal about Craig's family. His sister worked at the hospital they were heading to now, as well as his brother-in-law, who was a paediatric doctor. His dad still ran the plumbing business he had started twenty-three years ago, and mum stayed at home, but was right into the Country Women's Association. She apparently made a 'Bitching' lemon meringue and 'pretty damn good' lamingtons. Most of the conversation had been less random than before but occasionally the delirium kicked back in, and he wandered off.

As they turned onto the road that led them to the hospital, they passed a police car and Craig waved, as did Rebecca, but she was shocked when Craig's wave turned into a raised middle finger, that luckily was not observed.

"Pigs man. Oppressing our generation. Revolution is coming man."

"That's not nice."

Craig looked down, "Sorry Miss Wilkins."

"Who?"

"Oh shit. Sorry. Mrs Wilkins was my maths teacher. You look nothing like her."

"Ok. Well here we are. Hopefully we find your sister in there."

"Probably stealing body parts."

"Hmm. Probably not."

"Yeah, well she's not getting mine. Take photos of my legs and stuff, just in case she tries to sell them."

"Yep, okay. We'll do that."

She parked outside the Emergency doors and honked her horn at a nurse that was standing out front.

As the nurse came over, Rebecca climbed out of the car and walked around to Craig's door. The nurse stopped at the kerb just as Rebecca swung Craig's door open.

"Something wrong?"

"Maybe, maybe not. Just need a little help getting him inside."

"Drunk?"

"No. Got a nasty whack on the head, stung by wasps and took some tablets that are making him wacko."

Craig swung his legs out of the car but remained seated "Don't forget my fingernail. Oh and, she stole my ladder."

"Aren't you Tania Braye's brother?" asked the nurse.

"Yep. She sells organs on the black market you know."

"What?", the nurse's face crinkled up in shock.

"Take no notice. Like I said he's been a bit wacko since it all happened." apologised Rebecca.

"Ok. Best get him in and checked out then."

Craig was able to stand by himself, but balance was trickier. With Rebecca on one side and the nurse on the other, Craig's arms hung over their shoulders, they ambled into the emergency room. The nurse directed them to a seat and then went off to find a doctor. Around them about fifteen other people gave Craig a quick stare, then went back to dealing with their own pain or the pain of the loved one with them.

Ten minutes later they were in a small room. A doctor and Craig's sister rattling of medical terms as they checked pupils, pulse, temperature and whatever else they could prod, without opening him up.

Craig's sister, Tania came over to where Rebecca sat and looked down as she spoke.

"So are you...a girlfriend."

"What? No. Craig was just doing a job at my place when this all happened."

"Ok. He doesn't tell me much about his private life. He could be married with three kids...but thanks for taking the time to get him in here."

"So, is he okay?"

"I think so. Looks like just a combination of everything. The tablets didn't help but the doctor doesn't think they are going to be a problem. Much as I would have liked to get a stomach pump going on him."

Craig turned his head from the doctor and looked at Tania, a touch of panic in his voice. "What?"

"Settle down Mr Bean. I'm just kidding. Lay down and get some sleep."

Craig lay back and closed his eyes.

"Doc wants to keep him for a few hours in case of a concussion, so you're good to go when you're ready."

"I guess he's in good hands then. His van is still at my place..."

"And my ladder."

"Yes...and his ladder."

"It's okay I'll let dad know and get him or one of the boys to call in tomorrow and pick it up, if that's alright with you."

"Yeah. That's fine."

Rebecca approached the bed that Craig was lying on. She felt largely responsible for what had happened and felt the need to apologise.

"Listen, I really have to say sorry. The wasps, the falling pipe, and those pills. It shouldn't have happened."

"There's no way you could have known anything like that was going to happen. I'm the one that should be apologising. That pipe still needs fixing."

"I'm sure it will get done. I'm just glad you're okay."

"And I'm really sorry if I said weird stuff. I don't know what that was about."

"Are you kidding? Almost peed myself trying not to laugh."

Craig started to laugh himself but stopped suddenly.

"Damn. Laughing makes my head hurt."

"Then don't laugh. I'll let you get some rest now, and I want to get home before it gets too dark."

Rebecca looked back one last time as she left the room and headed out of the hospital. Craig was already laying back, closing his eyes, and drifting off to sleep. His sister, Tania gave Rebecca a nod of thanks as she headed toward the car park.

'Well, that was a day and half', she thought and exhaled deeply in relief. Outside the sun had already set. The wind had blown away any clouds that might have threatened rain and already the stars were shining, just not as brightly as back home. Once out of Tamworth, she flipped on the high beam, driving just a little more carefully. The last thing she wanted now to end her day was to hit a kangaroo. Without a bull bar, she knew a hitting a big grey, could prove disastrous for them both.

An hour later she pulled up outside Tracey's shop. She had seen several kangaroos, but none had been on the road. At one stage a fox had darted across her path, but it had been well ahead of the car.

The shop was shut now, but she knew Tracey would be around back in her flat. She stepped out of the car, instantly regretting not putting on a warmer jumper or jacket. Once around the back of the shop, she could hear Tony's voice and Tracey giggling. She knocked twice and Tracey answered.

"About time Miss Bec. We were going to send out a search party."

The warmth inside the flat was welcome, and as she stretched out her arms to soak in some heat, she saw Tony and Sarge sitting on the floor in front of the TV. Sarge was enjoying a belly rub and when she saw Rebecca she jumped to her feet, quickly brushing Tony aside.

"Sorry to interrupt you two. Should I come back later?"

Tony looked up, almost disappointed that Sarge had left him.

"Just keeping her occupied until dinners ready."

Tracey, standing in the kitchenette, tapped a spoon against the side of an old cooking pot.

"Speaking of which. Tony, grab an extra bowl. Bec's joining us for dinner, regardless of what she says."

Rebecca, exhausted from her day, accepted the offer without a fight. Within in minutes, three of them sat around the small, round table and dove into the steaming bowls of pasta and homemade garlic damper. Sarge had already finished the beef sausages that Tony had cooked up for her earlier and now sat on the floor at Rebecca's feet.

"Thank you so much for taking her. I was a bit frantic."

"Yes, you were. Seemed a bit concerned for just a run-of-the mill tradie."

"He...Craig, is a nice guy. I hardly know him, so don't get any ideas there, but he was easy to talk to and it's a bit quiet around the house sometimes."

Tony piped in, mouth half full of bread, "Desperate Housewife."

"Thanks for the support, Dog Napper."

Tracey gave Tony a slap on the wrist, "Despite what this Bozo might say, it's good to be making friends, and you're a good friend to have."

The meal continued with a mishmash of talk about Rebecca's hectic day, Tony's flat tire and Tracey's run in with a school age, shoplifter until Tony stood up and started taking the bowls away.

"Ok girls, Thursday night is my turn for the dishes and then I'm off to bed. Got to be at Port Macquarie by lunchtime for a meeting."

Rebecca stood as well, "Yeah. I should get going too, thanks for the feed and looking after Sarge."

"You know it's okay. It's been a while since I've had a bestie." Tracey stood and gave Rebecca a hug as they both walked toward the door. "Oh, and are you up for a Pub meal tomorrow night again? I think there's a big Trivia night planned."

"Trivia ? Yeah. That would be good actually."

"Ok see you there at seven. Now go get some sleep, you look exhausted."

It felt late when she got home to the cold and darkened house. She checked her phone for the time. Only Nine Thirty-Two, but it had been a long day, and she yawned as she opened the car door, drawing in a lungful of the frosty night air. Sarge jumped past her and started barking as something jumped from the old iron roof into a tree.

"Girl. It's just a possum. Please no more excitement tonight."

Sarge barked at the tree a few more times and then joined Rebecca as she unlocked the front door and stepped inside. The lights flickered on as she flicked the switch. The fireplace was just a blackened pile of charcoal covered logs, not a hint of warmth.

"Ok. Fire, Cuppa and Bed. Then onward to Friday."

It took almost half an hour to complete those three tasks but only five more minutes before she was overcome with sleep. Thursday was finally done and dusted.

Friday morning, one a.m. and as soon as he stepped out of the warmth of the car, the cold seeped straight through every layer of clothing. Breath turned to steamy mist and a deep inhale felt like a knife upon the inside of your throat. The road was dark, only a touch of moonlight filtered down from what was now a sky scattered with light cloud. He could not remember any night being so cold, but he had to do it. He would not be denied again.

He stepped around the old fence, tangled with jasmine, and stopped dead in his tracks. He stood in the middle of the driveway and would have been visible to anyone that had bothered to look, but he was fixated on what he saw and only one thought went through his mind.

'Bitch.'

In the front yard sat a van. A van whose side read 'Brayes Plumbing'.

How could she. This could not be allowed to be. I need to fix it. End it, and he knew just how.

He did not even feel the cold as he walked back to the car, his blood boiling in anger, his mind set on a new task. Murder.

28

Friday morning promised to be warm, for winter. The eight a.m. news teased a pleasant twenty-four degrees and similar across the weekend. Rebecca sat on the edge of the back veranda, sipping from the mug of milky tea, listening to the morning birds, and letting her skin soak in the sun. There were a few things she wanted to get done today. Amongst them the most highly rated was a good clean-up of the house. It had not seen a vacuum since she had gotten there and perhaps, she thought, she would stumble across the diary. She also wanted to check in on Nashy to make sure Liz was okay. She had sensed a bit of concern behind Nashy's cynicism. At some stage she assumed someone would come pick up Craig's van, and she wanted to make sure they did not forget that damn ladder. And finally, later tonight, dinner and trivia night, and she just might invite Matt and even Tate if she ran into them at the mill.

She stood, ruffled Sarges fur, waking her from the sunny slumber she had been enjoying beside Rebecca and headed back inside.

"C'mon girl we got some work to do."

The vacuum was ancient. Its hose had been patched in several places with electrical tape and one of the wheels looked almost ready to fall off, but it did what any good vacuum needed to do. She started in the bedroom, cursing as it took hold of a loose sock, which she managed to salvage before it disappeared to the innards of the old Hoover. She moved on down the hallway, turning into the kitchen, and finally ending in the lounge room. The floor here was covered in patches with a fine soot from the fireplace from when the door had been opened but surprisingly the vacuum picked it up with hardly any effort. She was about to do a quick sweep of the floor in front of the couch when she caught sight of a sheet a paper laying beneath the small coffee table. It was the photo of her dads winning football team, fallen from her mother's diary. She bent down onto her knees and looked under the table and couch hoping that the missing diary might also be there, but she found nothing. Once the vacuum was packed away, she took a seat in the kitchen and stared at the clipping from the paper. The photograph of the young men, her father, Uncle Paul and Nashy included, holding aloft the shield that they had won.

"Which one of you bastards messed with my mum?"

She continued staring at the photos trying to make out any features of anyone else that she might have known, but it was a long time ago.

Sarge, who had been sleeping as was her normal these days, jumped up and began to bark. A knock came to the front door and Rebecca heard a car running somewhere close by.

A sheepish Craig stood at the door. He gave Rebecca a crooked and almost cheeky smile that made her laugh.

"Seriously. Still laughing at me."

"No. No. Just remembering the good times, we had, way back yesterday."

"Yeah. Apologies for all that."

"How's your head?"

"Doc says I'm fine. No damage done that wasn't there already."

Behind Craig another older man, short but muscly walked over from the utility now parked in the driveway.

"This is my dad. Dad, this is Rebecca."

Craig stepped aside as his father extended his arm to shake Rebecca's hand.

"I hear you two got up to some mischief yesterday."

Rebecca took his hand and held on for the ride as Craigs father shook it like a can of paint.

"Dad settle down. You'll pop it off at the wrist."

"Oh sorry. Just wanted to thank you for what you did."

"I didn't do much. Probably caused half of the trouble."

"Not how he tells it. Anyways, thanks for watching out for him."

"It's okay."

"Now, Craig tells me we've got to fix a downpipe."

"But there's wasps."

"That's why I brought this little beauty along." Craig's dad held up a yellow and white can with an extended nozzle. "this'll sort 'em out."

He gave it a shake, almost as vigorous as his handshake and stepped back down the stairs.

"Well don't stand there gawping at the lady boy. Lead the way."

Craig led his dad around the side of the house. The ladder and downpipe still lay there, in the grass that seemed to have grown even longer in the past twenty-four hours.

"Lawn needs cutting Miss Rebecca. I know a good lawn guy if you want."

"No, it's fine. That's my weekend job."

"Right you are. Now let's get this pipe sorted."

Rebecca stood back as Craig and his dad firstly sprayed inside the pipe, stepped back and watched the wasps fly off drunkenly, then they righted the ladder, removed the downpipe and finally installed a new PVC pipe. All in less than half an hour.

"Well, that was impressive. What's the bill come too?"

Craig's dad shook his head, "No. Won't take your money. I look after those that look out for me and my family."

"You have to take something."

"Glass of water will do. Then Craig and I will be on our way. Got some catching up to do after yesterday."

"Thank you, Mr Braye. I really appreciate it."

"Call me Kev, and make sure you call us if you need any other work done. You'll get good rates."

Rebecca gave Craig a sideways glance and a tight smile, not knowing what else to say.

Craig gave her his big cheeky smile in return.

Kev caught them looking at each other and knocked Craig's shoulder as he lifted the ladder and headed back to the van. "Well boy, you going to ask her out or not. You haven't shut up about her since this morning."

"Seriously dad." Kev gave a laugh that trailed off as he walked away, "Sorry about dad."

"That's okay. He seems harmless. So.... you going to ask."

"I was trying to be professional. You know, work and all but yeah...I enjoyed chatting with you and if you wanted, I'd like it if we could catch up again...with less wasps this time."

"What did you have in mind?"

"If you like music and a bit of dancing, there's a B and S next weekend out near Kootingal."

"B and S?"

"Sorry. It's Bachelors and Spinsters. Just what we call a good old country dance party. Local bands."

"Sounds fun. Give me a call through the week. You still got my number."

"Yeah. In my phone."

"Cool. Now you best be going before your dad gets us married."

She watched them pack the van, asking Craig twice if he had his ladder, and waving bye as Kev took off in the Ute, closely followed by Craig. When they had gone, she headed back inside grabbed her keys, the newspaper clipping and called to Sarge. The two of them climbed into the Suzuki and took the short trip to the mill.

29

Nashy was upstairs as expected, tapping away at the computer with the phone pressed against his ear. Rebecca was sure he had not even seen her enter the office and gave a cough, so that she did not startle him.

"Got to go. Someone waiting to talk to me. Invoice is on its way. Take care mate."

He swung around in the chair, "Morning young lady. What brings you in today?"

"Just checking on ya. Checking on Liz too. Was worried she was alright."

"Yeah, she's okay. None of us getting any younger. Just another lot of pills to take every night. She'll be fine."

"Good. So...something else I wanted to ask you about as well."

"I see."

"Remember when you and dad won the footy comp."

"The glory days, or day I should say. Never won another one after that."

"Well, I found this old photo and was wondering if you remembered the names of the people in it."

Nashy grunted, "You doubting my memory girl? Let's see this photo then."

Rebecca pulled the folded clipping from her pocket and handed it over to Nashy, who held it up to his face and began squinting before finally pulling a pair of glasses from his pocket and putting them on.

"That's better. Okay, yeah, I remember all these blokes. Me at the end there of course. You dad and your Uncle Paul there in the middle of the top row, but you knew that."

"What about the rest? Any loose cannons amongst them?"

"Loose cannons? What you looking for? You don't want to go dredging up trouble young lady."

"Just something I read. Someone might have been hassling mum. Just tell me their names, write them down if you can."

Nashy looked Rebecca in the eye and saw just how serious she was. "Okay, but you know you can talk to me or Liz if somethings bothering you."

"I will, I promise. I just need to get this straight in my head."

"Right let's see. Top row, from the left you got Bill Nolan, think he's living in Western Australia. Eric Sutter, he was a real funny bastard, I mean made you laugh, not weird. He lost a leg in a farm accident, died a few years back, some say he might have killed himself, but I don't know for sure. Lou or Luigi Maritelli. Him and his wife got a little restaurant up in Narrabri. Then there's your dad and your Uncle Paul. Bernie Patterson. He runs a little property out west of town. Doing it tough with the drought. Good bloke though. Real decent."

Nashy looked up from the photo and found Rebecca staring intently at him.

"Bloody hell girl. You're making me feel like I'm being interrogated."

"Sorry. Just keep writing and talking, then I'll leave you alone."

Nashy gave a cough, "Where was I? Okay. Jack Davies, or Davidson. Davies that's it. He was a rough nut. Bit of a crim they say. Got shot by his own brother in some drug deal gone wrong or something. Killed him. Then me, good looking bloke wasn't I."

"Not too shabby at all."

"Bottom row Trent Simmons, Patrick Collison, John O'Hennessy, Ed Shaw, Billy Cole, Arnie Ambrose and Stephen West. Phew, how's that for memory."

"I'm impressed. Pretty good for an old bloke."

"Watch it missy. Some life in this old bloke yet."

"I know. Thank you Nashy. So, of all those names...who would you think I should be concerned about. Is there anyone there that might have harmed mum?"

Nashy stood up and walked to the big pane of glass that looked down over the mill. He stood there silent for a minute before turning and looking at Rebecca. She gasped when she saw what appeared to be the beginnings of tears in his eyes.

"What? What's wrong?"

"You really don't know do you girly?"

"Know what?"

"Ed Shaw. Edward Harold Shaw. The bloke was an alcoholic. He...he's the bastard that got drunk and ran your mum and dad off the road."

Rebecca fell silent. She stood and walked towards the stairs, stopping to hold herself up against the wall. Her legs had suddenly become unsteady, and she could feel her skin tingling.

A thought filled her mind, 'Not an anxiety attack now, please.', but she knew it was too late.

She felt her legs go and suddenly she was falling. A set of arms grabbed her, and she looked up to see Matt's face. He had been coming up the stairs just as she had walked to them. Matt held her tightly and Rebecca wrapped her arms around him and began to cry.

Matt picked her up, effortlessly scooping her legs and carrying her to the chair she had been sitting in only moments ago. Nashy put his hand on her shoulder and looked Matt in the eye.

"Thanks Matt. Could you go make a cuppla cups of coffee. I need to get Rebecca settled down".

"Yeah sure. What happened? Is she okay?"

"Just got some bad memories that just won't let go of her. She'll be okay. I hope."

Nashy knelt in front of Rebecca's chair and put his hand on her knee. Matt headed over to the sink in the corner of the room.

"I'm sorry girl. I should have shut up, but you kept pushing. I didn't want to see you like this. It still messes me up when I stop and think of it too."

"I don't even know why I'm crying. I thought I had cried all that out of me years ago." Rebecca struggled to get the sentence out between sobs, but eventually drew a deep breath and found her centre. She wiped her eyes with the back of her hand and then put her palm on top of Nashy's hand.

"You were right to tell me. Don't be blaming yourself. I would have found out from someone else anyways, and the name I think I knew it. From all the stuff in the news and papers back then. Even though Grandma and Grandad kept most of it from me."

They both turned their heads toward Matt as they heard the kettle boiling. Matt felt the sudden attention and held up a cup. "Ready in two secs."

"Matt. I'm so sorry for acting like a blubbering idiot all over you."

"No. I'm just glad I stopped you from falling down the stairs."

"Yeah, me too."

Nashy butted into the conversation. "What were you coming up here for anyway?"

"Oh yeah. Almost forgot saw on bench two has seized up. Can't get it to release."

"Ok. Watch her for a minute. I'll go sort it out."

Nashy headed downstairs and Matt turned back to the coffee. "How many sugars and how much milk?"

"Two sugars and a gloop of milk."

"A gloop? What the hells a gloop?"

"Not too much but not too little. A gloop."

"Ok, I guess. A gloop it is." The teaspoon rattled in the cup for a moment and Matt carried the coffee over.

"Thank you, Matt."

"No problem. You okay now?"

"Yeah. I'm fine." She took a sip of the coffee, inhaling deeply as she drank. "Tell me something. Anything. Distract me."

"Umm. Let's see... The sister ship of the Titanic was the Oceanic...and some people say that it was really the Oceanic that was sunk. A big conspiracy for insurance or some crap."

"What? Where do you get that from?"

"Reading lots of rubbish. Lots of old magazines in the van." Matt gave his big smile.

"Hey." Rebecca paused for just a moment, "How are you a Trivia?"

"Not bad, I guess. Why?"

"Tonight at the pub. Tracey, Tony and me are going. You and Tate up for it?"

"Sounds like a plan, nothing else happening. So yeah, why not. We'll be there."

For the next twenty minutes she sat, drank her coffee, and chatted with Matt until Nashy came back upstairs.

"Right Matt that should be fixed."

"Keeps doing it though."

"Yeah. I'll get it replaced soon, but for now you can get back down there and do some real work."

"Yeah. On my way."

Rebecca watched as Matt headed back down the stairs. "Thanks Matt and see you tonight."

He gave a little wave and disappeared back down the stairs.

"Tonight?" Nashy raised an eyebrow as he questioned her.

"I invited him to the Trivia night at the pub. Tate too. Some other friends are going. Should be fun. You should come."

"Nah. Not my scene. Besides its Friday night footy."

"Fair enough."

"So girlie, is everything okay now."

Rebecca gave him a look of horror, "No...your coffee tastes awful."

"I'll take that to mean your good."

"Yeah, I'm good. Just surprised me is all."

"Righto then. You best be off."

"Trying to get rid of me."

"Yep."

"So, we on for the shop tomorrow morning."

"If you're up to it, but if not that's okay."

"Oh, one more thing. Do you think you could come over and install a dog flap on my back door? Just want Sarge to be able to get in and out without having to wait for me."

"You mean just a flap that she can push open." Rebecca nodded. "Ok I'll come over in an hour or so. I got some marine ply, some hinges that should do the job. Might not look pretty but it'll be solid."

"Cool. I can pretty it up with some paint later."

Rebecca stood up and surprised Nashy with a kiss on the forehead, before saying goodbye and leaving. Sarge was still sitting outside, in the shade of the building with a bowl of water, that one of the boys must have put there for her.

"C'mon girl. Let's go home."

CHAPTER THIRTY

30

The afternoon passed quickly, with Rebecca looking through old boxes of photos, most of which were of Jake and her. As promised Nashy turned up just over an hour after she had left the mill. The job took him forty-five minutes. Take the door down, cut out a square from the door, seal the wood, cut the ply to size, then attach it with the hinges to the door. The old door was back on in no time and Sarge wasted no time in checking it out. Nashy was gone before she even had a chance to offer him a drink. She returned to the boxes of photos until finally, late in the afternoon she folded the top of the box over and stepped outside. The sun was already low in the sky and the night chill had begun to rise from the ground. Sarge was wandering around the yard, sniffing, barking at birds and doing what dogs did. Rebecca let Sarge take her time before giving her a yell.

"Ok girl. Dinner time for you...and guess what...You're on guard duty tonight. I'm going out."

Sarge gave her the cocked head look, which seemed to hint at uncertainty and then followed Rebecca inside.

She was dressed and ready to leave by six thirty. Sarge was fed and lazing in front of the fire. She opened the door to the slow burner and threw in another log, poked at it a few times, then re-latched the door.

"Well girl. You be good. No parties. See you later."

Rebecca parked her car across the road from the pub. She wandered in, nodded at the bartender, who nodded back and headed out to the beer garden. She spotted Matt and Tate sitting at the same table the group had sat at the previous Friday. They seemed to be having a friendly argument and did not notice her until she stood at the end of the table.

"Evening boys. Got a spare seat for a lady."

Matt stood up, pulled out a chair for Rebecca and waved her in. "For the lady."

"Thanks. You two been here long."

"Just long enough for one drink. Tate's shout."

"Yeah. You owe me one ya' tight bastard. Oh, sorry. You tight bugger."

"Then I guess I best grab the next round so you don't keep harping on it all night. What would you like Rebecca?"

"I'm driving. So just a lemonade for me."

"Lemonade for the lady, and I'm guessing another beer for the boofhead."

"You won't be calling me a boofhead when we win this Trivia competition. I'm not as dumb as you look, you know."

Matt shook his head, laughed, and walked off to the bar.

"You pretty good at Trivia are you Tate?"

"Guess we'll find out. How about you?"

"Only ever been to one before, with a big group, we didn't win, but we did okay."

"Well, step up your game tonight. Winners are grinners."

"You like to win, don't you?"

"Yes indeedy ma'am. I surely do."

Matt came back from the bar with drinks and took his seat, just as Tracey and Tony turned up. Tracey joined them at the table, whilst Tony went to the bar.

"Well, hello everybody. Looks like we've got a diverse team for to-night. You guys ordered any food yet?" Tracey pulled in an extra seat for Tony as he spoke to the group.

"No. Well I haven't, but I only just joined Matt and Tate here. Did you two order yet?"

"We thought we'd wait for everyone else. I'm starving though." Matt patted his stomach.

"Well then, as soon as my man gets back from the bar, let's get some food."

Tony returned, and they all took a moment to browse the menu. The boys all ordered ribs, Tracey a pasta dish and Rebecca decided on a chicken Caesar salad. They added in three bowls of garlic bread, and all threw in some money. Matt and Tony took the orders to the bar and in no time the group was all back at the table chatting aimlessly.

Tate asked everyone what name their team should be, throwing in a few ideas of his own, which everyone sneered at. Eventually they agreed on the A-Team.

The smell of garlic bread found them before the waitress did, and the bowls of bread were half empty when the waitress returned with the first of the meals. It was halfway through their meal when the PA system began to crackle, and a booming voice invited teams to come up to the bar and register for the competition. All team members would have to pay ten dollars and tonight's prize was a fifty-two-inch TV with a three-month Netflix subscription, plus a handful of Bunnings vouchers.

"Not bloody bad for a town trivia night comp. Wonder who gets the money they make?"

The booming voice must have heard Tate asking, as the next thing through the speakers was that all proceeds were going to the Shattered Falls Junior Soccer Club. Someone, somewhere in the pub yelled out "Go the Brumbies."

"Ten stuffing bucks. Bloody hell." Tate looked shocked, eyebrows knotted, and lips twisted in a scowl.

"Don't be a doofus. Pay up, shut up and play. It's for the kids. You play footy and I'm guessing you know how hard it is for the teams to cover costs." Matt had put on his serious face.

"Yeah. I know but ten bucks...well since were going to win anyway." He pulled out his wallet and reluctantly dragged out a ten.

The rest of the team paid their dues and Tony took the fifty dollars to the bar, coming back with two pencils and three sheets of paper.

Rebecca took the sheets from him as he sat down. "I reckon you got ripped off at the newsagents Tony."

She took one of the pencils and wrote the team's name on top of each sheet. The pages all had different headings, and each one had one to ten written down the side.

"Ok A-Team. Looks like three rounds. Ten questions per round, and our categories are Numbers," everyone groaned, "Movies, Music and Mayhem and Captains."

Tate lent back in his chair and crossed his arms, "Numbers, I hate maths and what the hell is Captains."

Matt lifted his drink and drained the last drops of beer, "Probably cricket, AFL and League. We should be alright at sport."

Tate's face lit up, "Sport. That's more like it. Winner, winner, chicken dinner."

A waitress came and collected their finished plates and empty glasses. Tate gave her a smile and 'Thanks' then turned to Rebecca "I think she likes me."

"Everyone loves a winner."

"Yep they do. So how we going to split the telly?"

Everyone shrugged their shoulders in unison and then Tracey offered a solution. "If we win, how about we draw straws for the TV and the rest can share the vouchers."

They all agreed, and the announcer's voice proclaimed five minutes to game start.

Rebecca stood up, "Ok my shout. What's everyone having?"

She took a mental note of everyone's drink and headed to the bar with Matt along to help carry them back. Matt took the opportunity to ask Rebecca a question.

"So about today. Tell me to mind my own business if you want, but what happened."

"Oh. I'm so sorry about that. It was just a photo. An old photo. My dad was in it. It was his footy team and...well I didn't know that one of the guys in the photo was the one who caused them to run off the road...It was a long time ago and before you apologise for asking, it's okay, was just a shock."

"Ok. I'm sorry about your parents. Real sorry."

"You don't need to be sorry. You didn't do it, and thanks for catching me."

The bartender handed over the drinks and the two made their way back to the table.

The announcer gave a two-minute warning and gave some rules.

No Mobile Phones.

No arguing with the judges, and

Once again, No Mobile Phones or it was instant disqualification.

And then it was question one.

Ok Ladies and Gents. Let's get this started. Remember No Phones or you will be disqualified. Good luck.

Question One: To the nearest whole number in Kilometres, what is the speed limit within the city limits of Nutbush?

Tate mouthed a few obscenities then whispered, "Holy shit. That's a question?"

Tracey leant forward toward the rest of the group. "Well think about it. Nutbush. You know the dance, the song by Tina Turner, I think. Doesn't it say what the speed limit is?"

Tony joined in with her, his voice a little too loud and everyone at the table shushed him. "Yeah. Nutbush city limits. Twenty-five was the speed limit."

Tracey sang along "Motorcycles not allowed in it."

"So, twenty-five." Tate prompted Tony to write it down.

Rebecca stopped him, "No. It's a trick. That's twenty-five in America, which is miles. So, we need to change it to kilometres. I think multiply by one and a half."

Matt put his hand over hers and whispered, "It's one point six, which would be... forty kilometres."

The A-team all looked at each other and gave a knowing nod to Matt. Tony wrote the answer down.

Question Two: What number Olympics was held at Sydney in Two Thousand?

Tate began to curse again, this time without a whisper "Shit. We're stuffed."

"Thought you were a winner. You give up a bit too easy." Rebecca scolded him.

"Well, I don't know this shit."

"You're forgetting we're a team. One person's weakness might be another one's strength." Rebecca looked at the others but could see by their faces that they had no idea either, "or not."

Tony gave it his best shot. "I think it's XXV something something."

Matt did the math, "So that's twenty-five plus something something."

"Twenty-five. I'm detecting a theme." Tracey added.

"Shall we vote?" Tony held the pencil up as he asked the question. "Raise your hand for twenty-six." No one put their hand up. "Twenty-seven." Only Rebecca put her hand up. "Twenty-eight." The rest of the team raised their hands. "Ok twenty-eight it is."

Rebecca gave a shrug.

Question Three: How many inches are in the horse measurement of one hand?

Tate's jaw dropped, and he blurted out "I know this one. It's four inches. Dammit I know this one." He looked around the beer garden realising he had almost shouted the answer.

Matt slapped him in the head, "So does everyone else now boofhead." Matt made sure this was said loud enough for most people to hear, and a round of laughter swept across the crowd.

Question Four: What number was written on the side of the General Lee?

Tate whispered this time "Who the hell is General Lee?"

Rebecca answered "It's not a who, it's a what. It's a car. From 'The Dukes of Hazzard'. The old TV show. It was a red car. A charger, I think."

Tracey joined in, "Yeah, Yeah. With that cute blonde guy. Which one was he, Beau or Luke?"

"But ladies." Tony interrupted them, "What was the number?"

Rebecca gave a big smile as she answered, "It was one, or zero one to be precise."

Question Five: How many letters in the Hawaiian alphabet?

The group all took turns looking at each other, exchanging shrugs.

"What Hawaiian words do we know?" Rebecca asked.

"Honolulu, Oahu, Lei." Tracey rattled off. "anyone else got any?"

"Mele Kalikimaka." Tate surprised everyone.

"And what the hell does that mean?" Matt asked. "And how the hell do you know it?"

"Means Merry Christmas. Read it in a book. Les Norton."

"Well that gives us about ten letters, but there must be more. That's not much to work with." Tony was itching to write something down before the next question.

"Ok how's about fifteen then?" Tracey asked the team.

Everyone nodded.

Question Six: How many stars appear in the current Paramount logo, as seen at the beginning of a Paramount movie?

"Well, this is getting bloody hard. Anyone need a drink?" Matt looked around the table.

Everyone lifted their now empty glass toward him.

"I'll take that as a resounding yes."

Tony stood up to go to the bar with him, "It's my shout Matt." He handed the pencil to Tracey and said, "I got no idea about the stars.", then headed to the bar with Matt.

"Ok. Me and Bec will figure it out then. Unless you got something Tate."

"Nah. Stuffed if I know."

"Ok then. So Paramount is the mountain logo with the stars over the top." Tracey started.

"And sometimes they come down from the sky like shooting stars and skim the water before they go on top of the mountain. There's a few of them." Rebecca added.

"Want to take a guess?" Tracey pointed the pencil at Rebecca.

"Twenty?"

"Twenty will do." Tracey wrote it down as the boys returned with the drinks.

Question Seven: Halley's comet passes the earth every how many years?

Tony wrote it down straight away, without even consulting the team, then whispered to them "It's 76 years."

Tony seemed so confident that no one argued with him.

Question Eight: Opposing sides of a Die will always add up to what?

"What's a die?" Tate scanned the team looking for someone who knew. It seemed he was the only one who did not.

"Two dies are Dice." Matt answered.

"Seriously. Dice and die. Does that mean one mice is a mie?"

The group chose to ignore the question from Tate and instead began hushed conversation about the answer to question eight.

"Let's see. I'm pretty sure the six is opposite the one but the rest...well I don't know." Rebecca looked at the others seeking confirmation.

"I think so too, and that would mean five and two, and then three and four. Holy crap. I never noticed that before." Matt backed up Rebecca's answer.

"So, then it's seven." Tony wasted no time writing it down.

Question Nine: How many pairs of chromosomes in a normal human cell?

"Well, I think I know." Tony bit his bottom lip as he answered, unsure of his answer "If my memory is holding out, and I actually listened in Uni Biology, it's forty-six chromosomes to make twenty-three pairs."

"Well, I don't think any of us has got anything better." Rebecca looked at the team, and they all shook their heads.

Tony added the answer to the list.

And final question in Round One. Question Ten: What is the postcode of Noosa Heads? There will be a short break now. Answer sheets for round one need to be handed in before Round Two starts. If you don't have it in before it starts...sorry to say but you will be disqualified.

"It's Queensland. So, it will start with a four." Matt whispered. Tate leant forward and nodded. As the two Queenslanders in the team, the remaining team members put their trust in them.

"Damn. I can almost see it. It's a weird number." Matt looked up to the roof, shaking his head.

"Weird how? Like double numbers, or triples?"

Tate slapped his hand down on the table and whispered just loud enough for the group to hear "It's running numbers."

"Yeah. That's it Four five six seven. Good work Tatey." Matt gave Tate a congratulatory slap on the back.

Tracey stood up and grabbed the sheet of answers and gestured to Rebecca "I'll hand this in and then take a ladies break. You coming?"

Rebecca stood too and smiled at the remaining males at the table "Back in a tic."

By the time Rebecca and Tracey had returned to the table, they found another round of drinks sitting on table. Matt and Tony seemed to be now on soft drinks, but Tate still held a tall glass of beer. Rebecca gave him a motherly look "Don't you get too drunk young man".

"It's light and anyways, I'm not driving, and I can sleep in tomorrow morning."

"You won't be sleeping too long. You got cleaning to do. I'm not living in a pigsty." Matt berated Tate.

"Whatever."

Ok. We seem to have everyone's answer sheet. So, lets kick of Round Two. Movies, Music and Mayhem.

Question One: What was Bruce Willis's characters name in the Die-Hard movies?

Tate was first to speak, whispering to the group, fully aware that last time he had made a fool of himself by talking to loudly.

"This is more like it. John McClane. Easy as."

Question Two: The jewelled necklace in Titanic was known by what name?

Rebecca and Tracey knew instantly and whispered to Tony at the same time.

"The Heart of the Ocean."

Question Three: What are the names of the parent dogs in 101 Dalmatians?

Tracey gave a muffled squeal "Oh my god. I'm a Disney freak. I know every movie...almost. It's Pongo and Perdita."

OK, before we move on to question four, lets check the scores from Round One. And, yes, I'll run through the answers.

The voice read through a list of team names and scores. Highest to lowest. The A-Team, much to Tate's displeasure were equal fourth. One team had gotten a perfect score, which had roused a call of 'Cheats' from the front bar. The A-team sat on seven points, which they all agreed 'was not a bad spot', with eight other teams behind them. Finally, they read out the answers to Round One, with the players all yelling 'yes' or 'no' as they found they were right or wrong.

Question Four: What band sung the lyrics "I didn't ask him his name, this lonely boy in the rain"?

Rebecca just beat Tracey to the answer "Heart. It's from, All I Wanna do is make love to you."

Tony made everyone laugh when he replied, "Settle down girl. My girlfriend might hear."

Question Five: What is the only day of the week mentioned in Van Morrisons "Brown-eyed Girl"?

Matt closed his eyes and the team could see him mumbling as he started singing the song under his breath.

"Tuesday. Write it down. We are on a roll."

Question Six: What is the only toy mentioned in Billy Joel's 'We didn't start the fire'?

Tate looked to Matt, "Do this one Matt?"

"Well I don't have a Billy Joel tape collection in the truck. Van is the man."

No one had noticed that Rebecca had been doing Matt's trick until she quietly blurted out "Hula Hoops."

Question Seven: What three alphanumeric characters were used to represent the computer bug that threatened the world in 2000?

Everyone in the team agreed on Y2K.

Question Eight: From what German city did the ill-fated airship The Hindenburg depart from on its last journey?

Matt leant forward, "Well it was landing at Lakehurst just south of New York when it exploded...and if I remember right, it left from Frankfurt in Germany."

Tate began laughing "Frankfurt. Stop making shit up, we're trying to win."

The team all gave Tate a death stare until he stopped laughing and asked, "So it's a real place?"

Rebecca asked Matt "How do you know this stuff?"

"Like I said before, I read a bit."

Question Nine: What year did the Newcastle earthquake occur?

Tony was first to talk, "Late eighties wasn't it."

"Yeah. Wasn't eighty-eight, that was the Bicentennial. So probably eighty-nine." Matt added.

"I remember Grandad talking about it. It was near Christmas. Boxing day, yeah that's it boxing day eighty-nine." Rebecca added, which confirmed it for the rest of the team.

And last Question for Round two: Question Ten: What is the name of the Oscar winning song from the original 'Poseidon Adventure' Movie?

Tracey almost yelled but Tony realising what she was about to do, put a hand across her mouth.

"Oops. Sorry...but holy shit. We watched that DVD on Wednesday night. Something like 'there has to be a morning after.'"

Tony wiped his hand on his shirt front, "Yeah but I think its just called 'Morning After'".

Ok Ladies and Gentlemen...and you ratbags in the front bar. We'll have another break while you hand in your answer sheets, have a toilet break, and grab another round of drinks, then on with Round Three.

Matt, Tony, and Tate all stood up together and headed to the men's room. Tracey called after them "I thought it was us girls that went to the loo in packs."

Not one of the three men turned, taking the veiled jab in their backs.

"Guess they didn't hear me. So, you need a drink?"

Rebecca drank the last drops from her glass and placed it back down on the table, "Just a glass of water for me, I think. I would say I'll be up all night going to the loo as it is."

"I know what you mean. I'll be back in a tick. I'll hand these answers in and grab the drinks. The boys can get their own."

As Tracey left, Rebecca looked around the room. The tables in the beer garden were occupied by mainly older couples, with a smattering of younger ones. She tried to spot a familiar face but could find none, and she turned her head toward the entrance to the front bar. She found a young man, sitting on a bar stool beside the door who seemed to be staring at her. When their gazes met, he raised his glass to her and took a drink. Rebecca lifted her empty glass back at him. He seemed to take that as a cue to approach, and he stood from his chair and began to walk over. Rebecca turned her head away, regretting what she had done. This guy, she thought to herself, thinks I've invited him over. Just as he was almost at the table Tate flung himself down into his seat.

"Jesus Christ. Friggin' packed as, in the dunny, and none of the bastards can piss straight. Lucky I'm wearing shoes."

Matt followed and sat down in his seat. "Bloody hell Tate. You pissed on some poor old guys shoes. He nearly tripped over coming out of the toilets.'

"Wasn't me."

"Luckily I think he was too drunk to know any better."

Rebecca looked back around toward the front bar doorway. The young guy had disappeared, and Rebecca breathed a sigh of relief.

Matt gestured at Tate and Rebecca, "So round of drinks for you two."

Rebecca blurted out "Tracey's gone to get one for me and her."

"For you and her...Nice." Matt replied sarcastically.

"Sorry."

"It's okay. I'm just on water now anyway."

"I'll have a light." Tate added.

"Well you can go bloody get it…and a water for me."

Tate stood up, mumbled something, and headed off to the bar just as Tony reached the table. Tony yelled after him, "Tate, can you grab me a coke?"

Tate threw his hands up in the air and answered without turning back to the group "Yeah. Sure. Why not?"

Five minutes later they all sat back around the table waiting for Round Three to commence. Tracey had bought two packs of chips, Salt and Vinegar, opened them both and sat them in the middle of the table. "Dig in if you've got the munchies."

Tate reached over grabbed a chip and shoved it into his mouth, "I prefer chicken."

Ok. Let's get this done. Round Three. I'll give the score in just a moment but let's commence. In this round I'm going to give you the name of ten Captains and I need you to tell me the name of what they captained. For example, Captain Cook captained the Endeavour. And I realise some may have captained more than one thing, but we want the most famous thing they captained. Any questions? Well too bad.

Captain One: Captain James T Kirk

Throughout the beer garden whispers of 'Star Trek' could be heard. Tate leant in toward the group "Did you hear that? 'Star Trek'."

"But his ship is the Enterprise." Tony added.

Tate looked at him questioningly "You sure? I thought that was a Space Shuttle."

"It was, but it was also Kirks ship. Didn't you ever watch Star Trek?"

Captain Two: Captain Nemo.

"Ok. He's the guy from 'Twenty Thousand Leagues under the Sea', and it's…damn it…something to do with fish or a sea animal." Matt looked frustrated as he tried to pull the name from his memory.

Rebecca tapped him on the hand, "It's okay smarty pants. It's Nautilus."

"Oh shit. That's it. Good work."

"You're not the only one who likes to read."

Just before we go on to Captain Three, we'll run through score and answers again.

The A-Team listened patiently as the answers were read out. Ticking off correct answers by counting on their fingers. By the end of the read of answers they all triumphantly held ten fingers in the air. A perfect score. They were now sitting in equal second, with the top team getting another perfect score.

"Ok A-Team. We can't afford any errors. Put your game face on." Tracey did her best to give them a pep talk.

Captain Three: Captain Feathersword.

Matt chimed in first, "Ok he's the pirate in the Wiggles, but his ships name...I got no clue."

"Luckily, I do." Rebecca gestured for the pencil and paper from Tony and wrote it down on the sheet, passing it back via the rest of the team.

When the sheet got back to Tony, he read it and screwed up his nose as he asked Rebecca "Are you sure? Sounds too easy."

"I'm positive.", and so the Good Ship Feathersword made it to the list.

Captain Four: Captain Ahab.

Tracey did not hesitate, she grabbed the pencil and scribbled down the answer and showed it to Tony.

"Wow. Awesome baby. How did you know that?"

"It was in a crossword I did on the plane back from Bali last year."

"When I was sleeping?"

"When you were snoring your head off."

Tony tilted the answer sheet so the rest of the team could see. The Pequod.

Captain Five: Captain Pugwash.

"Ha. I know this show. Hasn't been on in a long time, but they used to have it on the ABC." Tate proclaimed to the rest of the team.

"Well...what's his ships name." Rebeca asked.

"Oh…Got no idea. I just remember the cartoon."

"Jesus Tate. You had us thinking you knew." Matt went to slap Tate on the back of the head but stopped himself. "Guess we have to figure it out. Anyone else know of this cartoon."

Tony and Rebecca knew the name but had no idea of any cartoon and certainly not of his ship.

"Leave it blank. If we come up with anything, we can come back to …"

"Black Pig. Ha. Not as stupid as you think am I. It's the Black Pig." Tate obviously happy with himself downed his beer, before banging the glass on the table and declaring, "I'll have another one of them thanks."

Matt obliged.

Captain Six: Edward Teach.

"A teacher. What the hell? What's he Captain of the school or something?"

"Helps if you listen to the question Tate. They didn't say he was a teacher. That's just his surname." Tony tried not to sound like a know-it -all but failed.

"Alright then Mr Braniac. What's the answer?"

"Sorry Tate. Didn't meant to sound like an ass. Edward Teach was the real name of Blackbeard. The pirate."

"Yeah. Yeah. Blackbeard's treasure and all that. So, what's his ship?"

"Queen Annes Revenge."

Captain Seven: Captain Solo.

Every person in the pub seemed to know the answer, or at least someone in their team did, and the room went quiet as they waited for the next question.

"So, did you write it down Tony." Tate asked.

"It's cool. We got it. Millennium Falcon."

Captain Eight: Captain Flint, and I'll give you a clue. Think Treasure Island.

"Ok. Treasure Island. That's a book. You two bookworms got any-thing." Tracey's question was directed at Rebecca and Matt.

"I know the book and I know the name Flint, but I haven't read it." Matt shrugged.

"Me either. I think there was a movie at some stage too, but no. I got nothing." Rebecca mimicked Matt's shrug.

Tate shrugged as well, "Well the only Treasure Island I know is the Muppet movie one. That had a Flint in it, but it didn't say his ship. I remember watching it with mum. She read a bit. She might have said something about Flint and a Walrus."

"A Walrus. Like the big, fat, tusked seal thing." Tracey probed Tate for more info.

"Yeah, but not a Walrus. The Walrus."

"Well Ladies and Gentlemen. It's worth a shot. Write it down honey." Tony wrote down The Walrus, almost sure it would be wrong.

Captain Nine: Captain Edward Smith.

"Pretty common name Smith. Any ideas team." Tony asked.

Tate felt eyes on him, "I got the last one. You guys figure it out."

"Nothing to figure. It's pretty easy. Only the most famous ship around." Matt offered.

"Really." Everyone asked the same question.

"Yep. The Titanic."

And finally, the last question. Captain Ten: Forrest Gump.

Tracey twisted her lips and raised her eyebrows, "Umm, I'm pretty sure he was just a private. Gary Sinise was Captain Dan. The one that got his legs blown off."

"Ok so there must be some sort of trick here. We got Captain Dan, Private Gump. What was Bubbas last name? He was a private too, though." Tony tried to figure it out.

"Actually, I think in a roundabout way you just pointed out the answer. Forrest was on a boat. Remember, Bubba wanted to catch shrimp, and Forrest did that on a trawler. So, if he was the only one on the boat, at first anyways, he would be the Captain." Rebecca rubbed her fingers together as she explained her logic to them.

"So did the boat have a name?" Tony asked.

"Yep. It sure did. It was called Jenny."

If I could get you all to bring your answer sheets up as soon as possible, we'll get them checked and get final scores. In the meantime, we might draw the Meat Raffle.

Rebecca looked at the others, puzzled. "Meat Raffle. I don't remember any Meat raffle."

Tony, Matt, and Tate all pulled ticket stubs from their pockets and placed them down on the table.

"Sorry forgot to mention that. Some guy got us when we were headed to the dunnies. I got a couple. You can have one of mine." Matt offered.

"What's the meat?"

"Looks like a big Sunday roast. If you win, I reckon Sunday dinners on you."

"Ok. You got a deal." Rebecca took one of the tickets from the two that sat in front of Matt and gave him a smile. Matt just nodded in return.

Tickets ready Ladies and Gentlemen. Green Ticket K 27. Green K 27. Have we got a winner?

Tate swore, then apologised to the ladies, "Sorry. Bloody K 25."

"Which means." Rebecca was almost laughing, "Da dada da." She lifted her ticket K 27 into the air and shouted. "WINNER."

She took her ticket to the bar and the announcer came back from the front area of the pub to confirm.

Meat Tray won. Congratulations to the young lady from the beer garden.

Rebecca returned to her table with a small voucher in her hand.

"Did you get it?" Tate asked.

"It's in the cool room. Pick it up later with this." She waved the voucher at him.

"Cool. Can almost taste it. Baked taters, gravy, and you got to have peas."

"Inviting yourself are you."

"Umm...sorry...I just thought."

"Just kidding. You're welcome. You can all come if you want. How about it? Sunday arvo roast."

Tracey looked upset, "Well we can't make it. We got a birthday in Tamworth to go too, but you guys enjoy."

"You sure? I can make it next weekend."

"No. Use it while it's fresh."

Ladies and gentlemen. We have final scores. Close finish but we have a winner. So, if I could get you all to be quiet for just a minute. Seems to be a bit of noise from the front bar, but we'll continue anyway.

Taking the wooden spoon on eleven points is the Upstarts. Twenty-dollar voucher for meals at this fine establishment for the Upstarts.

The announcer ran through a list of the other teams and their scores. The A-Team all sat patiently waiting to hear their name called out. Tate seemed to be holding his breath and only released it when the announcer continued.

And now for the top three teams.

"Shit we made top three...Didn't we? Did I miss our name?" Tate looked round at his teammates, and they all shook their heads in response.

In third place on a score of twenty-six points, The Chosen Few. Congrats to The Chosen Few. Hundred-dollar voucher for your table.

Second place goes to the A-Team. Twenty-seven points. One Hundred and fifty dollars of Bunnings vouchers.

And in first place with an unbeatable perfect score. The Misfits. The major prize. Widescreen TV and two hundred and fifty dollars of Bunnings vouchers.

There was a roar from the front bar, which Rebecca assumed was The Misfits. "We did alright. Second place."

"I wanted to win the bloody thing. Second is okay but..."

The roar from the front bar grew louder and a chant seemed to be rising. At first, it was hard to make out, but it soon became a cry of "Cheat, Cheat, Cheat."

Rebecca stood and looked through the door from the beer garden and saw the announcer talking to someone, who was showing them something on a mobile phone.

"Somethings going on."

After a few moments, the announcer began to speak again.

Seems we have a dispute. As mentioned earlier, the use of mobile phones will result in disqualification, and as seen in this video I have just been shown The Misfits appear to have broken that rule...Misfits disqualified.

The roar from the front bar came again, this time louder. Cries of "Suck it", "Cheating dogs" rallied around the room and slowly died away.

First prize now goes to the A-Team, second to The Chosen Few, and Third will go to.... The Farmers Daughters. And NO. Judge's decision is final, you cheat you lose end of story.

Tate looked confused, "What the f' just happened?"

"I think we just won. We did. We won." Tracey jumped up and gave a bellowing "Whoop, Whoop."

The team shared a celebratory drink. Even Rebecca downing a glass of light strength beer. The crowd began to thin out almost immediately. A few of the other teams came over to congratulate the winners as they left, one group offering to buy the TV. Tate was first to answer, "No bloody way."

"So, who gets the TV?" Matt asked.

"We already have a big screen, so we don't mind." Tracey offered and Tony nodded in agreement.

"I don't need one. I've not been watching much TV." Rebecca looked to Matt.

"Cool. So, it's ours Matty boy."

"Seriously Tate. We live in a caravan. Where we going to put it? Hardly room to cook dinner let alone a big ass telly."

"But we won...well stuff it. We win, and we can't even take the frigging prize. That's crap."

Rebecca leant forward to the group "I got an idea. We could do something nice, but we all have to agree."

"Nice? Sounds like a shit idea already." Tate murmured.

"Listen to the lady for a second you arsehat." Matt scowled at Tate.

"How about we donate it back for a raffle for their next fundraiser...What do you think?"

Tracey, Tony, and Matt all gave big smiles, obviously happy with Rebecca's plan.

"It's a shit plan, but...ohh...stuff it...do it." Tate was not happy.

"Thanks, Tatey. I'll make sure there's extra baked taters for you on Sunday."

"Bloody well wanna be."

Rebecca got up to go to the bar and Matt stood up to join her. She spoke to the announcer who was by now behind the bar and told him of their plan. Several minutes later the two returned to the table, Rebecca carrying several Bunnings gift cards and Matt holding a large platter of meat.

"Ok A-team. I think we're good to go."

Before everyone heads off tonight, just a quick announcement. Seems we have some philanthropists amongst us tonight.

Tate screwed up his face "Stuffing stamp collectors. Who gives a shit?"

No one said a word, but all gave him a death stare.

The television has been donated back and will be major prize in a raffle. I reckon we'll draw in two weeks' time. Proceeds will go once again to the footy club. Tickets will be available from tomorrow. Now you can all piss off but drive safe.

Rebecca shared out the gift cards and the A-team made their way out of the pub. Several other patrons congratulated them as they left.

Outside there was a light but icy breeze. Rebecca turned up the collar of her jacket and made her way to the car as she said good night to the rest of her friends. Matt walked to the car with her and placed the meat tray on the passenger seat.

"Thanks Matt. See you about four, maybe four thirty on Sunday."

"You know you don't have to do that."

"I want to. I enjoy chatting with you, even Tate."

"Then you have got a problem lady." Matt laughed, said "Goodnight", and caught up with Tate, whom Rebecca could have sworn was urinating on a tree. Matt gave him a shove and the two headed back down the road toward the caravan park.

It was just after ten thirty when she walked back through her front door. Sarge had not moved until she had caught sight of the meat tray. The smell had caught her attention and once she had investigated, which involved a sniff of the underside of the tray and a whimper at Rebecca, the dog climbed back onto the couch and fell asleep.

Once the tray was in the fridge, Rebecca made herself a cup of tea, sat down beside Sarge and let the chill from outside disappear from her body as the heat from the slow burning fire slowly warmed her up. With her feet up on the coffee table, a warm cup in her hand, a warm fire in front of her and a warm furry friend beside her, she smiled. 'Life is good' she thought to herself, 'Good friends, good times. This place is going to work out just fine.'

She found her bed twenty minutes later, curled up inside it and fell asleep. She failed to wake even when Sarge climbed onto the end of the bed just before midnight. It was not until eight the next morning that the alarm woke her from the best sleep she had enjoyed in a long time.

31

Saturday was overcast and cold, despite the prediction of warmer weather. She made it to the joinery just after nine or more precisely a quarter to ten. Nashy stood by the counter as she walked in, tapping his wristwatch.

"What's all this about? Think you can turn up whenever you like."

"Sorry. I slept better than I have in a long time. Was hard to get out of bed."

"Heard you had a good night at the pub."

"Who told you that?"

"No secrets in a small town."

"Well then yes I did. Sorry about being late."

"Don't worry about it. Nothing much happening here today I don't think. Too damn cold."

Rebecca peeked back through the door. "You think it's going to rain?"

"Doubt it girlie. Don't let them few wet days fool you. We've been lucky here, being right up against the mountains. You drive half an hour west and rain is just a distant memory."

"Guess I haven't seen much of that yet."

"Let's hope we don't have too. You should check out the fundraising ball that's on next week, or the week after, sometime anyway. That's to help the farms that are doing it tough."

Behind the two of them the door creaked open. An older couple walked in trailing two disinterested children. It looked to Rebecca like Grandma and Grandad had their grandkids for the weekend.

The man smiled "Sorry. Are you open yet?"

"Yes. Come on in out of the cold. I'm about to make a cuppa if you would like one." Nashy greeted the group.

"See I told you kids. Country hospitality."

The older of the two girls lifted her head from her phone and asked Rebecca, "You got free Wi-Fi?"

"No. Sorry."

The girl rolled her eyes, "Ok then. Country hospitality."

Rebecca laughed quietly to herself, seeing just a little of her old self in these two. "I'll go put the jug on."

"Thanks Miss. We'll just have a look around if that's okay." The man replied and wandered off with his wife. The two girls sat down on the old couch by the door and tapped away on their phones.

By midday there had been another five lots of customers into the shop. Sales had been slow, although Nashy had taken a phone order for a bedroom suite, which he had told Rebecca consisted of bed, dresser, two bedside tables and a hand carved blanket box. From the smile on Nashy's face she could tell that it was a good sale.

At twelve thirty on the dot, Nashy closed the door and both headed off home.

Rebecca spent the afternoon tidying the house and yard. The lawn-mower had proved to be difficult to start, but after twenty minutes, enough language to make a pub full of patrons feel awkward and a wrenched shoulder, it finally kicked over. The front yard was done in no time but out back was more challenging. She started with just ensur-ing the paths were clear, then a section closer to the house. The rest would have to wait, 'maybe' she thought 'I could borrow a sheep from someone.'

At around five pm she called it a day, went inside, ran a bath, and spent the next hour soaking herself. Dinner was two cheese and tomato jaffles, something which she liked to claim as her own comfort food, even though she hated how some people had decided to call them toasties.

A quiet night in front of the fire followed, the TV on just as background noise until it became a distraction, and she turned it off. In silence now, she continued to read through some of the other paperwork in the boxes from the shed and somewhere amongst it all, she fell asleep.

She did not know what had woken her. Maybe the chill throughout the house, or a louder crackle from the dying fire, but she woke, neck sore from her head hanging to the side and was suddenly aware that something was wrong.

Sarge was nowhere to be seen. The fire was smouldering, throwing out just enough heat to make the thin blanket that she had thrown over herself seem warm. She checked the phone that sat on the coffee table in front of her. One eleven am. Outside she could hear the wind and something, a gate or a door shrieking as its hinges swung back and forth, occasionally banging against a wall and making her jump. Perhaps that was what had woken her.

As she swung her feet down onto the floor, she was thankful that she had thought to put a heavy pair of socks on. The small part of skin above her ankles that was exposed to the chill immediately got goose bumps. She stood and rubbed her eyes, rolled her neck to try and ease the muscle pain, and turned to head toward the bathroom. As she stepped into the hallway, still rubbing her eyes, and massaging her fingers into her neck, she froze, mouth agape trying to scream as a darkened figure stepped out of her bedroom and into the hall.

32

The scream slowly made its way out as a muffled gargle, but quickly turned into an ear-piercing shriek. The figure that had been hunched over at first, stood tall and stepped toward her, still hidden in the darkness with an arm outstretched as if trying to quieten her.

At that moment Sarge came running in through the doggie door, barking and trying find some traction, but instead skidding suddenly to a stop on the wooden hallway floor. She slammed into the legs of the intruder and both became a tangled mess on the floor. The intruder quickly righted themselves and ran toward the back door, flinging it open and disappearing into the night. Sarge gave chase, her barks echoing back as she too, was enveloped by the dark.

Rebecca just stood there in the hall. The chill of deep winter now overtaken by the cold fear of the intruder's presence. She was still standing there when Sarge returned, panting, and limping and only moved when the protective dog jumped up, trying lick her face in concern. She collapsed to the floor, knees to her chest, arms cradled around her lower legs and head tucked in. Sarge nuzzled her and eventually sat down beside her, sniffing, and prodding her.

Finally, Rebecca raised her head, placed her hand on Sarge's head and spoke. "It's okay girl. I'm okay. I'm okay." Whether she was talking to the dog or herself she was unsure, but it helped. She stood, wandered throughout the house turning on every light, locking doors and checking windows, turning on the radio and the TV, and then turning the volume on each up loud. Then she boiled the kettle, made herself a coffee, a strong coffee and sat in front of the fire, on the floor, thinking.

'Who? Why?', kept running through her mind, and it all kept coming back to one person. One person that she now knew she would have to face and deal with once and for all. Zak's time had come.

She finally looked at the time again and was surprised that it was after three am. She knew she had sat in front of the fire for a long time, stoking it and adding logs, but she had not imagined it had been just over two hours since she had woken. Sweat had beaded on her forehead from the heat thrown off by the fire, and she wiped it away with the back of her hand. Sarge had retreated to the hallway, obviously uncomfortable with the heat, despite the outside temperature being close to zero.

Rebecca stood and walked to the dog. "Sorry girl. I went a bit numb there for a while." Sarge just looked at her with big eyes, her muzzle flat on the floor. "But you did good. C'mon let's get a treat."

In a short time, the smell and sound of bacon cooking filled the kitchen, audible even over the sound of the radio and TV. Rebecca sat at the kitchen table, a plate before her stacked with perhaps a little too much bacon. She crunched through one rasher herself and handed two down to an appreciative Sarge.

"I should call Uncle Paul, shouldn't I? It's just, well the middle of the night. What do you think?"

Sarge just looked back at her with an expression that just said 'Bacon'.

"Ok. Close enough."

She rang the number, tensing as she awaited an answer. Cringing over what she would say, how she would not seem a weak little girl. The phone went straight to a message service, which she thought strange. It always rang, day or night, that was part of his role. Unless he was somewhere with no service. 'That must be it.'

Instead she rang another number on the list that Uncle Paul had left in her phone. Tamworth Police Station.

After taking down as many details as she could remember, the officer on the line told her a car would be there soon, and she should keep the lights on and stay indoors. She asked, before hanging up if Paul Caplan was on duty, but was told he was unavailable now. Then she returned to the bacon, feeding most of it to Sarge and listening to the early morning radio.

At around four, a car pulled up outside. She looked out the window and saw two men emerge from a police car, not a four-wheel drive. More likely a highway patrol vehicle. They turned on flashlights and one walked toward the rear of the house, whilst the other approached the front door.

The officer knocked, came in, inspected the house, looking for points of entry and anything out of the ordinary. The second officer joined them a few minutes later, after having checked the outside of the house and the yard.

After half an hour, they left. The whole process feeling almost as intrusive as the earlier incident. She wished Uncle Paul had been here. He would have made her feel safe.

They had asked if she had someone she could call, or someone with whom she could spend the rest of the night, but she hid her fears and told them she was fine. Told them she would call a friend if she needed them. Instead, she sat on the couch, pulled the blanket up over her legs and patted the spot beside her until Sarge curled up on the couch with her. She never thought she would fall back to sleep, but she did and when she woke to a ringing phone it was after sunrise.

It was Uncle Paul, returning the missed calls. He listened patiently to Rebecca's account of the night and then asked some questions to fill in the blanks. Had she recognised the intruder? Was anything left behind that could identify the intruder? And finally, was she alright? He had some things to do, but he promised he would be there by mid-afternoon, which struck Rebecca as strange. She had expected him to drop everything and run to her aid, but then he explained, and her heart dropped, and she felt guilty for monopolising his time.

Late last night, returning home after a late shift he had found Meg collapsed on the floor. He had rushed her to the hospital and had spent the rest of the night with her. Rebecca could hear the tremble in his voice as he told her,

"The doctors...they can't do much more for her. It's eating her away and I think I'm losing her."

"I'm sorry. Can I come see her?"

"Not yet. They said she needs rest. She didn't wake the whole time I was there."

"Are you okay?"

"As good as I can be, considering. Listen there's some stuff I need to do, and I want to get back to Meg, but I'll see you this afternoon to work out what went on last night."

Rebecca hesitated but then blurted out, "I think it was Zak. It has to have been him."

"Yeah. We need to talk about him too. I'll see you soon."

"Ok. Bye Uncle Paul...Love you."

The line went silent for what seemed an eternity to Rebecca and then finally, he hung up.

Rebecca sat for a moment holding the phone in her hand. Auntie Meg meant the world to her. Other than Grandad, Grandma and Jake, she and Uncle Paul were the closest family she had, even though they were Uncle and Aunty in name only. As she sat there worrying about Meg, she thought back to the conversation she had just had. 'Uncle Paul said he needs to talk about Zak. What the hell does that mean?'

She made her way to the shower and tried to clear her head beneath the warm torrent.

'Damn. I'll have to let Matt and Tate know this afternoon is off.', but then she reconsidered, 'I could do with some company. Stuff it. Let's cook up dinner.'

33

The morning was a blur, tidying, checking her cooking supplies and a quick trip to the store to get what she needed. She avoided talking to Tracey's mum by feigning a phone call and was back home by lunchtime. She had no appetite but forced herself to have a cup of tea and a sandwich, and then she began to prepare to cook.

After a few false starts, she got the roast into the oven, and began peeling the vegetables. Time seemed to pass slowly but when she had put the potatoes and carrots into the oven as well, she discovered it was just over an hour until she had told her guests to turn up.

They turned up fifteen minutes late, which Rebecca was thankful for. She had destroyed the first batch of gravy and was now making another. Warily she watched the stove top with elements that were older than her and three times as erratic.

She made Matt and Tate set the table as she carved the beef and soon, they all sat around the tiny kitchen table feasting on the winnings of Friday night.

"This gravy's a bit of alright Rebecca."

"Thanks Tate. Got the peas special for you too."

"Me and Tate don't get too many home cooked meals." Matt gave a big smile, with just a hint of gravy on his chin. "Makes home feel a little less distant."

"You get home much Matt."

"Every second weekend. Check on mum and the rest of 'em."

Tate added, "I ain't been home in a year or so. Dad told me not to come back till I had my nose straight." He screwed up his nose and lifted his head. "Only broke it once playing footy, but don't reckon I can afford to get it straightened out any time soon."

Rebecca gave a polite laugh, "I don't think that's what he meant. I think he means when you got your life sorted out."

Tate thought on it for a moment "I guess that could be it too."

"I reckon Rebecca's right. You should go home for a visit. Let them see the new you, the respectable working man."

"Yeah righto, don't get all bloody gushy on me."

The meal finished up and the three of them moved onto washing the dishes. Rebecca washing and Matt and Tate drying. They all heard a car pull up out front and Tate went to investigate.

"Shit. It's the cops."

"Tate. Settle down. It's my Uncle Paul. You remember him, don't you?"

Tate answered like a spoilt child, "Yeah. Kicked me out of your shed. It was nice and cosy in there...and free."

"Well he's a good guy. Been watching out for me for a long time."

"If you say so."

There was a knock at the door and Rebecca answered, drying her hands with a tea towel as she went. Paul stepped inside and gave a weak smile.

"Hey. How is she?" She did not wait for an answer, instead she wrapped her arms around him and gave him a hug.

"Sleeping. She woke a couple of hours ago, but the drugs have knocked her back out." He looked toward the kitchen. "You got guests?"

"It's Matt and Tate from the mill. I promised them a roast dinner and now they're helping clean up."

Paul raised his voice and directed it toward the kitchen, "Afternoon boys."

The boys both stepped into the hallway and nodded toward Paul "Sergeant."

"If you boys are nearly done, me and Rebecca have some stuff to chat about in private."

Matt answered for both. "Yeah. We were just finishing." He went back into the kitchen, hung his tea towel, and motioned for Tate to do the same before they came back out into the lounge room.

"Thanks for a great feed Rebecca. Me and Tate appreciate it. We owe you."

Matt nudged Tate, "Yeah. What he said. It was great." Tate seemed a little quieter around Paul.

"I'll catch up with both of you through the week." Rebecca opened the door, saw them out and shut it as the boys climbed into Matt's car and disappeared into the dusk.

Paul sat down at the kitchen table as Rebecca filled the kettle and put it on to boil.

"I'm guessing you'll have a cuppa?"

"Yeah. That'd be good. Hospital stuff was terrible."

"I'm sorry you had to come here. You should be back at the hospital."

"Doctors basically told me to piss off for a while. They've just got her sleeping, but we've got to talk business. I read the report and was hoping you might have remembered something else since then. Like did you see his face, or did he speak. Anything I can use to identify the bastard."

"It was dark, and I'd only just woken up. It was all so quick. All I saw was the black figure, but it has to have been Zak."

"No."

"Why? The only way you could be sure is if he was already locked up."

Paul took a deep breath, held it for a minute then began to speak again. "Yeah. Well, I don't know whether you heard about that fire at the Club at Willow Tree."

"I did. Just a bit about it on the radio. Last weekend or Monday."

"Yeah that's it. Well it looks like it was lit on purpose. Place burnt to the ground. Took them a few days to sift through all the shit."

"You think Zak started it. Why? Is that why you locked him up?"

"Slow down young lady. I don't know if he started it but it's more likely someone else did, and I don't have him locked up."

"I don't understand."

"The bar manager saw him there that night, and some of the patrons told us he had been trying to sell some drugs. Joints, maybe some ecstasy but we think he may have pissed off someone."

"Is he in hospital? Someone bashed him?"

"He's dead."

Rebecca's face froze. "What? How?"

"In the remnants of the club they found a body. Badly burnt. Took most of the week to identify him. Stabbed three times... Zak was murdered."

Rebecca sat silently, the kettle began to whistle, and Paul got up and made the tea.

"Oh my god. I hated him for what he did, but dead...that's a shock."

Paul placed two quickly made cups of tea down on the table and sat back down.

"But the thing that I'm trying to work out...the thing I'm worried about amongst all this stuff with Meg is...if Zak's dead, who was in your house?"

"Oh my god, that's just sinking in now."

Paul lifted the tea to his lips, took a long sip and looked Rebecca in the eye. "How well do you know Matt and Tate?"

"No, not them. Well I don't know them that well, but it couldn't be one of them. They're friends...the first new friends I've made up here."

"Well...I'm telling you now, I'll be checking them out. Just watch everyone."

Paul finished his tea, then went to check out the house. He went outside and Rebecca followed, with Sarge close behind her. They walked slowly around the outside of the house until they got to the bedroom window.

"Look at that." Paul pointed to the window frame. There were marks in two places where it seemed some sort of tool had been used to pry the window open.

"So that's how they got in."

"Most likely. Looks like they used a screwdriver to force it. Was it locked?"

Rebecca answered sheepishly, "It's too hard to turn the latch thing."

"That's not helpful at all. I'll be making sure it's locked before I leave, and you get Nashy to fix it tomorrow. Promise."

"Ok. I promise. I'm just glad I was sleeping on the couch when he got in."

"If it was up to me, you wouldn't be sleeping here at all. There's a spare room at my place, just until this gets sorted."

"No. I'm not going anywhere. This is home. No one is chasing me out."

"Yeah. That's what I thought."

"Anyway, Sarge knocked him off his feet. Gave him a good old scare. Didn't you girl."

Paul stood silent for a minute. "I don't like it, but I know I'm not going to change your mind. Too much of your mum in you."

"I'll be okay."

"Yeah. Well let's go make sure this place is able to be locked up tight."

On the way back inside Paul stopped at the top of the back steps. "This pet door was a bad idea."

"It's hardly big enough for Sarge, and I'm going to put a bell on it. You know, so it tinkles every time it opens wide enough."

Paul frowned and went through the door and into the bedroom. He spent time struggling with the window lock before it eventually secured the window, then he wandered through the house ensuring every other window was locked.

Finally, happy with the windows, he made his way into the spare room and looked around for a moment before spotting what he had hoped to find.

"I remember your Pop used to keep this around. Well, I told him too."

Paul handed Rebecca a baseball bat.

"Use it wisely."

After a final walk through of the house and a check outside he made his way back to his car.

"Ring me if you need me, and if you can't get me ring the station. I've told them all to give you priority."

"Thank you."

"I'm heading to the hospital now, so…well just promise me you'll be safe. Don't take any risks."

"I promise. Now go. Give her my love, and please let me now when I can go see her."

Rebecca gave him a kiss on the cheek and a hug. She could feel the big man trembling and it almost made her cry.

With one last "Ok", he climbed into the car and headed off, and then she was alone again, or so she thought. A wet nose touched her hand, and she felt a warm feeling of security as Sarge rubbed against her legs.

"C'mon girl. Let's go watch a movie."

34

The remainder of Sunday night was uneventful, Monday morning even more so. The boredom gave rise to questions that she could not answer. 'Who would break into her house? Why?'. She had nothing of any great value, but she guessed an intruder would not know that until they got inside. Suddenly a thought dawned on her, 'What if this had not been the first time?' Her mother's diary had gone missing, and she was now sure it was nowhere in the house, but why would anyone want it.

Could it be someone she knew? She rattled off a list of names in her head. Matt, Tate, Tony, Nashy, Craig. But none of them made any sense. She had been sure Zak had been the dark figure she had seen, but now she knew that was impossible. He had been killed days before. 'Killed', that scared her. He must have made some enemies out there that night, but he always did. Arrogant and overconfident, full of his own shit and that always seemed to piss people off.

Rebecca jumped as her phone rang. It was a voice that she had not realised she had been longing to hear.

"Grandad. God it's good to hear your cranky old voice."

"Love you too my girl."

"Sorry. I love you too."

"So, how's things up there."

"Yeah. Interesting." The last thing she wanted to do was have Grandad and Granma worrying, "but good interesting. How's things down there?"

"Same old stuff. Just wanted to ring and check in with you before we head up on the weekend."

"Yeah. Almost forgot about that."

"Well, just want you to know that Gran and me have got a room at the pub, so you don't need to worry about a bed for us, but Jake insists on staying at '*his place*'."

"Ha, well I guess it's as much his as it is mine. I think there might be an old fold out bed in the one of the sheds. Pop used to keep a few for unexpected visitors."

"Good, because he'd whinge like an old woman if he had to sleep on the floor."

"So, what time you think you'll be here."

"Probably just before lunch on Saturday. Your grandma is making something to eat for the lot of us, so don't be doing any cooking. She misses cooking for you."

"And I miss her cooking, especially the lasagne."

"I'll remind her...so you can probably expect to have your fridge filled by the time we leave."

"Guess what...I got a dog. Uncle Paul gave me an ex-police dog. Her names Sarge and she's gorgeous."

"You sound like a giggling schoolgirl...so I'm guessing you like her."

"Yep, I do." Rebecca hesitated for a moment before asking something that she knew might bring up old wounds. "Grandad...do you remember anyone ever giving mum a hard time up here."

"Damn girl, that's a long time ago and you know I get all choked up when I talk about her."

"I'm sorry, it's just ..."

"Tell you what, we'll have a talk on the weekend. I don't want to keep any secrets from you, so I'll tell you what I know then, just don't let your grandmother know."

"Ok, you've got me worried now."

"No need for that. Not much to tell."

"Thanks Grandad."

"Ok my girl. I'll get going, but we'll all see you soon. Love you."

"Love you too."

She hung up the phone and walked to the back door, opened it, and took a deep breath. She was curious as to what Grandad knew about someone harassing mum years ago. Maybe, she thought, it would be the missing piece that would make sense of what had concerned her mother all those years ago.

Sarge barged past her, barking at something in the back yard and running down by one of the back sheds. Rebecca followed out, calling after the dog and finding herself running as well. She stopped when she reached an old fencepost, which she remembered at one time had been part of a fence line that had been covered in passionfruit vine. Sarge was sitting just beyond it, challenging several Corellas that had perched in the dead branches of an old tree. The birds ignored Sarge and continued their squawking, but the dog did not give up until Rebecca's hand rested on the dog's head.

"Noisy little bastards aren't they girl... but then so are you."

Sarge looked up at her, almost apologetically and gave another round of barking. The Corellas took to the air as if tied together with an invisible net and flew further towards the scrubby Grey Gums at the base of the mountains. Pleased with herself Sarge sat down on her hind legs and looked up at Rebecca.

"Ok. I'll give you that one."

Rebecca turned and found herself looking at one of the sheds that she had not been into since coming to her new home. The walls were a patchwork of fibro sheeting and corrugated tin, but all of it was painted a pale blue. Two small windows sat in between some of the sheets of fibro and drawn on the glass were various styles of flowers. Some drawn better than others, and as Rebecca smiled, she remembered which ones were hers. Her Nan had drawn the intricate blossoms of roses, orchids, and other plants that Rebecca could not even guess at. The more childish ones were hers, but they were also the most colourful. She remembered this shed was Nan's pottery shed, and with a sad smile she remembered Nan.

Nan had passed away when Rebecca had been only eight. A woman that loved creating things. Painting, making decorations for Christmas, Easter or any event, and the thing she loved most, pottery. In the shed would be her potters' wheel and the old stone kiln that Pop had ordered from overseas. The day that it had been delivered was Nan's birthday and Rebecca could still remember how much she had smiled and cried and thanked them all for the present. Two years later, to the day, Nan had gone in her sleep and Pop had locked up the shed, and as far as Rebecca had known, it had not been opened since.

She had always been fascinated with Nan's pottery and now as she stood in front of the blue door, she began to remember the pride she had taken helping Nan mould clay into shape, set it in the kiln and hold the finished plate, cup, vase or whatever else they had made. Maybe, she thought, this could be her thing, her focus. Firstly however, she would have to find a key.

Beside her Sarge began to bark again as the Corellas returned. Whether it was the same flock or another, she could not tell.

"Ok girl, inside now. I've got to find a key.... oh shit, I've got to find a bed too."

Once back inside she grabbed a jacket, the car keys and put more wood into the fire.

"You coming, girl?" she asked of Sarge.

Sarge climbed up onto the couch and curled up, answering Rebecca's question.

"Ok then."

The trip to the mill was short, and she could have walked it, but she wanted to get back home and find the key quickly, after solving her other problem.

Nashy sat in the office upstairs, steaming cup in one hand and the phone glued to his ear with the other. When he saw Rebecca, he nodded and finished up his call.

"Ok mate. Got to go. Business partner just turned up.... Yeah...Nah...For sure...See ya."

The old corded phone clicked as Nashy put it back down onto the holder.

Rebecca smiled and pointed at the old phone.

"Are you scared that thing's going to run away. You got it chained up to the holder."

"What...What the hell you on about? Oh...Yeah, well it works fine. Don't need one of them cordless things...and anyway, I'd just forget where I put the bloody thing. Already lost one."

"Listen, I need a favour?"

"Oh...this'll be good. What you need?"

"How quick can you make a bed? I don't mean tucking in blankets and stuff. I mean the frame and all that."

"What the...You broke your bed?"

"No...Jake's coming up on the weekend and I've got no bed for him."

"Oh, in that case, I'll have something brought over...probably Thursday morning if I can get the boys sorted."

"Sorted? Is something wrong?"

"Just that bloody Matt didn't turn up this morning. Tate said he didn't come back to the van after he had the feed at your place. What did you feed 'em?"

"Funny. Should we be worried? Where would he go?"

"He goes home to Queensland every now and again, but he's always back for Monday morning. He's a big boy so I wouldn't be too concerned. It just stuffs up my workday."

"Weird. Have you got his phone number?"

"Not answering?"

"I hope he's alright. Give me the number I'll try again later."

"Well since you're his boss too I guess it's okay." Nashy scribbled a number onto a post-it and handed it to Rebecca.

"Ok. I'll let you know if I get him....and thanks for the bed." She headed down the stairs, stopped and turned to ask one more thing. "I might need a mattress too."

Nashy swore as Rebecca continued down the stairs but just before she went out the door, she heard him yell. "Lucky I got a spare at home then."

As Rebecca stepped back outside, a car pulled into the parking spot beside her Suzuki. It was Uncle Paul in the Police Landcruiser. She stood and waited at the mill door as he climbed out of the car.

"You look in a hurry. How's Aunty Meg?"

"She's fine. I've been trying to ring you, but it just rings out."

"Oh Sorry. I had it on silent last night. Must have forgot." Rebecca pulled out the phone and slide the switch back to normal. Half a dozen missed call notifications flashed up at her. "What's wrong?"

"I just needed to know where you were. Can you hang here a minute? I need to go talk to Matt."

"Sure. I can wait, but you won't find Matt in there. Didn't turn up for work this morning."

"Shit. Do you know which van he was staying in?"

"No, but he shares with Tate. He's in there."

"Ok then I need to go talk to him."

Rebecca stood in front of him as he tried to enter the door.

"First you need to tell me what the hell's going on."

Paul stared into her eyes for a moment before speaking. "You know much about Matt?"

"Not really. He's from Queensland."

"You know his last name?"

"No."

"It's Lonergan, and he used to live just north of Tamworth when he was a kid..." Paul paused, "but he wasn't a Lonergan then. That's his mum's maiden name. They changed it when the family moved up to Queensland. Changed it because the family was getting too much heat from people. Before that his name was Matthew Shaw...Shaw. Rebecca...Matthew is the son of Ed Shaw... The man that ran your mum and dad off the road."

Rebecca stopped breathing and felt her head begin to spin as thoughts raced through her mind, none of which she could make any sense of.

She felt dizziness taking her, and she reached out to support herself on the door frame at the same time as Pauls arms grabbed her, and then she collapsed.

35

Rebecca groggily opened her eyes and found herself sitting in the front seat of the Police car. It was parked but no longer in front of the mill. Instead, it was now down on the main street of Shattered Falls, almost directly across from the pub. She shook her head, trying to shake of the grogginess and reached up the rub her eyes just as Paul opened the door.

"What the hell happened?"

"You fainted. Lucky the door and me caught you. Could have taken a nasty knock on the head."

Rebecca looked around again "What are we doing here?"

"You're going in to see the doctor."

"I didn't think we had a doctor in town."

"Mondays and Thursdays. Doctor Braggman comes out from Tamworth. I told him you need to be checked."

"I just fainted. I'll be okay."

"Don't fight me on this. You're going in to get checked."

"Okay. Okay."

Paul helped her from the car and with his support she walked into the front rooms of what she remembered was a small community hall. The doctor was waiting at the door. Paul got her into one of the side rooms where an examination room was set up and sat her down on the edge of the bed.

"The sergeant tells me you fainted. Had a fall. How are you feeling now?" The doctor was looking into Rebecca's eyes as he spoke.

"Ok, I guess. Bit groggy, maybe a splinter in my palm, but nothing major."

"Well let's do a full check anyway. Blood pressure, heart, lungs."

Paul stood back and waited a moment before speaking. "Doc will she be right here for half an hour. I got something to check out."

"Yes, of course."

"Uncle Paul? Where are you going?"

"Just going to pick up Tate and go check out that van that Matt and him are staying in. I'll be back soon." He did not wait for Rebecca to reply, instead he turned his back and walked out the door.

The doctor regained Rebecca's attention with a tap on the shoulder.

"Let's take a look at that splinter first."

An alcohol swab wiped across her palm, and she turned her head as the doctor poked at her palm with a pair of tweezers. With only a small amount of pain he had the small splinter from the mill door out of her hand, followed by another wipe of some antiseptic solution.

"Ok. Let's give you a proper check-up now."

Over the next half hour, the doctor shone a light in her eyes, strapped a blood pressure cuff to her arm and held a cold metal stethoscope against her chest and back.

"Well your heart's still racing, but you've had an eventful day it seems. Everything else is fine. I would like you to have a restful remainder of the day and an early night, a good meal would help too. You're not a vegan are you."

"No. Not a vegan."

"Good. Not that there's anything wrong with that, but I think you could go for a nice steak and vegies. No salt though."

"I think I can manage that."

"You know if there's something bothering you, I can refer you to someone. Maybe a psychologist, and that doesn't mean you're crazy, just sometimes we need help or guidance to deal with things."

"I know. I'll be okay, but I'll keep it in mind."

"Ok. Well he should be back soon. Would you like a coffee?"

"No. I'll just wait. Thank you. I don't have my Medicare card."

"No problem. Call it an introductory free consult."

They both looked to the door as they heard an echoing bang, which Rebecca assumed was Paul coming back into the hall, slamming the front door loudly. The doctor opened the door to the examination room and gestured to Rebecca.

"You're free to go Miss Ford."

Paul spoke, "She okay doc."

"Yes. Yes. She's fine. Next time it's your turn to get a check-up. Don't recall seeing you this year."

"When I have time. I'll add it to my list."

"Make sure you do. Now I have to get some home visits done, so I'll say good day."

"Thanks again for seeing her doc."

The doctor nodded to Paul and smiled at Rebecca before returning to the examination room to collect his belongings.

"Uncle Paul, can you take me home...actually, back to the mill. Have to get my car."

"Nashy already took that home for you."

"Ok. Home then."

"Home it is. As long as you can be trusted to stay in and get some rest."

"I promise. So, did you find Matt?"

"No. A contact up north said his vehicle was seen in Queensland this morning. So, you won't be seeing him today or hopefully ever."

"It doesn't make sense."

"Just stop. Stop thinking about it. Rest is all I want you doing. So, jump in the car and I'll get you home."

Rebecca climbed into the four-wheel drive as Paul held the door open for her. He slammed it shut, and she closed her eyes, waiting for him to get into the car himself. She heard his door open and close but continued to keep her eyes closed, taking a deep breath, trying to centre herself. When she finally opened her eyes, she found Paul staring at her, a creased brow and a look of concern in his own eyes.

"You okay there. Thought you'd gone into some weird state there for a minute."

"Yeah. Just getting my shit straight."

"Ha...Getting your shit straight. You sound like your Grandad, but seriously girl, are you okay."

"Yeah. Just starting to feel the cold a little."

"I'll put the heater on and get you home."

She gave a forced smile, buckled her seatbelt, and wrapped her arms around herself trying to shake of the chill. She looked down beside her seat, at the central console noticing a yellow all-weather jacket, emblazoned with police insignia, and grabbed for it to throw over her legs. As she lifted it, something fell that had been wrapped up it. It was something she had not expected to see, not here.

"Geez girl. Can't you just leave things alone."

"I'm sorry. I was cold." She lent down and grabbed the item that had fallen to the floor of the car and held it up. "Why have you got this?"

In her hand she held up a small red leather diary. Her mother's diary. A diary that had gone missing from her home.

Paul hesitated answering, looking out the window as he drummed his fingers on the steering wheel.

"Found it...Found it in the van. I thought it was his but the stuff inside...well I knew that it belonged to your mum. I'm sorry. I don't know how he got it. Stole it from your house I'm guessing."

"But that went missing days before the intruder. My god ... how many times has he been in there?"

Paul put his hand on her leg, patting it twice. "Hey. Hey. He's gone. He knows I'm after him now. Doubt he'll be back in town any time soon."

"But why? Why would he?"

"Guess he's angry about his father doing time for what he did, the accident. Can't even guess what goes through the mind of someone like that."

Rebecca took another deep breath. "Take me home."

She flicked through the diary as Paul drove. Pages had been creased, smudged and some torn out leaving angry, ragged edges. She closed her eyes and held back the tears that she knew were coming.

36

They were back at the house within five minutes. Her Suzuki was parked in the driveway and Nashy was sitting on the front steps, cigarette hanging from his mouth, which he quickly stubbed out as Rebecca and Paul climbed out of the car.

Nashy walked toward the car, coughing and met the two.

"So, you alright?"

Rebecca kept on walking, not ignoring Nashy, just not hearing.

"She'll be okay, but I need you to keep an eye on her. I'd do it myself, but with Meg..."

"Don't say another word mate. I'll watch her. I'll get the neighbours watching too."

"And if you hear anything from Matt Lonergan, you need to ring me straight away."

"Of course. Shit, I never imagined him to be the type. He always played by the books."

"Doing this job, you learn that people are rarely what they seem."

Rebecca made her way up the front steps and was greeted by Sarge. She sat down on the top stair and wrapped her arms around the dog, giving her a huge hug. Nashy and Paul both stood on the lawn in front of her, watching her for a moment until Paul spoke.

"Nashy is going to be checking in on you. I wish I could, but I got to get back to Meg."

"It's okay Uncle Paul. I'm alright, it was just a shock."

"And I believe you. I know just how tough you are, but that doesn't change the fact that I care, and I think I can speak for Nashy too. We both care, and we will not stand by and not do anything. We will be checking in on you, and that's just how it is."

Paul had been expecting Rebecca to put up a fight, but she just smiled, looked up at them both and answered "Yeah, that'd be good, but right now I just want get inside, have a shower, have something to eat and maybe have an early night."

"That sounds like a plan, and if it's alright with you I'd like you to come visit Meg tomorrow."

"Of course. I feel so guilty, making this all about me when she's...well...tomorrow I'll be there. What time?"

"Any time. I'll make sure they know you're family."

Rebecca stood and gave Paul a hug. She put her hand on Nashy's shoulder "...and thank you for bringing the car."

"That's okay girlie. You want me to hang around?"

"No. Just want some space and some rest."

"Ok then. I'll be checking in though, just like Paul said."

"I know. It's okay."

After saying goodbye to them both, Rebecca headed inside put the kettle on and filled a bowl with food for Sarge. She sat down, took off her shoes, and gave the dog a serious look.

"You and me girl. We got this under control. Am I right?"

Sarge answered with one short but loud bark and then went off to eat.

Rebecca followed her plan to the letter. After a shower and a meal, she made her way into bed. It was earlier than she usually tried to sleep but her body wasted no time, and once engulfed in the warmth and comfort she fell fast asleep.

She woke early, showered, made a big country style breakfast, and took a long walk around the backyard, cradling a steaming mug of tea in her hands. Hands which were just barely visible, hanging below the long sleeves of one of Pop's old hand knitted jumpers. A heavy dew still clung to the grass, but she had worn a set of gum boots, Pop's again for that reason. She looked up at the crystal-clear blue sky, holding the mug of tea to her lips, drawing in the aroma, and breathing it out again in a cloud of misty breath. Yesterday she had doubted whether she should stay, in fact had almost resolved herself to leaving but now, just standing here, feeling part of the country, she knew she would not give in. She was here to stay.

37

Just after ten a.m. she climbed into her car, stopped to fill up the petrol tank in town and then headed into Tamworth. It took just under an hour, not driving fast, just enjoying the countryside until she pulled into the parking lot of the Hospital. The receptionist directed her to Meg's room, and she wandered down the hall, buying a bunch of flowers at a kiosk near a stairwell.

After climbing a flight of narrow stairs, Rebecca found the room and found Paul sitting beside an empty bed, half asleep. She placed her hand gently on his shoulder, not wanting to startle him and disturb one of the other people in the room. There were curtains drawn around the three other beds and Rebecca assumed there were other women in them. Paul woke without jumping, which Rebecca knew would be from years of being alert for anything as part of his job. She smiled at him and gave him a kiss on the cheek, which brought out an even bigger smile from him.

"Where's Aunty Meg?"

"They had to take her for some scans." He looked at his watch. "That was a while ago, so I reckon they should be back any moment."

"How is she?"

'Yeah. She's in Hospital, so good as can be expected."

"What about you? You really should be taking a break from work."

"I'm okay, and they understand. If I need to be here, I'm here. How about yourself?"

"I made a decision."

"You're going back to Newcastle aren't you."

Rebecca crossed her arms defiantly. "No way. My decision is that this is my home. Feels like it always has been and there's no way I'm leaving."

"Good. I like having you around."

A noise in the hallway made them both turn in time to see Meg, seated in a wheelchair, being pushed by a nurse back into the room. Her face, aged since Rebecca had last seen her, lit up when she saw her visitor.

"Aunty Meg."

"Hey sweetie. You are a sight for sore eyes. Best thing I've seen in days. Give me a hug. Just watch out you don't get tangled in all these tubes."

The two gave each other a careful hug for a moment, stopping when another nurse came into the room.

"Mrs Caplan. Let's get you back into bed, then you can catch up with your visitors."

Rebecca stepped out of the room with Paul while the two nurses helped Meg into the bed, attached tubes and wires to monitors and finally made some notes on the charts.

"Ok. That should do it. Your visitor can come join you now, but not for too long. You still need to get some rest." The two nurses then headed back into the hall.

"Don't you listen to them. You stay as long as you like, you'll be better company than Paul."

Paul shook his head and rolled his eyes.

"I know. He can be a bit dry, can't he."

Paul pretended to be offended. "Well if that's how it is, I'll go get myself a decent cup of coffee." and ventured off into the hallway as well.

"He's a tough old bugger, but I know all this stuff I'm going through is hard on him too." Meg whispered.

"He keeps busy. Been helping me with things, but yeah, he worries. He loves you, so of course he worries."

"So, my dear, what's been happening with you?"

For the next twenty minutes Meg and Rebecca chatted. Rebecca left out details of her intruder and the details of Matt's identity, but Meg seemed to love hearing about every little thing that Rebecca had been doing. She lit up again when she heard Jake would be visiting Shattered Falls on the weekend, smiled widely when she heard about Rebecca's plans to do some pottery and gave a deep sigh when she heard about Sarge, which reminded her of her own dog at home.

Paul returned, sat on the edge of the bed, and took hold of Meg's hand. "You need to get some rest now. I know how much you're enjoying having Rebecca visit, but the nurse spoke to me in the hall. We need to give you a break."

Rebecca stood from the chair, taking the hint that she should go.

"Yeah. I got a heap of things I have to get done anyway." Paul looked at her and could tell that she did not have a heap of things to do but gave her a thankful smile.

"And I've got to check in at the station."

"You two aren't much of the rebel, are you? Doing exactly what the nurses tell you to do."

Rebecca and Paul both shrugged and said their goodbyes. Rebecca leaving first giving Paul a chance to say goodbye properly. As she stepped into the hall, she almost walked into a tradesman moving quickly with a toolbox. The toolbox fell to the floor and the noise was enough to bring heads from every door in the hall. Rebecca looked the man in the eye and began to laugh. It was Craig.

"Oh my god. I'm sorry." Rebecca giggled as she helped him put a few scattered tools back into the toolbox.

"My fault. What you doing in here? You're not sick, are you? Did the wasps come back?"

"No. No wasps. Just visiting a friend. What about you?"

"Leaking toilets. Loads of fun. Listen I been meaning to call you about the dance. I got tickets, so wanted to make sure you were okay to come along with me. Not a date or anything. Just friends."

Rebecca noticed most of the hallway heads had retreated to whatever they had been doing before the toolbox had crashed to the floor, except one. Paul, Uncle Paul still stood there watching them both, like a father watching his daughter with a new boyfriend. The protective look on his face made even more ominous by the uniform. Rebecca gave him a death stare and turned back to Craig.

"Well, a lot's being going on...but yeah. It'd be great, and you know what..." She spoke just a little bit louder so Paul would hear. "Let's call it a date."

"Umm...ok. You going now? I can walk you to your car if you like."

"I think I would like."

She did not look back as she walked away, but she could feel Paul's stare every step of the hall.

Craig stopped in front of the elevator bay, which Rebecca had missed the first time.

"I took the stairs before."

"We can do the stairs if you prefer."

"No. Elevator is fine."

The doors opened, and they both stepped in and Craig reached to press the button.

Rebecca said something that she had always said in elevators since she was young. Something her mum had taught her. "Elelator go down."

"Ha. Unbelievable, you're quoting Tiny Toons."

"You know it?"

"I push the button. You no push the button."

Rebecca laughed, feeling comfortable in the moment. "That is so cool."

The elevator took only a moment to reach the ground floor and as the doors opened, Rebecca smiled at Craig.

"You know what. I am really looking forward to this dance. I think it's going to be fun."

Craig nodded "Well I hope so. Wouldn't want to let you down now."

Rebecca headed toward where she had parked her car, with Craig walking along beside her. They stopped when they reached the Suzuki and chatted again. Rebecca had the feeling they were being watched and looked up at the window where she assumed Uncle Paul would be standing, doing his best to supervise. She even waved up at the window.

From another window, eyes that were watching her however did not look on with fatherly care. The eyes burned with rage, jealousy, and deadly intent. The eyes, unblinking were a grey shadow compared to the dark thoughts that ran through the mind behind them. A mind that still carried hate toward anyone that came between him and her. 'Someone', he thought, 'needed to be taught a lesson, and this lesson…this one needed to be final. They would learn from this. Murder was absolute understanding.'

38

It was mid-afternoon when Rebecca arrived back home. She had not hurried, instead enjoying visiting the local shopping centre. Not expecting to buy anything, only intending to browse but coming home with three bags full of things she had not previously known she needed. Sarge came walking up the driveway from the backyard when Rebecca parked the car. From the raucous squawking that met Rebecca's ears when she stepped out of the car, she guessed that Sarge had likely been at the back-fence line voicing her disapproval at the flock of Corellas that had returned to the old gum tree.

"They been giving you the irrit's girl?"

Sarge gave a low growl and sat down, sniffing at the bags that Rebecca had placed on the ground.

"You're a busy body...but yes I got something for you. C'mon. In-side. I need to get these shoes off."

Once inside it was shoes off first, then bringing the fire back to life, which seemed to be an easy chore for her now. The fire was soon glowing with warmth and the afternoon chill drifted away. The kettle went on and was boiling in no time, and a packet of chocolate biscuits that had somehow found its way into Rebecca's shopping was opened.

"Oh. I promised something for you too didn't I."

Rebecca dug into the shopping bag and pulled out a rubber chew toy, shaped like a bedraggled chicken. She threw it into the air and Sarge snatched it instantly, Outside the Corellas screeched and as Sarge began to chomp down on the chicken's head, Rebecca was sure she saw the canine equivalent of a smile of satisfaction.

Once coffee and biscuits were finished, she grabbed something else from the shopping bag, found an old pair of work gloves from under the sink, whistled to Sarge and together they both headed outside. The sun was low now, but what she was planning would not take long. She made her way down to Nan's pottery shed, took a last look at the padlock that held it shut and lifted her brand-new set of bolt cutters into the air. The lock offered no resistance at all and for the first time in who knew how many years the pottery door swung open.

It surprised her that the lights still worked, the globes did not even flicker. They burst to life, bathing the room in clean white light. Everything had been covered in old calico sheets, which themselves were covered in a layer of dust, webs, leaves and what was most likely dried possum droppings. She pulled a sheet from atop two chairs, one high with a footrest and the other a small yellow plastic stool, emblazoned with Smurf's stickers. She felt tears welling in her eyes as a flood of memories came back to her. She could almost hear Nan singing and despite the years, the room still smelt of her perfume. She removed the other sheets of calico, folded them roughly and flung them into an empty corner.

Everything in the room was exactly where she remembered it should be. Brushes stood in an old vase, lengths of wire with handles at either end hung from an old towel rail, knives with plastic covers in a wooden case, pieces of towel and chamois, pencil like instruments with what looked like thick needles on the end. In the centre of the room was the wheel, still stained with clay but otherwise remarkably clean and at the rear of the room the huge kiln, that Pop had always said was a pizza oven, all the way from Italy. She knew that it was not, but she still smiled when she thought of Pop saying it.

She found the switch for the potter's wheel and turned it on. Nothing happened, and then she remembered the foot pedal that controlled the speed. Pop had made it from bits and pieces. An old washing machine engine, parts from one of Nan's broken sewing machines and the turntable from a record player, all took their place in the machine. Rebecca sat on the chair, not the yellow stool, her legs were too long for that now, and pushed down on the foot pedal. The old engine kicked in slowly, but the wheel remained still, so she pushed the pedal all the way down and it burst to life. A thin layer of dried clay went flying, and she was engulfed in a cloud of gritty, grey dust, some of which found its way into her eyes.

"Ok. Guess that works. Pity I'm blind now." She gave a cough, wiped what she could from her eyes and stood, closed the door, and made her way back inside.

After a quick wash, she stepped back into the hallway and found Sarge sitting just outside the kitchen, giving her the best 'Why are you starving me?' look she could do.

"Yeah. Me too girl. How about an early dinner? Steak for me and I bought some chicken for you."

Sarge gave a whimper and padded into the kitchen and waited.

Dinner came and went uneventfully with the later evening spent in front of fire and two episodes of Gilmore Girls, and then Rebecca settled in for the night. Strangely after the events of the week she felt safe in her home, in her bed, in her life. Sleep found her quickly and soon the house echoed with droning rumbles of two snoring girls.

That night two things happened.

A car, a van more precisely was run off the road by another vehicle. A vehicle that had seemed to have done so intentionally. The van returning from a late evening, emergency job just east of Gunnedah. The other car waiting in a rest area beside the road, driving with lights off, coming almost noiselessly until right behind, and then all lights blinding, overtaking and sliding sideways to just touch the van enough to send it into a ditch, and come to a sickening halt up against an old but hefty stump. Glass shattered, engine stopped, radiator fractured and steaming. The other vehicle, just a flash of light disappearing into the distance, uncaring. The injured driver would sit there until the following morning, breath shallow, bleeding from a head wound and unconscious.

One hour and eighty kilometres away, Megan Caplan passed away in her sleep.

39

It was Nashy that brought her the news of Meg's passing. He had parked his car in the heavy fog, in the driveway and sat there for a long time. Engine idling, heater washing warm air over him whilst he ran over how to break it to her. When he finally decided that he had no idea of what to say, but knew he had to say it anyway, he climbed from the car and knocked on Rebecca's door. He woke her and it took her a while to stumble down the hall and fumble with the door, opening it slowly. She shielded her eyes from the morning light, even though it had been dimmed by the fog and shielded herself from the cold by pulling up the collar of the old dressing gown she had pulled from amongst Pops things. When she saw Nashy, she knew something was wrong, his eyes were downcast, trying to avoid hers.

"Nashy. What's going on? You look like you ran over someone's dog."

He looked up at Rebecca, and she could see the glint of a tear in his eyes.

"I'm sorry Bec. It's Meg. She's gone. She...Damn it."

"No. I saw her yesterday. I know she was sick, but...she." Her breath caught in her throat.

"I know Bec. I know. It's all fucked up...sorry for swearing, but it is."

"Where's Uncle Paul?"

"Not sure. Hospital, I guess. He left a message on my phone. Sounded in a bad way himself. Not answering his phone now."

"I've got to get ready and get in there."

"I thought you might. That's why I'm here. I'm driving you. Get changed. I'll wait in the car. I got a thermos of hot tea out there and I hope you like it milky and sweet."

Rebecca reached out and put her hand on his shoulder. Nashy looked her in the eye again and just nodded. It meant more than he could find words for, and Rebecca turned and hurried back to her room to get ready. Sarge sat in the hall, sensing something was wrong. As Rebecca came out of her room, she let her hand fall to the dog's head.

"I'll be back soon girl. Be good."

The trip to the Hospital was one of silent sadness. The tea, sweet and milky as promised, still tasted bitter to Rebecca, but she knew it was just the overwhelming shock and grief that had put a sour taste in her mouth. Nashy spoke to her a few times, but she hardly took it in. Staring instead out the window into the mist shrouded gullies, and farmland that lay beside the road.

The Hospital was a hive of activity when they arrived. From what little they had overheard a head-on crash between a semi-trailer and a car had brought in four people in serious condition, and another single car crash had another person on their way in, in an ambulance. She could see the focus and concern on the faces of the nursing staff and felt guilty when she stopped one of them to ask about Meg, and Paul.

"Are you family?"

Rebecca knew the real answer was no.

"It's my Aunt. Aunty Meg."

"I'm so sorry. She was peaceful when it happened." The nurse paused for a moment. "I think her husband is still upstairs with the Doctor."

Rebecca did not hesitate to head for the elevator, Nashy following close behind and when they both stepped out into the upstairs corridor, they saw him. Rebecca held back her tears as she stepped toward him but could hold them back no longer when she heard the sobs coming from Nashy behind her. She ran the last few steps and wrapped her arms around her Uncle Paul, burying her face in his chest. He held her tightly, and she could feel him trembling slightly as he too began to sob.

It was only when a Nashy joined the tearful hug that they both drew a breath and Paul spoke.

"It's okay you two. I'm glad you're here, but I'm okay."

Rebecca drew back, still holding Paul's hand to look into her uncle's eyes. Reddened and puffy, but still, as always, a steely grey that commanded authority. The tremble in his hand gave Rebecca a true sense of what state he was in. She broke the stare when Nashy spoke.

"I'm so sorry mate. I can't begin to imagine how you're doing but..."

"Thanks, but...yeah it's a bastard to get your head around, but she's not in pain anymore. She went in her sleep, just wish..." his breath caught in his throat and between some choked sobs he continued, "wish I'd been here with her when she went."

"She loved you Uncle Paul and I know you loved her. We all did."

Paul gave a fractured smile, while a tear ran down his cheek. Rebecca wiped it away with the back of her hand.

"Is there anything we can do mate? I know all you coppers help each other out when you need, but I...we want to help as well. Don't we Bec."

"Yeah. We do."

"I know, and yeah I think most stuff will be sorted. She planned for this you know. Ran all the plans by me but I didn't want to listen, so she made me. So, I reckon other than feeling like shit, everything is almost sorted."

A nurse stepped up to them, giving the impression she needed to talk.

"Listen you two, thank you but I reckon the plans she made ,still need me to do some stuff. Megsie said I'd have to get my shit together and get stuff done, so I best go do it."

Rebecca could tell the Nurse needed him, so wrapped her arms around him once again.

"I love you Uncle Paul."

"Love you too Missy."

Nashy not wanting to feel left out added, "Yeah me-too mate. Love you."

"You're a good mate Nashy. Now do me a favour and get this lady home."

"Done."

Paul turned and followed the nurse back down the hall and into a room. The heavy wooden door closing behind them.

Rebecca smiled at Nashy. "You're a big softie. Lots of love in that big old heart I think."

"Yeah. Maybe. Just don't go telling anyone I said I love a copper."

She put her arm around his shoulder and together they headed back to the elevator.

Downstairs nurses and doctors moved with purpose. All seeming intent on the critical patients that had come in this morning. Rebecca spotted Craig's sister, Tania and gave a quick wave, not wanting to distract her from her duties. Tania looked up at Rebecca, a look of puzzlement on her face as she came toward her.

"How did you get here so quick? How did you find out?"

Rebecca answered hesitantly, "Nashy. He came over this morning told me. Brought me in."

Tania seemed more confused now than earlier. "Umm...Ok. Well he's been taken into our critical care unit. It's scary. Mum and Dad haven't even got here yet."

"He? What? I came in to see my Uncle. My Aunt passed away last night."

"Oh my god. I'm so sorry. You haven't heard then. It's Craig. He was in a crash. Struggling to keep things together at the moment but it's all staff on deck."

Rebecca stopped and stared, mouth half open. "Is he okay?"

"Doctors are with him. Don't know much more now, other than they found him crashed into a stump. Ambo's said looked like someone ran him off the road. Someone just left him there to die."

A buzzer rang somewhere, and Tania turned to look. "I got to go. I'm sorry about your Aunt." She hurried off and was lost amongst a swarm of medical staff.

"Who's Craig?"

"Oh. Sorry Nashy. Craig Braye. He came to fix the downpipe."

"The plumber. Yeah, I know his dad. Shit, hope the kid's alright."

"This is turning out to be a really shit day."

"Yeah. Well, nothing we can do here now so let's get you home."

"Ok...actually do you think we could make a detour."

Nashy raised his eyebrows, the tangled mess they were at the best of times, knitting together, errant hairs pointing in all directions. Rebecca swore they were alive.

"Detour?"

"Yeah. Someone else will be missing Aunty Meg."

40

They pulled into the Caplan's driveway. The morning fog had burnt away leaving a cold but clear midday sky. Rebecca climbed out and spoke to Nashy before she closed the door.

"I won't be long. I just want to feed her and give her a bit of attention."

"Ok Bec. I might hang out here if you don't mind. Don't feel right me heading into a coppers house uninvited, even if it is a mates and...I know you're going to tell me otherwise, but I need a bloody smoke."

"Yeah I think I'll allow it. Just one though."

"Deal."

As she ventured up to the front door, Rebecca stopped and lifted a flat white rock from beside a sun-bleached bird bath in the garden. Beneath it was a spare key to the front door. The same hiding place for the past ten years. As she unlocked the door and stepped inside, the darkness enveloped her. Like it had Aunty Meg since the disease had started. Aunty Meg had hidden from the world in her last years, seemingly embarrassed by the waif like woman she had become. Rebecca pulled the cord on a blind and the room seemed to burst to life with an explosion of light. Everything had a place, and everything was in its place. Aunty Meg had always been one for being tidy, but it seemed in the last few years it had become her obsession. Rebecca inhaled, taking in the smells, closing her eyes, and imagining her doting Aunt still dusting the furniture or cooking Lemon Meringue Pie in the kitchen.

Rebecca made her way into the kitchen, noticing a small pile of dirty dishes in the sink and unlocked the back door. Sitting on the back veranda, almost unmoving was Peaches. A ball like bundle of white fur that barely lifted its head to Rebecca, but when recognition took hold, she stood and gave a friendly 'Yap'.

"Hey girl. You know, don't you?"

The dog stared back at Rebecca, giving a fretful whine that almost brought tears to her eyes.

Rebecca scooped the small dog up and carried her inside, cuddling her and scratching behind her ears and under her chin as she went.

"You hungry or is that a really stupid question."

Rebecca found tins of dog food and a bowl. Peaches despite her obvious depression, devoured it before running into the front room to bark through the now lifted blind, at the car in the driveway.

"You get him girl."

From her vantage point she could see straight down the kitchen hall and through the front window to the now seemingly sleeping Nashy.

"Okay, guess I got time to clean up these dishes while you nap then."

There were only a few plates, cups, cutlery items and a saucepan. Rebecca, despite not having visited properly in years remembered exactly where everything went, and she knew Aunty Meg would have approved of her cleaning up. She finished up and was hanging the tea towel over the back of one of the chairs surrounding the small table in the kitchen, when she noticed the jumbled mass of paperwork on the table.

"Well best tidy that as well."

At first, she regretted touching it, but curiosity soon won.

The symbols on the front of the folders told her that these were police files and the name on the front of the top one was Matthew Lonergan. She felt a chill rush through her body and her shoulders shrugged instinctively. Rebecca balanced herself by placing one hand on the table, not wanting a repeat of the last time she had been confronted by information about Matt.

She put her hand on the front cover of the file, wanting to open it but holding herself back. The folder slid to the side and those beneath it fanned out. Now she could see some of the names on them. Tate Sedgewick, Zak Thomson, Cameron Nash, Tony Higgins, and Craig

Braye. She drew a deep breath not realising for the past few moments she had been holding it.

"What the actual F..." The sharp blast of a car horn outside cut her words short. She desperately wanted to look inside the files. Her only explanation was that Paul suspected one of these people to be the one who had broken into her home. 'Obviously' she thought 'it's not Zak.' She was also sure, positive in fact that it was Matt, but then why were there files for Craig, Tony and even Nashy. She flipped open the cover of one the files, feeling like a criminal herself and started to read. The horn outside blared once again, so she pulled out here phone and took several quick photos as she flipped through the other files. As she opened the file that belonged to Cameron Nash, she jumped and screamed. Not at what she saw, instead at the noise of Nashy banging heavily on the front door.

"You done yet girlie. You alright. Haven't fallen down and can't get up have ya?"

"Sorry Nashy. I'm coming."

Rebecca tidied the files and table before giving Peaches a final rub behind the ear and locking up the house.

"What the hell took you so long in there? Did you do the ironing or something?"

"Sorry Nashy. Lots of memories of Aunty Meg in there."

"Nah, it's me that's sorry. You don't need to explain. I can be an impatient old bugger sometimes...but...it's gonna be hard for a lot of people. You, Paul. Even me...Let's get home, I need to give Liz a hug."

"Yeah. I need to ring Gran and Jake. I reckon we've all have got a few more tears to spill before the day is over."

41

It was early afternoon when they pulled back into the cracked concrete driveway that led to Rebecca's house. Nashy gave her a broken smile and then apologised as his stomach rumbled like a far-off thunderstorm.

"Sorry. Well overdue for a feed. You should get something too. If you want, I know Liz would be happy to have you over for dinner."

"No. I know she would too, but I just need some time to myself."

"Ok...but you call if you change your mind...or if you just want some company."

"Thanks, Nashy."

Rebecca watched as Nashy's car turned and headed back toward town, now with all the windows down to rid the vehicle of the smell of cigarette. She fumbled for keys in her pocket and stepped to the door, only to have it swing open. For a moment she tried to remember whether she had locked it or not but soon began to shiver when she thought of the other possibility.

"No. Not again." She took two steps into the house and stopped, listening for any movement. She heard a dog bark and then a male voice.

"You're a good girl aren't ya."

A figure stepped out of the kitchen. A figure clad in a black jacket, a hood still hung over his head. In one hand what appeared to be a half-eaten sandwich and the other holding a mobile phone. Rebecca recognised the figure instantly and the intruder turned to see her as well, jumping just a little in shock.

"What the hell are you doing here?" Rebecca's voice came stern and clear, like a cranky maths teacher.

"Shit…Scared the crap out of me sis."

"Jake." It was all she could say before she stepped to him and wrapped her arms around her little brother and hugged him tightly. Jake dropped the sandwich and it fell to floor but only for a moment as Sarge cleaned it up.

The tears came from Rebecca before she had a chance to say another word.

"Sis. Seriously, you didn't miss me that much."

She pulled back just a little, so she could see Jake's face and in that moment of sibling connection Jake knew that something else was wrong.

"It's Aunty Meg…She's gone."

As soon as those two words 'She's gone' rang out, Jake sat himself on the edge of the couch, closed his eyes, and tried, unsuccessfully to hold back his own tears.

After they had both shed a few more tears and comforted each other as only a brother and sister could, Rebecca stood.

"Now I need a strong cup of coffee and then I need you to help me."

"Ok. Coffee sounds good, but help with what?"

"We have to ring Gran and Grandad."

"Shit… We'll need some tissues then."

From the kitchen Rebecca asked, "So how did you get here anyway? And how come my dog didn't rip you apart?"

"I bought a bike. Been fixing it most of the week. Hundred and twenty on Gumtree."

"Gran wouldn't have liked that. You don't even have a licence. So, where's the bike?"

"Behind the toilets at a Rest stop near Wallabadah. Piece of shit. Had to hitch the rest of the way."

"Seriously. Why would you hitch? There's psycho's out there."

"I would have still been walking, and I only took rides from truckies. Slightly less psychotic."

"And...How did you bypass my security?" Rebecca put her hand down to scratch the top of Sarge's head, who was now sitting by her legs.

"Still had half a monster Sausage roll from Wallabadah servo. I wasn't a fan of it, but the dog loved it. Me and her are a team now, so you best get yourself another dog."

"God. I should be so angry at you...but I'm so glad you're here."

With two cups of coffee in hand, Rebecca sat down on the couch and together they made the call. For twenty minutes they talked, cried a little and somewhere near the end had a brief laugh. They said their goodbyes, and both drew a deep breath.

"Well sis, I need a shower. Being a truckies bitch for half a day leaves you a feeling a bit dirty."

Rebecca threw a cushion at Jake as he made his way down the hall.

"Ok, smart ass. Hope he at least gave you his number, but I bet he won't call in the morning...Clean towels in the cupboard...and don't use all the hot water."

Rebecca lent back in the couch and finally cast her gaze at Sarge.

"Traitor. Some guard dog you are."

The pipes began to squeal, and Rebecca heard running water and her brother singing some crude semi-rap song that seemed to get louder at any offensive word. It only made her smile.

She pulled out her mobile phone, thinking that now would be a good opportunity to browse the photos she had taken of the police files. Flicking from last to first, she was less than impressed by the information. Dates of birth, known associates, home addresses. It was only when she got to the second photo, she had taken did she stop and take any real notice.

It was a schedule of movements for Matt Lonergan. Uncle Paul had gone to a lot of trouble to track Matt and his vehicle. As Rebecca read the details, she stopped. Something was not right. She read again but still the details she read defied logic. At the time the intruder had broken into her house, whilst she had watched him in the hallway, Matthew

Lonergan had been getting a speeding ticket just outside St George, Queensland. A good four hundred miles away.

Sarge jumped suddenly to her feet a second before there were three heavy knocks at the door. Rebecca looked out the window, spotting a car that looked familiar. She read the number plate and realised she had read it not two minutes ago in the police report. It was Matt's car.

Holding Sarge tightly by the collar she stepped to the door and swung it open just a crack.

"Rebecca. I'm sorry. It's Matt. I need to talk to you. I need to explain everything."

"Fuck off."

"Ok. I deserve that, but you deserve the truth. You've been lied to almost all your life. I know you know who I am. My dad was a drunk. He threw his life away on booze and gambling...but he didn't kill your mum and dad. He didn't and I can prove it."

Rebecca felt her legs wobble, and she steadied herself on the door-frame, letting the door swing open. Sarge began to growl louder.

"Sit girl. Stay." Rebecca drew a deep breath, considering her next actions. "You've got one minute to talk before I let her do what comes natural."

"Shit. Hell...ok. When we got the car back from the police a month after the court case, Mum found this under the seat."

Matt held up an old mobile phone. It was one Rebecca recognised. One she had seen only days ago or a picture of it to be exact. The phone belonged to Cameron Nash.

"My dad wasn't driving. He told me the story before he died and its been eating me up ever since. I need to clear his name...but I need to tell you first. You deserve it."

Rebecca held back a breath and closed her eyes. Everything she believed was falling apart and the person she had been carrying so much hate for, most of her life was the wrong man. At least if what she was being told was true.

"I don't know if you're telling the truth or not...but I know it wasn't you that broke in. You weren't even in town."

"Someone broke in?"

"So why should I believe any of this?"

Matt held up the phone. "I can prove it."

"It's just a phone."

"It's not the phone. It's the voice message left on it. A fourteen-year-old message...and when the truth gets out, it'll turn this town upside down."

"A message? Who from? This is getting more confusing...I can't deal."

"My dad kept this phone charged for fourteen years because he knew one day, he would be able to do the right thing."
"OK." Rebecca hesitated. "Play it."

Another voice broke into the conversation from behind Rebecca.

"Becster. I might have used a bit too much hot water but damn it felt good. Oh shit, sorry. Didn't know you had a visitor. Who's this?"

Rebecca turned to Jake and motioned to Matt with an open hand.

"Jake this is Matt. He worked at the mill. Matt this is my brother Jake."

The two nodded to each other before Jake continued.

"Oh, and I rang Uncle Paul. He was okay considering...and he said he was on his way over soon anyway."

Matt turned and began to walk away from the door. "I can't hang around. Not with him coming, but I still need to talk."

"Matt. Wait...damn...meet me...half an hour...at The Pane."

Matt turned back and stared at Rebecca and after a minute nodded. "Half an hour."

He climbed into his car and disappeared up the road. The vehicle travelling at a speed which only added to Rebecca's growing anxiety.

"That your boyfriend sis?"

"No. It's...It's just a real long story. I have to go out for a while."

"Secret rendezvous?"

"Jake. Please. I'm just a bit on edge. Do you think you could organise some dinner for us? There's plenty of food. Your choice. I'll be back in an hour or so."

Jake spoke in a quieter but concerned voice. "You okay?"

"I don't know. I just need to talk to Matt. He knows something...and I think I need to know it too."

"Ok. I'll have a feed ready for you when you get back. Take the dog with you."

"Her name's Sarge."

"Ha...of course it is. Take Sarge with you. I reckon she would rip the arm of anyone that tries to mess with you."

"Or anyone that doesn't have dinner on the table when we get back."

"Ok. Hint taken."

CHAPTER FORTY-TWO

A country dusk had begun to settle over the town of Shattered Falls as Rebecca climbed into her car and patted the seat, indicating that Sarge should join her. The dog did not hesitate, jumping and landing clumsily before climbing into the back seat. She flicked the headlights on and reversed out of the driveway as Jake watched from the front door. Jake giving a teenage style non-committal wave, that was little more than a raised finger. Rebecca hardly noticed.

She could feel pins and needles in her hands and almost a tremble throughout her body, but her grip held steady on the wheel and her eyes on the road ahead. She seemed a picture of calm, despite the whirlpool of thoughts swimming in her head.

What the hell had Matt been trying to tell her? Why did he have Nashy's phone? A phone that had apparently been missing for fourteen years. Had Nashy been driving Matt's father's car when it had forced her mum and dad off the road? How could he do that and carry on hiding it all this time, and how could he bear to look Rebecca in the eyes?

The main street. Tracey's store. The pub. Everything passed by in a blur as the unanswered questions continued to spin through her mind and Rebecca felt a wave of nausea wash over her. She wound down the window and the chill breeze cleared her head. Sarge must have sensed something, or maybe she was unhappy with the cold air now spilling into the car as she nuzzled Rebecca's elbow and gave a soft whimper.

By the time they bumped over a potholed section of road which seemed to mark the boundary of town and bush, darkness had fallen. She flicked between high and low beam as other cars randomly passed by and hit the brakes suddenly twice, as kangaroos shot across the road in front of her, but they were far enough away not to cause any issues.

"It's okay girl." Rebecca did her best to reach back and pat Sarge but only managed to slap her on the nose.

"Sorry girl. We're nearly there. Make a deal with you okay. You look after me and I'll look after you."

Rebecca surprised herself when she almost missed the turn off to the camping grounds at The Pane. The car's back end slewed slightly to the left on the darkened road, but she safely made the turn onto the rough dirt track that ran around both sides of the dam. The Pane was uncommonly quiet. She had expected to see several campfires but tonight there was no one. She sat, idling the car, wound up the window and looked down the long stretch of water, its calm surface disturbed as a flock of wood ducks settled beside the old jetty. She smiled as she remembered the pocketknife that she had lost from that jetty. A gift from her dad, with a plastic, mother-of-pearl like handle, which despite its true fifteen-dollar value had been the most valuable treasure she had owned at the time. She had heard her Mum call after her as she had run off with it. "Be careful now." And then she had heard a much quieter Mum say to her father "My god, did you see that smile? That's one proud girl."

When it had fallen from her pocket, weeks later, through the cracks between boards in the jetty, whilst she had been soaking up the mid-day sun, watching a yabby crawl in the shadows, she had been devastated. They had tried to recover it, but the soft mud and occasional smashed beer bottle hidden below, made the search impossible. She thought of that even now. Loss was a bitch and sometimes, it took a lot more from you than a fifteen-dollar pocketknife.

At the far end of the dam she saw another set of lights. Parking lights, and through the dim red shine she could just make out the motion of a car sitting idling just like hers. It was, she could now tell, Matt's car and despite a growing feeling of apprehension, she took her foot of the brake and began the last hundred metres to what would hopefully be the truth.

Matt was leaning against the front of his car, staring to the west, catching the last few moments of the dwindling twilight. He turned as Rebecca's car came to halt beside his and Sarge began to growl.

"Easy girl. Easy. I'll leave the window down for you. Just stay."

Rebecca opened her door and forced herself to get out and take steps that felt like walking through boot-sucking mud. She knew it was all in her head but just knowing that did not seem to make it any easier. She looked back toward the car to see Sarge, with head and front paws hanging out the passenger window, ready to spring out at the first sign that she was needed. She turned back as Matt spoke.

"I wasn't sure you would come...and I'm sorry I had to take off. That coppers got it in for me. Ever since he worked out who my dad was."

"He's just watching out for me...and I don't think you can blame him."

"I know. I've been keeping secrets, but I had too. I didn't know who I could trust. But I think it's time you knew everything."

"Then tell me."

Matt took a few steps forward and sat on a long log that acted as a barrier for cars and looked up at Rebecca. She took a seat at the other end of the log.

"Ok where to start."

"My Pop always said the beginning is a good place."

"Yeah. I reckon he's right. Well you know who my dad was. He was a drunk lots of the time but he was my dad all the time. He was never violent. Not like some of the drunks that beat their kids or their wife. Dad had a lot of issues when he was young with one of them type of drunks, and I reckon that's a big part of why he turned out like he did. His dad, who I never met, well dad didn't talk about him much, but mum knew about him. Let's just say he was one the worst type of drunks. Dad did his best to grow up and not be that sort of person, but things got him down and it was a way out for him. When he met my mum, he was as clean as could be, but he slipped a few times, lost his job and that was a spiral he couldn't escape from. Even did a couple of stints in jail."

"I know your Dad wouldn't have caused the accident on purpose, but..."

"That's just it Rebecca. He didn't cause the accident. I came down here, got the job at the mill. Stayed down here, away from my family to prove it."

"Family?"

"Yeah. I never let on to anyone. I got twin girls and my wife back home. We're separated now but we're working things out. Guess the anger in me from what dad told me wasn't healthy for our relationship."

"That's why you rushed back to Queensland straight from the pub the other night."

"Yeah. Gracie, she's the oldest of twins had broken her arm. Climbing a big old plum tree at her Aunties place. She's fine...but I had to go. Needed to go."

"I'm sorry. I didn't know."

"It's okay. Anyways back to what Dad told me. Damn I don't reckon you will believe me. It's probably best you listen to this."

Matt pulled the old phone he had shown Rebecca earlier, out of his jacket pocket.

"This phone. It's been a mission to keep it charged. But the message on it...well you need to hear it."

"I know who's phone it is. Are you saying Nashy had something to do with this?"

"Just listen. Like I said we found it in dads' car when we got it back from the police."

Matt punched at the buttons on the phone and held it in front of him.

Rebecca listened to the message that seemed to boom in the stillness of late twilight and within seconds began to sob heavier than she had in a long time, right up to the last words, when it felt like her body turned to ice and her world turned black.

"Rebecca. Rebecca."

When Rebecca focused again, Matt was crouched in front of her with his hand on her shoulder but was pushed aside when Sarge pushed her way between them.

"Ok you two. I'm okay."

"Thought you were going to faint then. You lurched forward like you were going to fall on your face."

"I'm okay." She rested her palm on Sarge's head and nodded to Matt. He stood back up and sat back down on the log.

"You need to play that again. I heard it but... it must be wrong. Something I misunderstood."

Matt once again punched at the buttons on the old mobile phone and sat it on the log between them. Rebecca calmed herself this time and listened intently as her mother's voice began to speak.

'Hello.'

'Cameron?'

Another voice, her fathers *'Just call him Nashy.'*

'Nashy it's Karen Ford. David was going to ring, but he's in a bit of a state. We just need you to do us a favour. Can you keep an eye on David's Dad? We have to go down to be with the kids at my mum and dads, and we've got some legal stuff to look into to.'

Rebecca's father cut in again. *'Got to get a lawyer.'*

'Just keep an eye on Pop for us.'

'and if that prick Caplan comes anywhere near him...just...shoot the bastard.'

'David.'

'He's been trying to steal my wife behind my back. My best friend for Christ's sake but he's gone too far now.'

'Nashy, just look after Pop. We'll be back as soon as we can. I just need to get to my kids'

The message ended and silence enveloped them.

"My god. Uncle Paul. He was harassing mum. That's who she was talking about in her diary."

"Yeah about that." Matt walked back to his car and returned with a plastic sleeve filled with papers.

"This is probably the most illegal thing I've ever done."

Matt handed the sleeve to Rebecca. "What do you mean?"

"I stole these out of his cop car while he was searching my caravan. They've been ripped out of another book...and I'm sorry but I read them. They just confirmed everything."

Rebecca pulled the pages from the sleeve and for the next fifteen minutes she read snatches from pages torn from her mother's diary in the bright headlights of Matt's car.

"It was him. All the time...but how does this prove your dad wasn't driving."

"Well, that's where you are going to have to put a little faith into what my dad told me."

"Faith? Just tell me."

"After the accident Mum took us kids back to Queensland to live with her parents. Dad did a couple of years in prison and eventually he came up too. He got a job with the council and stayed sober until his last breath."

"He died?"

"Yeah. Punished his body too much with booze and smokes...but before he went, he told me he needed to clear something up. Needed to restore some small piece of personal dignity.

The night of the accident he was drunk as usual and was driving home or back to the pub. He doesn't remember which, but he does remember driving along and seeing a police car at the side of the road. At first, he thought it was an RBT but when he got closer, he could see the car had hit a roo or something and had swerved off the road. It was just near where you turn onto the highway. It was Paul. The car had a flat and probably a broken axle. Paul was flustered. Like a mad man, dad said and in a hurry. That's when he took over driving Dad's car, and they took off chasing something. Guess now we know he was chasing after your mum and dad. They caught up with them just before crossing the range and Paul tried to get them to pull over, but they just kept driving. Paul was screaming how sorry he was. How he would lose his job, lose his wife. Lose everything...and then he tried to force them to pull over...but it went all wrong.

After the crash...Paul and dad tried to get down to them. Other cars had stopped. Paul turned to dad and said, 'You were driving and if you ever say any different, I'll make sure your kids end up spending their lives in prison just like you' and then he took off."

"Your dad should have told the truth about what happened...shouldn't have let it go this far."

"My dad was drunk. He had a reputation. No one would have believed him and the only good thing in his life was his family. He would have given up his freedom to make sure we were safe."

"I'm so sorry. I've been so angry at him for such a long time."

"You don't need to be sorry. It's not your fault but, hopefully you believe me now and you know whose fault it was."

"It's a lot to process. A lot. I need time...and his wife just died. I don't even think I could face him now."

"You should keep this for now too." Matt handed the phone to Rebecca.

They sat silent for a moment until the lights from another vehicle shone down over the dam.

"Ok Rebecca. I've given you a lot to think about. Maybe a night to get your head straight will help."

"Maybe. Maybe not, but yeah, I think it's time to head home."

They stood and turned back towards their cars and the dam. The lights from new vehicle at the other end of the dam were on high beam, and they had to shield their eyes.

"Just pick a place to camp dickhead." Matt muttered as he squinted at the headlights, and then as the flashing blue lights on the roof of the car began to strobe and the siren sung, they both swore.

"So much for having time to process. You should go Matt. It could get ugly."

"I've been hiding from him for too long, and there's no way I'm leaving you with him."

43

The big four-wheel drive pulled to a stop behind Matt's vehicle, blocking any chance of him leaving. The door of the Police car swung open, and Paul stepped out, engine running and headlights still beaming across the dam.

"Matthew Lonergan." Paul bellowed and his voice echoed throughout the campground. "You're under arrest. Put your hands on the bonnet of your vehicle."

"Seriously. What's the charge?" Matt stepped to his car and laid his palms flat on the bonnet.

"Break and enter for a start."

Rebecca stuttered at first, almost scared to speak. "N-N-N-NO."

"It's okay Bec. I'll make sure he doesn't bother you again. I don't know what he did to make you come out here, but I'll be adding that to the charges." A pair of handcuffs rattled in Pauls hands.

"Leave him alone. Just leave him alone. You can stop this act. I know everything. I know it was you that broke into my house. I know it was you that stole the diary...and I know it was you that killed Mum and Dad."

Paul continued with his back to Rebecca, as he slowly cuffed Matt's hands behind his back.

"Bet he told you that didn't he. Do anything to get himself out trouble. His old man was good for nothing and as far as I can tell so is he. You don't seriously believe a word he says, do you?"

"I don't have to believe him. I heard the truth from the two people I trusted more than anyone else."

"What are you talking about girl?" Paul turned back to face Rebecca.

Rebecca turned on the phone and started the message, making sure its loudspeaker was on.

Paul stared at it and in a broken and slow voice asked.

"Where...did you get that?"

"You left it in Ed Shaw's car that night. How you got Nash's phone I don't know but the message says it all."

Paul did not stop to listen to the message. Instead, he stepped toward Rebecca.

"Give it to me. You have no idea what happened."

Paul reached for the phone and Rebecca pulled away, but he grabbed her arm and pulled her toward him.

"You're hurting me."

"Just give me the pho...." Paul's words were cut short as he was knocked sideways by Sarge as she jumped and latched onto his arm, but he regained his footing and spoke in a stern voice to the dog.

"Aus. Platz. Sitz."

The dog released his arm immediately and sat on her haunches, growling but now unmoving.

"That's how you managed to sneak into my house isn't it. Of course. She's a police dog, and she'll do whatever you say."

"Enough of this rubbish Rebecca. Give me the phone now."

Paul was knocked off his feet again but this time by the handcuffed Matt from behind. He staggered to the side and Matt, unable to manage his balance with his hands behind his back, fell to the ground.

Paul stumbled and turned to face Matt, who was now laying in the short-tufted grass, trying to get back to his feet. Rebecca screamed as Paul pulled his gun from the holster on his waist and pointed it at Matt.

"Stay on the ground Lonergan."

"Put the gun away. I'll give you the phone. Just put the gun away."

Paul turned back to face Rebecca, and she immediately saw something different in his face. Some different shine in his eyes. Something not good.

"You don't get it do you Rebecca. I was in love with your mother. Always was, but she fell for David. I know there was something between the two of us. We kissed once. We…"

"Bullshit. She loved my dad."

"Rebecca he's just trying to justify himself. I read the diary, same as you. Your mum had too much to drink after the team won that Grand Final. She regretted it straight away, but this prick took it for something more."

Paul pointed the gun down at Matt. "Shut the fuck up."

A blur of fur bounced up from the ground and took all of them by surprise. Sarge snapped at Paul's arm and narrowly missed, and then a gun shot rang out. Sarge yelped, fell to the ground, unmoving and then to the sound of Rebecca's screams, lifted her head, growling at Paul.

"Sarge." Rebecca moved to the dog sprawled on the ground. "You shot her." With the dog's head cradled in her lap Rebecca turned up to look at Paul. Hair that had fallen across her face, blew to the side as an icy breeze began to sweep in, and as it did her eyes became visible. Narrowed, piercing eyes that held nothing but hatred for the man that stood above her.

"Everyone needs to calm down. I didn't want to shoot her. This is getting out of …."

"But you did shoot her you bastard. You self-righteous prick"

"Rebecca. Seriously. Everything I have done since you got here, has been for you."

"What breaking into my house and stalking me. What the hell is wrong with you?"

"You have to understand. When you turned up…Everything came back. You're the image of your mother. When I drove you out to Shattered Falls that day and gave you the keys to your Pop's house. Your house… Rebecca, I fell in love all over again."

Rebecca's eyes changed from hate to shock in an instant. "You're out of your mind."

Matt grunted as he attempted to roll over from his bound position on the ground. "You're old enough to be her dad, you weird prick."

Paul pressed the boot of his shoe against the back of Matt's head and pushed him back into the dirt. "I won't warn you again Lonergan. Shut up and stay put."

"Just take the phone and go." Rebecca held the mobile up.

"I wish it were that easy, but he's stuffed everything. I tried to protect you. Thought I had made sure this idiot stayed away. Took care of your ex-boyfriend."

"Took care of. Did you...?" Rebecca's hand dropped back to the ground still clutching the phone.

"You and me both know he was a waste of space. Junkies like him wouldn't have stayed away. He's gone now. I made sure."

"You killed him?"

Face down in the dirt, Matt seemed to have gone rigid. As if he were not wanting to draw any attention.

"My job is to protect people. Especially you. To know where you are and who you're with."

"Oh god. I'm so stupid. You gave me the phone. You even told me you could track me."

"It was for your protection Rebecca."

"My protection? More like it was all for you."

"Maybe, but it's true. I am in love with you and I'm not going to let anyone get in the way of that again. I lost you...your mum. It's not happening again."

"You're a married man...were a married man. And what do you mean by anyone?"

"Meg was dying. You knew that. You could see it. She was in pain. I loved her too, just in a different way. I couldn't let her go on like that and I needed...I needed to make space for you."

Rebecca stared at Paul, both her mouth and eyes wide open and struggling to find words.

"It was the hardest thing I have ever done but I had to do it...and the other guy. He was getting too close."

"You killed Aunty Meg? How could you even do that?... and what other guy are you talking about?" Rebecca could sense that the man that for years had been like family, her Uncle Paul was on the brink of cracking.

"I know he liked you...and I could tell you liked him too...and in a weird way it helped deal with what I did to Meg."

"Holy shit." Rebecca almost choked as she realised but managed to spit out the words. "You ran Craig off the road. You tried to kill him too. Just like you killed mum and dad."

Paul raised his voice, anger snorting through his breath. "It was nothing like what happened with your mum and dad. Nothing."

Rebecca went silent. Her head hung low, and her arms wrapped around the bleeding dog on her lap.

"Just give me the phone. Then we'll work this out."

Rebecca looked at the phone in her hand.

"How did you even get it? It's Nashy's phone."

"That day. The day of the accident. I went looking for your mum. To make things right... but she had already told your dad. I went to the mill looking for them. It was close to lockup time. I was in the office when it rang and saw it was Karen. It went to the message, and I listened to it and I knew I couldn't let Nashy hear it...and I knew then exactly where they were. Heading south. Heading to you...and to a lawyer. So, I took it and went after them. I got a flat just short of the highway and knew I had lost them and that's when...that's when Ed Shaw tuned up."

"You fucking asshole." Matt screamed into the dirt and then gave a grunt as Paul kicked him in the side.

Rebecca felt her fingertips begin to tingle and struggled to draw a breath. Anxiety was beginning to overtake her and this time all she wanted to do was curl up in a ball on the ground and disappear. Instead, she placed Sarge's head carefully down onto the ground, stood and looked Paul calmly in the eye. She held out the phone.

"Take it. Just take it and go. Some part of you has to understand that what you want is never going to happen."

Paul said nothing.

"Take it. Leave me the keys for the handcuffs and go."

Paul reached out and took the phone, his hand brushing against Rebecca's. The simple touch stopped the tingling in her fingers and sent a wave of revulsion surging through her body. She pulled away and stepped back.

"Rebecca. I'm sorry. I'm sorry for everything." He took two steps back and rested against the trunk of a giant Blackbutt. The phone dropped from his grip onto the stony ground and his boot smashed down on top of it.

"Now give me the keys to the cuffs." She held out her hand, trying desperately to disguise the trembling that she could feel within.

Paul stood up straight, the gun still clenched in his hand.

"You know I can't do that." He drew a deep breath and held it, closed his eyes, and tilted his head from side to side until an audible crack sounded.

"What? What does that mean?" Rebecca's voice began to rise. "Are you going to get rid of us too?"

"Go home Rebecca. Go home and stay home."

"What? You think you can shut me up?"

"Go. Home. Stay with your brother. It would be a shame if something happened to him."

"Don't you threaten him. What's happened to you? You said you loved me. You were family to me and Jake."

Rebecca could hear the laboured breath coming from Paul. Could see the gun trembling in his hand. Could smell the sweat that was now staining his shirt.

"JUST GO."

Matt had rolled over and was struggling to get to his feet.

"Don't do it Rebecca. He's going to put a bullet in me. He's gone mad. Don't leave me with him."

Paul lifted the gun and fired a shot in the air, which echoed across the dam and then stepped to Matt. A swift, forceful strike with the gun connected with the back of Matt's head, sending the handcuffed man crashing to the ground, unconscious. Somewhere a flock of ducks took to the air, a whirr of wings over water and for a fleeting moment, Rebecca wished she had taken flight with them.

"Enough of this bullshit." Paul grabbed Rebecca by the upper arm and pushed her toward her car. "You're going home and you're going to forget you were ever up here. Do you under-."

Lights appeared at the top end of the dam and the shape of a car became visible.

"What now?" Paul released his grip on Rebecca's arm, and she rubbed where his fingers had dug into her muscles. "Sit. If of either of you try anything...Shut your mouths and sit still."

Rebecca sat on her knees between the unconscious Matt and whimpering Sarge and studied them both in turn. Matt was breathing but clearly, knocked out. Sarge flinched as Rebecca's hand touched her muzzle and the patch of blood on her leg still seemed to be flowing.

At the top end of the dam the new vehicle turned and began a slow crawl toward the three cars parked at the dam's base. Shadows grew and twisted as headlights stabbed through the dark.

Rebecca shook Matt. One hand on his shoulder, pushing softly at first but getting no response she began to push at his arm roughly. "Wake up. We have to get out of here."

The car crunched through the dirt and gravel until it came to a stop several metres away and over the sound of all the running motors, Rebecca heard the whir of a window rolling down.

"I'll have to ask you to move along. Police operation underway here...Oh. It's just you. What are you doing here?"

Rebecca knew the voice instantly. It was Nashy and she wanted to yell out, but instead crawled toward the parked cars slowly.

"Where's Rebecca?"

Paul lent down to Nashy's window. "Should be at home. She...I found her car. That Lonergan bastard stole it. He's here somewhere. Armed, I think. You need to leave. Backup is on its way."

"What the hell are you talking about Paul? That's Matt's car there, sitting right next to Rebecca's. That doesn't make any sense."

"Like I said. Police Operation."

"Police Operation my ass. I got some half assed message from Matt. Pocket dialled I reckon. All I could hear was muffled shit from the three of you. Sounded like Rebecca screaming at one point."

Nashy pushed his door open and stood, surveying the area.

"Just let me take a look around mate."

Nashy only managed to take three steps before another gun shot rang out, and he fell to the dirt. His face smashing into the gravel between the two cars. His eyes looking just for a moment, beneath Rebecca's car and directly into Rebecca's eyes. She screamed and jumped to her feet just as Nashy's eyes closed.

Amongst all the action, none of them had noticed the fifth car, sitting in near darkness. It's headlights unintentionally dimmed as if its battery had not been fully charged in ten years, or more. The driver had pulled into the dam grounds just after Nashy, cursing as the antique stick shift had dropped out of gear, and then they had sat, watching as the brutal scene had unfolded.

After what had seemed an eternity for Jake, he slipped the stick of the 1951 FX Ute into gear, cursing as it caught up and the metal squealed, and then hit the accelerator. He moved through the gears smoothly now, building up speed as he sped down the track with one purpose in mind. Saving his sister.

He had heard the gun shot. Seen Nashy fall. Heard the scream and seen his sister spring up from the ground amongst the group of cars parked at the end of the dam. The flashing light told him one of them was a police car.

Now he could see a man, who looked familiar walking back toward Rebecca with a gun raised in his hand. It was all the encouragement he needed to push his foot further down on the accelerator and the car obliged by jolting and racing forward.

Paul paced between the cars, nudging Nashy with his foot.

"Why didn't you just drive away for Christ's sake?"

Nashy did not move and as Paul eyed the pool of blood that soaked into the dirt he looked around, muttering to himself loud enough for Rebecca to hear.

"Lonergan. He shot him. I can take that bastard down now." Paul turned on the spot as he heard the approaching vehicle and saw the dim headlights. In an instant he raised the gun again and fired three shots. One of the headlights turned dark and the sound of bullets hitting their mark filled the night air.

Jake ducked as he saw the man fire. The shots smashed into the front of the car, and he heard shattering glass. He pushed his foot down on the pedal even further and lifted his head just in time to see the man standing beside the police car. Gun raised and lit by the one headlight that had now burst to full life.

"Uncle Paul? What the actual f..."

Jake slammed his foot onto the brake and all he felt was spongy resistance. He ducked again and braced himself between the seat and dashboard as the 1951 FX Ute slid at almost full speed into the side of the Police Landcruiser.

The force of the collision pushed the Landcruiser sideways, which in turn hit Paul with enough force to fling him backward. His legs crumpled as his shoulder hit Matt's car with force and as he fell, he slammed his face and hand into the rear of the vehicle. The gun dropped to the ground.

44

Rebecca spun around. Matt was still laying bound and unconscious in the scrubby grass behind her. Beside him, Sarge was curled up, whimpering, and barking at any movement. Less than four steps away from her, lying on his back was Paul. Unconscious or momentarily stunned she could not tell. She did notice that his gun was nowhere to be seen, possibly under the car. She knew that Nashy was also lying in the dirt, face down on the other side of her car and now, she assumed Jake was in the old car smashed into the side of the police Landcruiser.

She was torn between checking Jake or Nashy, but family won out, and she made her way to the door of the old Ute. Through the window she could see Jake laid out across the bench seat, moaning, and holding one hand to his forehead and the other across his chest. Rebecca pulled at the door, but it failed to budge, until she pushed it back in hard and the lock released. It now opened with only a small amount of grunting and pulling.

"Jake. Jake." She climbed into the car, across his legs and pulled the hand from his face.

"Ahhh. Shit. That stuffing hurts." There was a thin scratch across his forehead that seemed to extend into his scalp. It was bleeding but not gushing.

"It looks like just a scratch. You'll be okay."

"Not my head. Get your knee of my ribs. Probably smashed them up something horrid against the steering wheel." He tried to sit up but laid back down, groaning.

"Just stay here. I have to check on Nashy."

"What the frig is going on? Was that Uncle Paul?"

"He's gone crazy. I have to check Nashy and try to call an ambulance or the police."

"He is the police."

"I know. I know. Just stay."

Rebecca climbed out of the car, carefully avoiding touching Jakes tender chest, and made her way to where Nashy lay. She knelt and put her hand out toward him, scared at what she might discover. Her hand pushed against his neck, and she gave a sigh of relief when she felt a strong pulse.

"Thank God. Stay with me Nashy. Help's coming."

Rebecca stood, fished her mobile phone from her pocket and dialled 000. It did not connect, and she checked the phone screen.

"No bloody reception." She looked around. They were in a tight valley and she knew reception up here could be hit or miss depending on where you stood. The slopes on both sides of The Pane were heavily forested and the nearest land line was a fifteen-minute drive.

She held the phone high in the air, swinging it around trying to find any signal. As she turned and faced the track that led to the top of the waterfall, for the briefest moment she saw a single bar flash on the screen. It was gone straight away.

She followed the source of the signal toward the top of the waterfall, until she stood looking over the valley below. The town lights of Shattered Falls lay to the west and far off she could make out the glow of the brighter lights of Tamworth. The phone now showed two bars, and she gave herself a congratulatory "Yes" and began to dial again.

"Don't do it Karen. "

Rebecca's shoulder dropped and she turned back around. Paul stood only two steps away, one arm hung limply beside him, and blood smeared across his face. His gun now back in his other hand and holding it clumsily in front of him.

"I love you. You know that and for once in my life I have got a chance to make a real life for the two of us. Just don't make that call."

Paul reached out and wrapped his arm around Rebecca, which at first seemed like an embrace but instead it pinned her arms to her side.

"I'm not Karen. Karen was my mum...she didn't love you either. You need to stop this. You need to end this now."

"End this...end this...end this now."

He released his bear-like grip of Rebecca's arms and swiped at the phone with his gun. It fell and clattered over the rocks, lost immediately amongst the shadows and water.

Paul lifted the gun. His face lit by the pale moonlight, a jigsaw of blood, dirt, tears, and madness. "We end it together."

Before either of them had a chance to do another thing, a low black form came running from the darkness and leapt at Paul. A ball of black and grey fur that had now decided which master it served. Sarge hit him in the chest with all the power an injured but determined ex-police dog could muster.

Rebecca instinctively reached out, her fingertips brushing at Paul's shirt as both dog and man sailed over the falls. As she rushed forward, she saw the police uniform hit the rocks below and bounce over them to fall the final drop to the base of the cascade. She screamed out despite the terror. "SARGE. UNCLE PAUL." The last two words more forced than ever.

She jumped when another voice came from behind her.

"Sis. Are you okay?"

She closed her eyes when she saw Jake and wrapped her arms around him, eliciting a cry of pain.

"Ease up there."

She pulled away and looked him up and down.

Jake tilted his head and raised his eyebrows. "Where is he?"

Rebecca just nodded toward the edge of the falls. "Gone...I hope...and Sarge as well."

"What are you talking about? That's Sarge right there." Jake pointed to the dark form on a narrow ledge just below them, struggling to make her way back up.

"Have you got your phone?"

Jake pulled an old flip phone from his pocket and handed it to Rebecca.

45

The next few hours were chaotic but seemed a relief to the madness they had all just endured.

Tony in his National Parks vehicle had been first on the scene with blankets and hot coffee for everyone and the ambulance had shown up minutes later. Nashy had been their first patient. Stabilising him and taking both him and Jake off to Tamworth Base Hospital. Matt had come around and had suffered some head trauma. His main gripe was the handcuffs which would not be able to be removed until another police vehicle turned up.

Tony had retrieved Sarge from the waterfall washed ledge and carried her up to the back tray of his car. Wrapping her in blankets, before doing his best to patch up the wound on her leg.

Once he was confident there was nothing else that he could do to assist at the top of the falls, Tony grabbed a torch and coil of rope from the back of his vehicle and began the difficult but not impossible climb down to the base of the falls. He found Paul, a broken and tangled mess pushed up against a boulder, his head in the water and his neck twisted like a pretzel. Dead. It was just after lunchtime the following day that his body was finally retrieved from its final resting place.

When the police had arrived, they immediately began to arrest Matt. With a dead cop and a man in handcuffs, he was their obvious target but as he was bundled into the back of another car he called to Rebecca.

"Don't let them take the dashcam until you've copied it. I set it up to record before you got here...Sorry, but I just wasn't sure how this would all go...and...well..." Rebecca had followed his whispered instructions and handed the SD card off to Tony.

Rebecca spent the next hours giving statements, taken to hospital, and checked by medical staff and finally being released the next morning.

Jake had only bruised his ribs and had two stitches in his scalp. Nashy had taken a bullet in his left shoulder and lost enough blood to ensure a prolonged stay in hospital. The complaints from that hospital room would be a never-ending string of curses and blasphemies all revolving around being unable to smoke.

By later that day Tony had copied the memory card from the dashcam and handed the original into the police. By late afternoon Matt walked out of the Police station a free man.

After the long night and day, the only thing Rebecca wanted to do now was go home. She collected Jake but before leaving she checked in on Craig. Nurses told her that he was doing well and would be released late next week if all went well. She peeked inside his room to find him sleeping, a thin line of dribble running down his chin. She sighed, feeling envious of his ability to doze, but she was mindful that Craigs sleep was drug induced.

"Gotta get me some of them drugs." She muttered.

A voice behind her made her jump. "You've just got to know the right people."

Rebecca turned to find Craig's sister, Tania standing behind her.

"How's he doing?"

"He's going to be fine, but more importantly, how are you? The whole thing last night...well you know how gossip is."

"I haven't really had time to stop yet. My head is still racing, and my anxiety, even though I think I deserve a medal for keeping it under control, I can feel it bubbling just below the surface."

"Ok. Wait right here. I'll get one of the doctors to prescribe you something." Tania headed off down the hallway and was only gone a minute before she came back with an older man in tow.

"Rebecca. This is Doctor Cooper."

After a few pleasantries and some personal details, Rebecca was off to the local pharmacy and on her way home, with Jake in the seat beside her.

"What a night sis. I can't get my head around it. Grandad didn't like him you know, but I think that was just a cop thing."

"Oh shit. We need to ring them as soon as we get home...but first we need to make a stop."

"I like the way that sounds. Home. I reckon I should move up here too."

Rebecca was about to chastise Jake about school but hesitated before she finally spoke.

"You know what. That's probably the smartest thing I've ever heard you say and Nashy is going to need help at the mill."

After a few minutes she parked the car and climbed out.

"Umm...sis. This is..."

"I know. I'll just be a minute."

It was closer to ten minutes before Rebecca returned to the car. The house whose driveway they had parked looked cold and grey in the afternoon light. Jake remembered it well. He remembered Aunty Meg and the swimming pool, and he remembered the man he had called Uncle Paul, and it nearly brought a tear to his eye. He snapped back when Rebecca came out through the front door with a ball of white fur. It growled and snapped at Jake as Rebecca opened the passenger door but instantly began to whimper and lick Jakes face as soon as the dog was placed into his lap.

"Jake. Meet Peaches. She's ours now."

"We got TWO dogs?"

"Yeah...and right now we have to go check on the other one."

The drive was filled with the distraction that was Peaches. For just a short period they forgot what they had just been through.

Sarge was recuperating at Tracey's house and that was where they headed next. Tony had refused to let the dog out of his sight and Sarge had shown the same feelings. That was quick to change when Rebecca and Jake drove down the driveway of Tracey's studio unit. They did not even have time to get out of the car before they were met by Tracey, Tony and even Tracey's mum. Words were useless, and the only thing they could do was hug each other.

"Ok. Everybody inside out of this cold." Mrs Pearce waved her hands, ushering the hugging indoors.

'I just want to get home and sleep. We only came to pick up Sarge. How's she doing?"

Tony moved over to Sarge who was curled up on a blanket. "She's tough. Took a bullet through her left front leg and pulled a couple of nails when she went over that drop, but...yeah...she's doing good. Vet says she just needs rest."

"Well, I'm going to make sure she gets plenty of that. After what she did for me..." Rebecca felt her voice break and then a hand on her shoulder.

"Sis. We got to introduce her to her new sister. No time for blubbering now." Jake had Peaches cradled in his arms, and he knelt beside Sarge and let the two dogs get familiar. After a few muted yaps and a lot of sniffing, Peaches curled up beside Sarge and fell asleep.

"Now you two aren't going anywhere. I got dinner cooked for you and Tony's going to shoot up to your place and get that fire going. I won't have you going home to a cold house."

Tony just stood and nodded at Mrs Pearce's instructions before realising he was being told to go start the fire at Rebecca's.

Within minutes Mrs Pearce had Rebecca, Jake and Tracey seated around the small table and was ladling vegetable and beef soup into bowls in front of them, with a plate of sliced, warm damper.

Rebecca's eyes lit up, and she poked Jake in the arm. "We don't have a bed for you at home yet."

"Oh yes we do. Nashy brought it over just after you left last night. Took us a while to get it down the hallway, but his swearing seemed to help it along, and he brought a mattress and a load of blankets too."

Rebecca dropped her head, thoughts drifting back to the events of last night.

"Sis. He's okay. You know when we were dragging that mattress into the room is when his phone went off. Heard you and that Matt guy and a bloody scream. I'd already told him you went off to The Pane to meet him. He told me to stay put but...well I was going too, mainly 'cause I had no way of getting there and then I remembered the Ute. Guess that's stuffed now. I didn't even check it."

"You'll fix it. However bad it is. You're good with your hands...just like dad...and I reckon Nashy will help."

"Yeah, I reckon your right."

After the meal and all the attention, they could handle, Rebecca and Jake headed home. Sarge and Peaches on a pile of old blankets in the back of the car.

Tony was still there when they turned up, and they carried Sarge inside and placed her in front of the fire before Tony left them.

When all was done, they sat and watched the fire with steaming coffees in hand, while Peaches went about exploring her new home. Sarge slept.

"We need to ring Grandma and Grandad." Rebecca stood and picked up the old land line.

"Yeah, I know. I reckon they'll be here first thing in the morning once they know what went on. Guaranteed."

Rebecca drew a deep breath. "I sure hope so."

46

Six Months Later.

They were late.

Rebecca had planned for them to be on the road half an hour ago but here she was still standing in the kitchen, waiting. She was in no hurry and the reality was that they had plenty of time. She could hear the shower running and what may have been singing or possibly the summoning of a demon. She yelled down the hall. "You okay in there. Sounds like you're in pain."

There was no answer, so she poured herself a glass of juice, peeled off her shoes and sat down at the kitchen table. She lent back in the chair, stretching her neck, and looked up at the ceiling, spotting a tangle of cobwebs in one corner.

"Damn. How did I miss that?"

Over the past six months, she had cleaned every inch of the house, or so she had thought. Wanting to keep busy while the drama had slowly faded away and keeping busy had been exactly what she had done.

She had taken up pottery. Making use of Nan's wheel and kiln and found that she not only enjoyed it but was respectable at it as well. There had been a street fair three weeks ago and with the aid of a fold-up table and a pergola, she had sold almost two hundred dollars of vases, jugs, and bowls.

Jake had cleaned up the backyard or as he said, "It's not a yard, it's a bloody paddock."

Craig had finally gotten around to taking her out to a Country Ball, which had been more fun than she had expected. It had led to a second date, and a third and another, until finally they had become a thing. They had even tried another Trivia night, with Jake, Tate, Tracey, and Tony, but had come dead last when Tate had insisted on writing down the answers. His version of the answers.

She had taken up running most mornings, even when it was freezing. Sarge and Peaches always ran with her, sometimes all three of them coming home covered in mud. The two dogs had become best of friends, with Peaches mothering Sarge as if she could sense the injuries that the bigger dog still carried.

And now Craig was in her shower, or by the lack of sound coming from down the hall, he was out of the shower, and she hoped, almost dressed.

She walked down the hall and found him already in the bedroom, half-dressed.

"Almost ready."

"Almost."

"You might want to put some pants on. I think the bride is supposed to be the centre of attention."

"Point taken. Pants coming up...and I have no idea where my good shoes are."

"Seriously? I don't know how your girlfriend puts up with you."

Craig looked up at Rebecca with a huge smile. "So, it's girlfriend now."

Rebecca smiled back and began scanning the room for the missing footwear.

"Under the bed?"

"Looked."

"Haven't you got another pair?"

"It's a wedding Bec. Can't be wearing my grubby old plumber's boots."

"Fair enough, just look again. Don't be having a boy look."

Craig wandered down the hall, threading his belt through his jeans as he went. Rebecca watched from the bedroom doorway as he almost fell over a rubber chew toy and disappeared into the lounge room.

"Got them." Craig's voice echoed down the hall. "Under the dog's bed. Crafty buggers are trying to stop us from going."

Sarge and Peaches just looked on as Craig put the shiny, black shoes into the travel bag sitting on the coffee table, hoisted it over his shoulder and made his way to the door. "Let's go then."

Rebecca followed him out the door, and they found Jake standing beside the car.

"Now bro, are you sure you're going to be okay."

"Seriously sis. I'm not some little kid. I'll be fine. Me and Tate are having a feed at the pub tonight and tomorrow we're going to go out to Chaffey Dam and do some fishing. So, I'll be keeping busy."

"I'm glad you've made friends up here, but please be careful at the pub. And make sure you get up for work on Monday or Nashy will get even crankier than usual and don't forget to feed the dogs."

"I don't reckon they'll let me forget. Just go. Have fun and give my best to Tracey and Tony."

Rebecca gave Jake a quick kiss on the cheek, which he wiped away with a grimace on his face.

"Save that for your boyfriend."

"You jealous Jake?" Craig nudged Jake in the side.

"Will the two of you just go."

Rebecca threw the last bag into the back of the Suzuki and turned to face the two others.

"Okay quick checklist. Wedding clothes? Check. Invitation?"

Craig pulled the folded shiny, silver cardboard from his pocket and held it up.

Craig read, "Tracey Pearce and Tony Higgins request the pleasure of your company to celebrate their wedding. Ceremony King Edward Park. Newcastle. Blah Blah Blah."

"Check. Gift? Check. Flowers?" Rebecca peered into the back of the car at the bunch of wildflowers. "Check. Okay, let's hit the road. See you Monday bro."

Rebecca grabbed the keys from Craig's hand. "I'm driving."

"You sure? You do know where we're driving?"

"Yeah, like I don't know how to drive to Newcastle...but yes, I'm sure. Been carrying this weight far too long."

She watched as Craig shrugged and limped to the car. His limp was getting better, but it was still one of the many constant reminders of what had happened all those months ago. The story, the rumours and eventually the truth had burnt through the town like a wildfire for weeks until people had found something else to focus on. Now it was just the few ongoing things like Craig's and Sarge's limp, or the sight of Peaches, or Nashy's constant whine about his shoulder that took her back there. She had made a promise to herself not long after everything, that she would survive and now with her family, partner, pets, and friends she was doing just that.

The Friday afternoon summer drive was perfect. Sunshine, music, and laughs made the distance pass quickly.

Just before Murrurundi, Rebecca pulled the car to the side of the road. The siding here was narrow, but she was able to climb out, take the bunch of flowers from the car and with a few cable ties, attach the bunch to the guard rail.

She stood silent. No tears just a quiet smile and quiet words.

"I love you mum. I love you dad." Then she felt Craig's arm around her shoulder, and she slipped her arm around him, before wordlessly climbing back into the car.

She smiled, glanced at Craig, started the car, turned the music up louder and headed off, thinking to herself.

The road ahead held great promise and there was no way she was going to sleep through any of it.

ACKNOWLEDGMENTS

Acknowledgments

First off, I want to give a huge shoutout to my amazing family. To my incredible wife, Rachael, and my wonderful daughter, Jazmyn – you two are my rock stars. Your endless love and support have kept me going, and I couldn't have done this without you.

A big thank you to the Lake Macquarie Fellowship of Australian Writers. You guys are awesome! Special thanks to Jan and Pam for all your guidance and encouragement. Your insights have been invaluable, and I'm so grateful for your help.

And finally, to anyone brave enough to pick up this novel and dive into its pages – thank you! Your time and interest mean the world to me, and I hope you enjoy the journey.

Just a quick note: This work is purely fictional. Any resemblance to actual persons, living or dead, is purely coincidental. And any errors you find are entirely my own.

Wayne Russell resides in the suburbs of Newcastle, NSW, Australia, where he crafts tales of adventure from his bustling home office. As the author of the *Butterfly Quest Trilogy—The Butterfly Quest, The Ember Island,* and *The Underocean*—Wayne has captivated young readers with his imaginative worlds and engaging storytelling. His trilogy has taken readers on magical journeys through fantastical realms, earning him a dedicated following among young fantasy enthusiasts.

Now, Wayne is embarking on a new literary journey into the realm of adult fiction with his latest novel, marking the beginning of what he hopes will be many more thrilling adventures to come. This new venture allows him to explore deeper themes and more complex characters, all while maintaining the sense of wonder and excitement that his readers have come to love.

Despite his busy schedule, Wayne finds time to immerse himself in a good book and let his imagination run wild with daydreams of epic quests and heroic deeds. Though real-life adventures are rare due to his commitments, his stories are filled with the spirit of exploration and discovery. Wayne is currently working on developing his social media platforms, where he plans to share updates on his latest projects and connect with his readers.

Stay tuned for more exciting tales from Wayne Russell as he continues to weave new stories and explore uncharted literary territories.

Contact: Wayne.Russell.Author@gmail.com